continued . . .

Carolina Man

VIRGINIA KANTRA

BERKLEY SENSATION, NEW YORK

THE BERKLEY PUBLISHING GROUP
Published by the Penguin Group
Penguin Group (USA) LLC
375 Hudson Street, New York, New York 10014

USA • Canada • UK • Ireland • Australia • New Zealand • India • South Africa • China

penguin.com

A Penguin Random House Company

CAROLINA MAN

A Berkley Sensation Book / published by arrangement with the author

Berkley Sensation Books are published by The Berkley Publishing Group.
BERKLEY SENSATION® is a registered trademark of Penguin Group (USA) LLC.
The "B" design is a trademark of Penguin Group (USA) LLC.

For information, address: The Berkley Publishing Group,
a division of Penguin Group (USA) LLC,
375 Hudson Street, New York, New York 10014.

ISBN: 978-0-425-26887-2

PUBLISHING HISTORY
Berkley Sensation mass-market edition / March 2014

PRINTED IN THE UNITED STATES OF AMERICA

10 9 8 7 6 5 4 3 2 1

Cover art by Tony Mauro.
Cover design by Rita Frangie.

This one's for the boys.
To Andrew and Mark,
And to Michael,
their model of what a man should be.

ACKNOWLEDGMENTS

Thank you to everyone who made this book possible. To Angela R. Narron, for her legal expertise and creative brainstorming. To Carolyn Martin and Michael Ritchey, who supplied comments, encouragement, and coffee as needed. To Robin Rue and Beth Miller of Writers House, whose insights are always spot-on. Thank you to my editor, Cindy Hwang, for supporting this series; to Kristine Swartz; and to Rita Frangie and Tony Mauro, for creating such fabulous covers.

Thank you to my readers.

And a special thanks to the memory of Sergeant Major Paul W. Ritchey, USMC (Ret.), and to all the men and women who serve.

One

In Afghanistan, the kids threw rocks.

Staff Sergeant Luke Fletcher watched four boys in the street take aim at an oil barrel and counted himself lucky that today, at least, they'd found another target.

He didn't dislike kids. They were sort of cute under the age of five. From a distance. The kids in Iraq used to tag after the Marine patrols hoping for handouts, candy, maybe, or soccer balls or humrats—humanitarian rations.

A stone ricocheted off the metal barrel like a bullet, and twenty-three-year-old Corporal Danny Hill, sweeping the bomb wand at the front of the column, froze.

"Easy," Luke said. "It's just some kids throwing rocks at a . . ."

Shit. At a dog.

He could see it now, slinking in the shadow of the wall, just another stray: abused, malnourished, obviously feral. Nothing he could do about it. The weak picked on the weaker. Yelling at a couple of ten-year-olds wasn't going to make them respect the dog or the law.

The dog yelped.

"Hey!" The word jerked out of him.

His tone needed no translation. The boys scattered in a flurry of jeers and stones. Nothing Luke could do about that, either.

He and his men were here to provide training and support for the Afghan National Police who would replace them. For two days, their joint patrol had hiked from town to town, sweating through the afternoons, freezing through the nights, trying to buy the ANP time and breathing room to hold this desert province once the Marines were gone.

Sergeant Musa Habib, the Afghan team leader, met Luke's eyes. "You know they will be back."

He meant the kids with rocks. Or he could have been talking about their fathers. Their brothers. The Taliban.

"You do what you can do." Luke glanced at the dun-colored mutt shrinking behind the barrel. He had too many people depending on him already. The last thing he needed was to take on responsibility for a dog. "Maybe it will be gone by then."

The mutt didn't move.

Luke dug in his harness for an MRE. He'd eaten the snacks already. Ripping open the leftover meat pouch, he squeezed a chunk on the ground.

Lance Corporal Anthony Ortega, an ex-gangbanger from East Los Angeles, grinned. "I wouldn't feed that shit to my dog."

But the mutt wasn't so picky. It poked its head from behind the barrel. Its ears were cropped, one eye swollen nearly shut.

Nineteen-year-old Private First Class Cody Burrows whistled in sympathy. "They really messed that bastard up."

"Kids didn't do all that," Luke said.

Fresh blood oozed from a gash on its shoulder. But its other scars were older injuries, puckered and scabbed over.

"No," Habib agreed. "This dog has been used for fighting."

The mutt inched forward, quivering.

"No way that's a fighting dog," Ortega said.

"It's big enough," Hill said.

"Often the bait dogs, they are cut like that," said Habib. "To rouse the other dogs and make them fight."

Poor mutt. Luke threw another piece of MRE. The dog's eyes rolled toward him as it took the food. Its big, black-rimmed eyes made it look like a bar girl after a bad night.

"Gee, Daddy, can we keep him?" Hill said.

"He's a she, numbnuts," farm boy Burrows said. "Look at her belly. She's gonna have puppies."

They all stood around watching the dog, like feeding some pregnant stray was the best, most entertaining thing to happen to them all day. Which it was.

"We should take her back with us," Hill said. "You saved her life. That makes you responsible for her."

Luke shook his head. "Don't give me that Zen shit."

Rescuing strays was not part of his mission. He put the rest of his MRE on the ground, watching the mutt lap it almost delicately from the foil.

He liked dogs. His family always had a dog.

He pushed the thought of home away, rolling his shoulders to resettle his pack. "Break time's over." He looked at Habib. "What do you want to do?"

The Afghan sergeant looked momentarily surprised. But the rules had changed in the past few months. Now it was the Afghans who were supposed to step up and take the lead.

Habib cleared his throat. "We should patrol the market."

Luke nodded.

They walked the narrow alleys between residential compounds. Luke watched the doorways and rooflines, braced for sniper fire. Their survival depended on his ability to make snap judgments, to distinguish between a threat and a friendly, to react quickly and correctly in a crisis. Everything in the village was parched and brown, the color of the never-ending dust that hung like fog over the landscape. It was part of him now, engrained in his skin, choking his sinuses.

Sometimes he missed the blue Carolina sky with a long-ing that burned the back of his throat.

The squadron emerged into the bazaar. A few stalls were open for business. Motorcycles zipped by like wasps, kicking up clouds of dust. A circle of men—village elders—squatted in the shade, surrounded by a standing ring of boys. Always boys, never girls. They kept their women out of sight. Luke's sister would have had some-thing to say about that.

Habib looked at Luke, seeking guidance.

"Ask them how it's going," Luke said.

The new Afghan police force needed to build rapport with the community, to establish trust in the new govern-ment. He stood back, an itch between his shoulders, watch-ing their faces as Habib and the elders went through the usual bullshit.

No Taliban, the villagers said. They hadn't seen any-body. They just wanted to be left alone.

"Is there anything we can do for them?"

No. Nothing.

"They got kids?" Luke asked.

One of the younger men nodded.

"You tell him he can go to the base if they need medi-cal attention."

More nods, more smiles, more bullshit. It was the same in every village. The patrol moved on.

"Hey, look," Burrows said. "That dog's following us."

"Happens when bitch gets knocked up," Ortega said.

Laughter rippled up the column, relieving the tension.

Luke looked back. Sure enough, the dog had fallen in behind the last man like a member of the patrol.

She was still with them when they made camp that night on a plateau of hard-packed gravel. They could have shel-tered in the last town. But despite Luke's mission to improve community relations, he didn't trust their hosts not to report them to the Taliban while they slept.

As the temperatures plummeted, the dog crept closer,

drawn by the need for warmth or food or simple companionship. Luke could sympathize. He tore open another MRE and set it on the rocky ground.

"Why do you feed it?" Habib asked.

"Staff Sergeant's our den mother. He takes care of everybody," Burrows said.

He couldn't take care of everybody. But by tagging along, the dog had made herself one of them. Theirs.

After ten years at war, Luke wasn't fighting for freedom and democracy. He was in this for the guys next to him, to keep them safe, to bring them home alive.

The mutt licked the wrapper, her thin tail stirring cautiously.

Out here, it was the little things that mattered. Making the world safe from global terrorism sounded good, but these days Luke measured victory one step, one sunrise, and now one dog at a time.

"You ever have a pet growing up?" he asked Habib.

The Afghan smiled wryly. "We can barely feed our families. We do not think of animals as you do."

The dog sighed and settled her head on her paws, fixing her dark, mascara-ringed eyes on Luke. Like a hooker who'd been knocked around and still hoped this time would be different. Better. *Help me. Save me. Love me.*

He looked away.

"Think she'll make it back to camp with us?" Ortega asked, seeking reassurance.

Luke didn't know. He didn't know if any of them would make it. The weight of responsibility pressed on his shoulders.

No Marine left behind.

Or dog, either.

"Sure," he said. "As long as we keep feeding her."

"She's eating for two now," Hill said.

"More like seven," Burrows said.

"How many puppies you think she's got in there?"

Luke listened to their good-natured speculation, his

shoulders gradually relaxing. By the time they reached the forward outpost two days later, the mutt was taking point with Luke at the head of the column, barking to warn of the approach of other dogs or people, and Ortega was making book on the size of her litter.

No way was Luke enforcing the ban on pets on base. His men were denied enough of the comforts of home. No beer, no porn, no barbecue. Only a hard-ass would deny them a dog.

Luke had more important things to worry about.

His report made, he sat on his bunk, turning over the thin stack of MotoMail that had accumulated while he was on patrol. Three letters in five days.

The fine hair stirred on the back of his neck.

He got mail, of course. His mom, trained by twenty years as a Marine wife, sent plenty of care packages, tucking in notes with the eye drops and baby wipes, hard candy and homemade cookies. His dad always had a word during Luke's infrequent phone calls home. *Stay safe. Shoot straight.* But Dad wasn't much for writing, never had been, even when he'd been the one on deployment.

And it wasn't like Luke had a wife and kiddies back home, sending him love letters and complaints about the toilet and scrawled crayon drawings.

He flipped to the first envelope, glancing at the return address. Katherine M. Dolan, P.L.L.C., Beaufort, North Carolina.

His brows raised. *A lawyer.*

He didn't need a lawyer. He wasn't sixteen anymore, getting pulled over for drunk driving. Anyway, no Beaufort attorney was going to solicit new clients in Afghanistan.

He ripped the envelope open.

Dear Staff Sergeant Fletcher, he read in neat type.

Okay, so this Katherine Dolan wasn't some woman he'd met in a bar during his last leave. That was good.

This office represents the estate of Dawn Marie Simpson.

Dawn. Jesus. That name took him back. All the way to

high school. Pretty, blond Dawn, with her wide smile and amazing breasts.

His hand tightened on the letter. And now she was . . . ?

I am sorry to tell you that Dawn is deceased as of August 9.

Dead.

Shit. Ten years in the Corps had hardened him to violence. But death came to the battlefield. Not to girls back home.

His gaze dropped back to the letter.

I am writing to inform you that Dawn left behind a minor child, Taylor Simpson, born February 2, 2003. In her will, Dawn identified you as the father of her child . . .

The tent broke around him, a kaleidoscope of shards, as his world, his heart, stopped. His vision danced.

. . . and as such named you as the child's guardian and trustee.

His heart jerked back to uneven motion. His head pounded. He didn't have a child. He couldn't. It was a damn lie. A joke. He hadn't seen Dawn in ten years, since she dumped him at the end of senior year for Bo Meekins. No way was he the father of her baby.

He read the first paragraph again. *February 2, 2003.* Not a baby. It hit him like a kick in the gut.

I understand that you are currently deployed with the US military, the letter continued in crisp, impersonal type. *Pending instructions from you, Taylor is living with her maternal grandparents, Ernest and Jolene Simpson. Please advise me of your intentions for assuming parental responsibilities for your child.*

He dragged in an uneven breath. His responsibilities were here. His life was here. The familiar tent whirled and refocused around him, his surroundings assuming the flat, clear detail of a firefight, boots, locker, green wool blanket, everything coated in a fine layer of grit. Time slowed. The paper trembled slightly in his grasp.

I realize this news must come as a shock. In addition to her will, the deceased left a letter for you which may address some of your questions and concerns. I will be happy to forward it per your instructions. Dawn was ada- mant that you were the right person to care for Taylor in the event of her death.

Dawn was out of her fucking mind. That was the only explanation that made sense.

I hope that you will consider your response very care- fully in keeping with Taylor's best interests. Your present situation may not be conducive to the raising of a minor child. There are other options that you and I can discuss. I look forward to hearing from you. Sincerely, K. Dolan.

She was going to hear from him, all right, Luke thought grimly. As soon as he could find a damn phone.

"I WANT A paternity test," Luke said.

It had taken him four days to arrange transportation to the main camp, Leatherneck, so he could make this call. Another eight and a half hours waiting for Eastern Stan- dard Time to catch up with Afghanistan so that he could talk to this lawyer person, K. Dolan, in her office. His head throbbed. His mouth was dry. His nerves stretched tight with stress and fatigue. This was not a conversation he intended to have via e-mail. Not a conversation he wanted to have at all.

But he was determined to be responsible. Reasonable. He had no proof this kid was even his. Only Dawn's word, and Dawn . . . He blinked gritty eyes. Dawn was dead.

"That's understandable and practical," the lawyer said in a voice that matched her letter, guarded and cool. "If you're not a blood relative of the child, you have no real standing for custody."

Perversely, her attitude made him want to argue.

"Except for Dawn's will," he said.

"The court is not bound by Dawn's decision," the Dolan woman said. "If you want to renounce your claim to the child, her grandparents are very willing to take her."

Grandparents. God. How would his parents react to the

news? They'd already rallied once, to help raise his brother's child. He couldn't ask them to . . .

But she wasn't talking about his parents, he realized. She meant Dawn's folks, Ernie and Jolene Simpson. Were they even around anymore? He vaguely recalled his mom saying they'd moved off island when the fish house closed eight years ago.

"That's not what Dawn wanted," he said.

"I don't think Dawn truly anticipated this situation ever arising. Her death was very sudden."

Tell me about it. He still couldn't wrap his mind around the idea of Dawn, dead. There had to be something he should say, something he could do. "When's the funeral?"

"August thirteenth."

Two weeks ago. His throat tightened.

"I'm sorry." The lawyer's voice softened.

He swallowed. "Why the hell did it take you so long to contact me?" he asked roughly.

"I took the will to the clerk's office to be probated within a few days of Dawn's death. After which, I had to locate you."

"How'd you find me?" It wasn't like he and Dawn had kept in touch. He didn't even know she had a child. *He* had a child. Hell.

"Your parents still live on the island where Dawn grew up. I looked them up."

"Do they know?"

"Only that you've been named in a will that I'm probating and I needed to get in touch."

"Did you tell them it was Dawn?"

"I didn't see the need," the lawyer said, still in that carefully measured voice. Actually, he was grateful for her restraint. This wasn't the kind of news you wanted to spring on somebody.

Luke winced. The way she'd just sprung it on him.

So it was up to him to tell his folks. To explain that while he was overseas, they had suddenly somehow become grandparents again. "How did she die?"

"An aneurysm. A ruptured blood vessel in the brain," Dolan said, as if using little words would help him understand. "The doctors said it was probably the result of a congenital condition."

"Did she suffer?"

"As I said, her death was very sudden." Did he imagine it, or did her voice shake slightly, as if she was suppressing actual emotion? "Dawn had a headache, a bad one. I told her to take the afternoon off. And then . . ."

"Wait. She worked for you?"

"Yes."

"Where was the kid?" *The kid.* His kid. He didn't believe it. Dawn would have told him.

Wouldn't she?

"In school," Dolan said.

Yeah, sure, the kid would be school age. Nine? Ten?

Dawn had written to him in boot camp, he remembered suddenly. Once, ten years ago, the summer after high school graduation. But try as he might, he couldn't remember anything beyond some hello-how-are-you kind of bullshit. He'd had other, more important things on his mind than a remorseful ex-girlfriend. He'd been too exhausted, or too pissed off still, to reply.

And when he'd gone home for his ten days of leave before his unit was deployed, Dawn had already left the island with ol' Bo.

Part of him had been disappointed she wasn't around to admire him in his new uniform. Maybe he'd even been hoping for one more hookup for old time's sake, a little pre-deployment action. But he'd been relieved, too. Dawn had made it clear when she dumped him that she didn't want a boyfriend in the Marines. She was already part of his past, part of the life he was leaving behind.

How the hell was he supposed to know she was pregnant?

He struggled to organize his thoughts. "You said she left a letter. What did it say?"

"It was sealed."

"But you're her lawyer. You could open it."

"I would have, if there had been no other way to find you. Since I was able to locate you through your parents, that wasn't necessary." The lawyer had this precise, deliberate way of speaking, like she charged by the word instead of by the hour.

Her lack of drama actually made this easier to get through. But she was so guarded that Luke wanted to reach through the phone and shake her, the way she'd shaken him.

He bit back his impatience. "Well, can you read it to me?"

"If that's what you want."

His teeth clenched. What he wanted didn't enter into it. This was about what needed to be done. "Yeah."

"One moment. All right. Here we go." A rustle of paper—or maybe that was just the connection—before she took a breath. "'*Dear Luke, I guess you never expected to hear from me again. But Kate says every parent ought to have a will naming a guardian, and I couldn't think of anybody better to raise our baby girl than you.*'"

Oh, shit. He cleared his throat. "Who's Kate?"

"Me." *Yeah, definite emotion there, under the professional act.* "When Dawn came to work for me, I told her that a lot of cases I see . . ."

"Yeah, okay, I get it. Go on."

"Er . . . '*Her name is Taylor. She's wonderful, Luke. The best thing that ever happened to me. I feel bad because you haven't had a chance to see her, how special she is. Maybe you never will. I didn't figure I'd ever have to ask you for anything. We've never needed anybody, Taylor and me. But if you're reading this, then she needs you now. I love her more than anything. I hope you can, too. Take care of her for me. Dawn.*'"

No explanations. No excuses. None of the answers Luke craved. Just the faint, remembered rhythm of her speech and the weight of expectations reaching across the years and miles.

His blood pounded in his head. *She needs you.*

"It'll take me a couple days to get there at least," he said.

"Excuse me?"

"I'll get emergency leave. But even with a good connection through Ramstein Air Base, it's thirty hours from Kandahar to Lejeune."

The phone was silent. Then, "I appreciate the thought. And your effort, Staff Sergeant," the lawyer said carefully. "But there's no need to act impulsively. We need to find a long-term solution for Taylor."

"That's why I'm coming home," Luke said. "I can't take care of this over the phone." *Take care of her for me.*

Another measured breath. "I hear what you're saying," the Dolan woman said almost gently. "But we have to think practically. Taylor has no relationship with you. You're a stranger to her."

I feel bad because you haven't had a chance to see her.

"So she'll meet me now," Luke said. "If she is my kid, she's entitled to military benefits. I can take her to the base, get her ID."

"Obviously, it's in Taylor's best interest to have health care," the lawyer said. "I can ask the court to grant you temporary custody, which would allow you to remove her from the Simpsons' home. But the issue of long-term care still has to be addressed. You have options. Dawn's parents . . ."

"We'll talk about it when I get there," Luke said.

After the paternity test. After he'd met her, this daughter. The daughter he'd left behind.

Two

KATE DOLAN LEFT the courtroom, flushed with victory.

"That's it?" Her client, twenty-seven-year-old Libby Brown, sounded dazed. "We can go home now?"

Her bewilderment tore Kate's heart. It had taken her almost eight months to convince Libby that she had the right to live free from abuse. Painstakingly, Kate had laid out the other woman's options, encouraging her to look beyond her husband's threats, promises, and emotional appeals to the real, recurring harm. Even so, if Will Brown hadn't finally hit her in front of the kids, if he hadn't gone after their oldest when he tried to intervene, Libby might never have found the courage to leave. Her decision had probably saved her life. It had also left her and her children homeless—at least until today.

"Your husband's been ordered to vacate the residence," Kate assured her. "And to stay away from you and the children. As soon as we verify that the house is safe, you can move back in."

"He won't go," Libby said.

"Then he'll be evicted," Kate said with grim satisfaction. "By the sheriff, if necessary."

The courtroom doors opened behind them as more people filed into the lobby.

"Good job, Kate," Susan Bennett, another attorney, murmured as she passed.

Kate nodded in acknowledgment, but her focus stayed on Libby and the kids. The two older ones waited with Libby's sister in the chairs in the center of the room. The youngest, a five-year-old with shadowed eyes and a chipped front tooth, pressed against his mother's side.

Kate kept a jar of candy on her desk for her clients alongside a big box of tissues. The Brown boy liked Smarties, she remembered. Her gaze dropped to the ugly purple bruise on his arm.

She took a deep breath. Outrage would not help her client. Preparation would. "I want you to stick with your safety plan," she told Libby. "The act of taking legal action can spur—"

"You bitch!"

Kate braced. Turned.

Will Brown looked ready to bust the seams of the shirt and tie his lawyer had almost certainly ordered him to wear to court. His fists were clenched, his face dark with anger.

Kate almost flinched before she got a grip on her emotions. Contrary to popular belief, most abusers *could* control their actions. They didn't blow up at their bosses. They beat their spouses instead.

Kate moved to put Libby and the child behind her. Brown would not hit her. Probably. Not in front of witnesses. She hoped.

"You've got no right to interfere between a man and his wife. His property," Brown said, his voice thick with violence. "Them's my kids. That's my house."

Kate's heart rate kicked up. She stood her ground, her armpits damp, her stomach cramping with tension. "You heard the judge, Mr. Brown. For the next twelve months, you are barred from the house and ordered to stay away from Elizabeth and the children."

"I'll make her sorry. I'll make you sorry, too, you interfering bitch."

Behind Kate, Libby made a choked sound, as if her husband's hands were already around her throat.

Where the *hell* was a deputy?

"Don't you threaten me. One more word, and I'll have your ass arrested," Kate snapped. "Mr. Reynolds."

Brown's lawyer hurried over, hovering ineffectually around the big man like a cocker spaniel with a pit bull.

"Control your client." Kate stepped away, lowering her voice so that the children would not hear. "Mrs. Brown hasn't pressed assault charges against him, but I will."

ALL IN ALL, a good day's work, Kate thought later as she walked back to her office, two blocks from the courthouse.

Her heart still raced. Raised voices still had the power to make her sick inside. But she wasn't a cringing child any longer. She had learned to fight back, to channel her fear into action.

Five cases, she thought with satisfaction. Five successful outcomes that she and her clients could live with. She couldn't save every battered or betrayed woman, every bruised or abused child who came through her doors. But that only made today's victories all the sweeter.

Kate liked helping people. It made up for all the years that she felt helpless.

She unlocked the front door of her house, a 1930s bungalow she'd converted into an office with an apartment upstairs. Quiet enveloped her. The air was chill and stale. No point in wasting heat when she was gone all day.

After graduating from law school, Kate had done her time as an associate in a big Charlotte firm. But protecting the rights and privileges of the powerful wasn't her idea of the law. She wanted her own practice. The freedom to choose her own cases, to control her own schedule, to order her own life, was worth the financial risk. No partners to placate. No egos to manage. She *liked* living alone. Her home was her castle, defended against all invaders.

Still, on days like today, she missed having someone to share her successes with. Sometimes castle life was lonely.

She adjusted the thermostat. Maybe she should look into getting some fish for the moat. Except she didn't have a moat. Maybe a cat?

The truth was, she missed Dawn. She hadn't noticed the silence so much when Dawn came in every day with her cupcakes and holiday sweaters, her kitten videos and constant stories about her daughter.

A yellowing philodendron drooped from the mantel of the bricked-up fireplace. Kate sighed and picked a leaf off the beige carpet.

She had never been particularly great at making friends. Not close friends, anyway. By the time she was eighteen, she'd moved six times and attended eight different schools. Always adjusting, always being the new kid on the block, always having to prove herself, had made her cautious about letting people in. Her home life had choked off any attempts she might have made at friendship. No play dates. No sleepovers. No sharing secrets. Kate had carried that reserve into adulthood. *Fear of intimacy*, her therapist said.

But she'd genuinely liked Dawn, her sunny smile, her upbeat optimism, her devotion to her daughter. It was like having a friend at a slight, professional remove or a family from a safe, vicarious distance.

I love her more than anything, Dawn had written in her letter to her child's father. *I hope you can, too.*

There was a lump in Kate's throat. She swallowed, brushing the dead leaf into her wastebasket.

He'd sat right there, she remembered, on the other side of this desk. Staff Sergeant Luke Fletcher, stiff and unsmiling as a soldier on a war monument, his blue eyes alive and focused on Kate with breath-stealing intensity. He made her uncomfortable, with his broad shoulders and lean, almost gaunt face, crowding her safe, neutral office, his large, spit-shined shoes touching the legs of her desk. Totally in command of his space. Her space.

Not her type, she told herself firmly, ignoring the stupid flutter of her pulse. She went for men who were more . . . cerebral. Not men who rode in tanks or sprayed villages with automatic-weapon fire or flew for thirty hours on a plane when any normal man would have simply picked up the phone. That whole "see the hill, take the hill" Marine thing he had going on made her prickle like a cat confronted by a large dog. But despite her distrust of his gung ho approach to Dawn's letter, there was something pretty great about his willingness to take responsibility for Dawn's child. His daughter.

Maybe an unmarried staff sergeant wasn't the best person in the world to raise a ten-year-old girl. The Simpsons— Dawn's parents—certainly hadn't thought so. *He doesn't know her*, Jolene Simpson had wept. *He can't love her like we do.*

And maybe he didn't, yet. Kate hadn't observed any evidence of an instant father-daughter bond during their brief meeting in her office. The little girl had been sullen and mistrustful, the man awkward and clearly frustrated.

But at least he was trying.

Kate booted up her computer.

Anyway, a judge had awarded the Fletchers temporary custody while Staff Sergeant Fletcher was in Afghanistan. Taylor was their responsibility now.

Kate scrolled through her in-box. Time to concentrate on the mothers she could help, the children she could save.

The subject line leaped out at her. *Taylor Simpson*.

Frowning, she clicked the e-mail to open it.

Her stomach dropped as she read. She should have seen this coming.

It's not fair, Jolene Simpson had cried in the courtroom. *Taylor's all we have left of our little girl.*

Your little girl didn't want you to raise her kid, thought Kate, staring at her computer.

Her thoughts beat like moths against the back-door screen.

Dawn had never explained *why* she would entrust her only daughter to a man she hadn't seen in ten years rather than her own mother and father. But Kate's imagination—and experience—could supply plenty of reasons, all of them bad. Maybe Dawn and her parents were simply estranged. Maybe Dawn had been motivated by guilt at keeping Taylor's existence a secret from Luke all these years. And maybe . . .

Kate read the e-mail again, resolve balling in her stomach. She was *not* reacting emotionally, she told herself. Taylor had told the judge at the temporary hearing that she wanted to stay with the Fletchers.

Kate reached for the phone to call them.

HOMEMADE BANNERS FLUTTERED for miles on the chain link fence along Highway 24, dazzling against the bright green grass and tall dark pines.

Through the windows of the charter bus carrying Luke's squad to Camp Lejeune, he could read the hand-painted signs.

WELCOME HOME.
MY HUSBAND. MY HERO.
WE ♥ DADDY. I MISSED YOU.

Ortega gripped the seat in front of him. "Man, I can't wait to see Kendra." His girlfriend.

"I want to see my daughter," Danny Hill said. "Stephanie was still pregnant when I left. I mean, I've seen the baby on Skype, but it's not the same as being there, watching her grow up, you know?"

Luke nodded tightly. At least Hill only had eight months to make up for. Luke had missed *ten years* of his daughter's life.

"Better hope you don't drop her," Ortega said.

Hill turned pale.

"You'll do fine." Luke intervened before Ortega's teasing created a situation. After a ten-month tour and over thirty hours of nonstop travel, they were all on edge. "Babies aren't so hard to figure out."

At least babies cried when they needed something, when they were tired or wet or hungry. They didn't scowl at you with big, wounded eyes, leaving you to wonder what the hell you were supposed to do differently.

Luke's gut clenched.

"So you're some baby expert now?" Ortega asked.

"I have a nephew." Luke stared out the window. And a daughter he'd met exactly once.

Luke was twelve years old when his brother, Matt, dropped out of college and showed up on their parents' doorstep holding a three-month-old son and a world of hurt inside. The Fletchers had rallied, as they always did, to care for their own. *Back to back to back.*

Luke admired his brother for stepping up, his parents for stepping in, but he'd never figured on following in Matt's footsteps. He'd never planned on dumping another grandchild on them to take care of. Mom and Dad weren't getting any younger. They had their own business to run, a bed-and-breakfast on North Carolina's Dare Island. Luke didn't like adding to their responsibilities.

But he didn't have a choice.

He was a Marine, first and foremost. Who was going to take care of Taylor while he was away?

And now that he was back, what the hell was he supposed to do? He didn't know the first thing about raising a kid on his own. Especially not a daughter.

The bus rumbled through the main gate, following the trucks that carried the gear.

Cody Burrows grinned. "My mom's going to flip. She and Dad drove all the way from Texas to meet the bus."

Luke had told his family not to come. It wasn't like he was returning from his first deployment. Anyway, his father, Tom, would be out on the boat with Matt. His mom was still recovering from a car accident a couple of months ago. The last thing they needed was to battle the traffic around base and then stand around for hours waiting for Luke to show up.

As for the kid, his daughter, Taylor . . . She barely knew him. She might not even recognize him. She definitely didn't need to take a day off from school to see him get off some damn bus.

So, yeah, better for everybody if Luke collected his Jeep from the Privately Owned Vehicle storage lot and drove his own ass to Dare Island.

He exhaled. And maybe sometime during the hour and a half it would take him to get home, he'd figure out what the hell he would say when he saw her again.

Small signs driven into the ground directed traffic to the unit's homecoming area. All around Luke, Marines shuffled their feet, shifting their weight, leaning forward in anticipation. The few who had been sleeping were nudged or kicked awake. Luke's heart sped up, just as if he had somebody waiting for him. Or was going into combat.

The brakes squealed. The bus gusted to a halt.

After the dust haze of Afghanistan, everything out the windows looked sharp and clear. Blue-and-white event tents and Porta Potties bordered the arrival area, full of balloons and handmade signs. And people. Families. Lots and lots of families eagerly awaiting the one hundred and seventy five men and women finally coming home.

Luke took his time getting off the bus. His men came first. Anyway, nobody was waiting for him.

There would be no formations or welcoming speeches today. The tents, the music, the balloon vendors, were there to entertain those waiting. For the Marines, this was Standard Operating Procedure. The brass recognized that those lucky enough to return from combat just wanted to find their families and go home.

Luke shouldered his bag and climbed down from the bus into the milling, calling, crying, kissing crowd.

"Do you see him?"

"Dad-deee . . ."

"Steven! Steve!"

He was bumped, jostled, and thanked by complete strangers. He stopped to shake hands with Cody Burrows's parents, saw Ortega stagger as his tiny girlfriend launched from four feet away into his arms.

"Welcome home, honey."

"There he is!"

Danny Hill's wife cried into his neck, their infant daughter crushed between them. Hill bowed his head against his wife's hair, his face raw with emotion.

Luke blinked and looked away from their private moment.

He had served seven deployments in ten years. He'd never sought—or missed—the distraction of a family. But watching the joyful reunions all around him, he felt . . . *Not sorry.*

Alone.

A familiar whistle pierced the hubbub.

Luke stiffened like a dog on point. "Dad?"

And heard it again, the same shrill note that always announced his father's return, whether it was from Beirut or the grocery store.

Luke pivoted, scanning the sea of people waving signs and flags and cell phones, searching for his father's face.

There. The red Vietnam vet ball cap, the shock of gray hair, the tanned face, and faded blue eyes. *Dad.*

And big brother Matt, tall and broad with big hands and weathered jeans, his normally serious face split in a wide smile.

Luke started forward, an answering grin working its way from deep inside. His gaze dropped. His throat constricted. *Was that . . . Between them . . .*

Tess Fletcher had always been short. Now, since the accident, she seemed to have shrunk even further. But her eyes were brilliant, her smile as warm as ever as she waved one hand above her head. The other rested on a cane. "Luke! Over here!"

He reached her in three strides. *"Mom."*

He put his arms around her slender shoulders, careful not to hug too hard. Small as she was, Tess had always been the family's rock. Their anchor. But now she felt so frail.

She squeezed back hard, her arms, her love, as strong as ever.

"Hey." Luke swallowed and drew back to smile into her face. A little paler than before, he thought. A little more lined. "You look great."

Tess ran her fingers through her short cap of dark red hair. "Do you like it?"

Luke blinked. "Sure." He wasn't sure. His mother's hair had been salt-and-pepper as far back as he could remember. "What does Dad think?"

"It's all good." Tom Fletcher winked. "I get to sleep with a redhead for the first time in forty years." He grabbed Luke in a one-armed hug. "Good to have you back, son."

Matt was next, dragging Luke into the family circle, gripping his hand, pounding his back. "You look like shit."

"You smell like fish."

They beamed at one another, reassured.

"I didn't expect to see you here," Luke said.

"Brought somebody else to see you, too." Matt reached down with one hand, nudging the somebody forward, producing her from behind his back like a magician with a reluctant rabbit. *Hey, presto, it's your daughter.*

Suspicious blue eyes regarded Luke from under the brim of a United States Marine Corps fatigue cap. His eyes, looking back at him from his daughter's thin, unsmiling face.

Emotion seized him by the throat. He couldn't speak. He couldn't grab her. From her point of view, they were practically strangers. She didn't, he remembered painfully, like to be touched.

But she was wearing his hat, the eight-pointed utility cover he'd given her before he went back to Afghanistan.

Maybe that meant something.

He observed the way she hung back, her skinny arms crossed behind her.

Yeah, and maybe not.

TAYLOR HELD HER breath, waiting to see what he would do. Luke, her . . . Well, her dad, even though she never called him that except sometimes in her head. Mostly, when she talked to him by Skype, she didn't call him anything at all. She didn't think he noticed.

All around them people were crying and kissing and stuff, babies bawling, fathers hugging their kids.

Taylor stuck out her chin. She wasn't going to cry. But she guessed it would be okay if he wanted to hug her.

He didn't.

Her stomach dropped in relief and disappointment.

He crouched down and looked her right in the eyes. His face was all serious. Taylor twisted her fingers together behind her back. When he first showed up on Grandma Jo's porch, tall and strong in his uniform, she'd felt a rush of relief so intense she'd almost cried. *Dad to the rescue.* And he *had* rescued her.

But then he'd gone away again.

Maybe he wasn't glad to see her. She wished, too late, that she had listened to Aunt Meg this morning and put on her new clothes, the ones they bought for her to wear to court.

Right. Like some dumb purple sweater would make him like her.

She scowled harder, swallowing the lump in her throat.

"Hey, kid," he said like he couldn't remember her name.

"Hi." *Dad.*

He tapped the brim of her hat with one finger, the way Uncle Matt did sometimes. The familiar gesture made her feel better. "Thanks for taking care of my cover."

Taylor's cheeks got hot. She hadn't let the hat out of her sight since he gave it to her. She even slept in it sometimes.

But that would be a loser thing to say. She didn't want him to think she was a baby. She jerked a shoulder instead. *No problem.* "Do you . . . do you want it back now?"

"Nah. You keep it." The corners of his mouth curled up, just a little. His big hand dropped on top of her head. He gave her a quick and careless rub, like she gave the dog at home sometimes, knocking the hat sideways, messing up her hair. The knot in her stomach eased. "It looks good on you."

Cautiously, she allowed herself to smile back.

Three

ALL THE VOICES in Kate's head were squawking as she sped across the bridge to Dare Island in her little red Mini Cooper.

Jesus, Kate, stop overreacting. That was her father.

I don't think it's wise for you to get too close. That was her mother.

It's important for you to accept that not everything is your responsibility. That was her therapist.

Kate turned up the volume on the radio to drown them out. Christmas music. She sighed. If you were a family lawyer, Christmas was not the easiest time of year. If you were also the adult child of an alcoholic . . . Well. You already knew that many families cracked under the expectations and disappointments of the holidays. Too much drinking. Too much stress.

Too many bad memories. She gulped in the fresh air rushing through her window. At least it was a nice day for a drive. Living above her office, walking to the courthouse, she didn't have many opportunities to get away. The waves on the Intercostal Waterway sparkled. The December sun shone. The jumble of shops along the Dare Island waterfront looked quite pretty with their lighted wreaths and garlands. The squat brick police-and-fire station sported a big red bow.

The buildings thinned out, the tourist shops and sidewalked streets replaced by cottages and then by oaks and pine.

Her errand wouldn't take more than ten minutes, Kate promised herself. Twenty, tops. The voices could hardly object to that.

And then she'd have another pleasant forty-minute drive back to Beaufort. Maybe she'd stop for Chinese on her way home to celebrate her successful day in court. *Because nothing says "victory" like eating takeout in front of* The Bachelorette. Just for a moment, Kate let herself imagine what it would be like to have someone waiting for her at home, someone to rub her feet or listen or laugh with. But the truth was she had no idea what that would be like.

She made the turn, peering for an inn sign.

The Pirates' Rest rose through the trees, perfect as a postcard. In Kate's experience, very little in life lived up to its advertising. But the inn looked remarkably like the photos on its website. Deep eaves protected the wraparound porch of the two-and-a-half-story house. Leaded glass windows reflected back the sun. A big American flag hung from the porch. A smaller one decorated the mailbox. Despite the patriotic-themed decorations—*more Fourth of July than Christmas*—the bed-and-breakfast looked elegant, comfortable, and solid.

Her heart tugged hard. She hadn't taken a real vacation in years. The whole concept of a B and B, of sharing someone else's home, of making normal conversation with complete strangers over breakfast, made her break into a sweat.

But even she could appreciate the care that had gone into the freshly painted green-and-white trim and edged lawn. Pink camellias and planters of cold-blooming pansies brightened the winter-browned garden. If she *were* going away for a weekend, if she bought into that white-picket-fence fantasy of home, she might actually want to stay here.

She parked by the front gate. Plenty of room, she noted. She imagined the Fletchers didn't get many guests midweek in the off-season.

Grabbing her briefcase from the passenger seat, she got out of the car, already regretting the impulse that had driven her here. She should have called. Again. Or waited until tomorrow. There was absolutely no reason to interrupt the Fletchers' evening and risk her own careful emotional detachment with a personal visit.

Except that for the past five years, she'd watched Taylor grow in the school portraits framed on Dawn's desk.

She'd seen Taylor walk to her temporary custody hearing like a prisoner marching to her execution.

She'd held those bird-wing shoulders between her hands and promised Taylor that she would be fine. As long as she was honest about her feelings.

Kind of a joke, coming from Kate. But it had worked, hadn't it?

Kate rang the doorbell, two deep chimes.

A dog barked, and she stiffened. She was not a dog person. But having come this far, she certainly wasn't going to turn back now.

"Fezzik, stay," a deep voice commanded from inside.

The door cracked open, and Luke Fletcher stood on the threshold, a big black dog beside him and a bottle of beer in his hand.

Kate's heart bumped. She took a half step back from the dog and the man. "You're here," she said stupidly.

His brows rose, but he nodded. "Got back today."

He still wore the desert camouflage pants of the Marine utility uniform, as if he were on base or in transit. He'd removed his outer shirt, revealing an olive green T-shirt that clung to the planes of his chest, the ridges of his belly. He looked lanky, lean, and dangerous.

Standing in her court-appropriate navy suit and pumps, she felt overdressed and at a distinct disadvantage.

The door swung wider to admit her.

Kate hesitated.

The man glanced down at the dog beside him. "It's all right. He's trained not to bite visitors." He glanced up, his lips curving in a slow, devastating smile. "So am I."

Kate exhaled. "I didn't expect to see you."

He tipped back his beer, regarding her over the bottle, his eyes joltingly vivid in his hard, tanned face. "I wasn't expecting you, either." The smile faded. "What's wrong?"

She ignored the pang in her chest. Naturally he associated her with bad news. Like a casualty assistance officer coming to the door. *I regret to inform you . . .*

"I came . . ." It wasn't just the color of those eyes, piercing blue, that tangled her tongue. It was the way he looked at her, completely focused. Intense. "I tried to call your parents."

He nodded once, stone-faced now. Total Marine. She recognized the look from her childhood. "They're in the kitchen. Want to tell me what this is about?"

She could. He was Taylor's father. Now that he was home, she really should share her news with Luke rather than his parents.

But not all at once. And not on the front porch. "Is there someplace we can talk?"

"Sure. This way." And before she could object or explain, he turned and disappeared into the shadows of the hall, leaving the door open behind him.

The dog padded after him, its nails clicking as it crossed from the faded antique rug to the hardwood floor.

Leaving her no choice but to follow them into the house. Not the alpha dog, obviously. Somewhere at the back of the pack.

The entry hall of the Pirates' Rest was warm with woodwork and rich with color. A square, spindled staircase wrapped around a built-in bench. Garland decorated the bannister, filling the air with pine. A banner draped the second-floor landing.

WELCOME HOME.

Got back today, he'd said.

Kate winced. Homecomings in her parents' house had rarely been joyous. That didn't mean she should spoil his. "I'm sorry. I can come back another time."

"You're here," Luke said over his shoulder. He pushed open the door at the end of the hall. "You might as well say what you came to say."

And go. Her mind supplied the words he was too polite to say. He must be looking forward to time with his family. He could hardly welcome a visit from his baby mama's mainland lawyer on his first night home.

Kate squared her shoulders. She owed it to Taylor—she owed it to Dawn—to finish what she started. She walked past Luke's outstretched arm, his stretched-out T-shirt, his muscled chest.

And stopped dead on the threshold.

The kitchen was full of people. Family. Fletchers. She recognized the broad-shouldered man with the big hands and quiet eyes as Luke's brother, Matt, the charter boat captain. The petite brunette in designer jeans and boots was their sister, Meg.

All of them subtly united, looking at her with nearly identical blue eyes and identical expressions of surprise.

She felt like a crasher in a Norman Rockwell painting.

"Luke? Is everything all right?" asked the thin, auburn-haired woman at the head of the table.

"Everything's fine. This is Kay Dolan," Luke said. "My mother, Tess."

Kate hid her wince. "Kate. We spoke on the phone."

The older woman's smile crinkled the corners of her eyes. "Dawn's lawyer friend. It's nice to finally meet you."

"You, too. Please don't get up," Kate said, observing the cane resting against the arm of Tess's chair.

"My father, Tom," Luke said, indicating the spare, gray-haired man beside Tess.

"We've met. Hi, Mr. Fletcher."

Luke's sister Meg stepped forward. "Kate let us wait in her office the day we went to court. Thanks for that, by the way." She smiled at Kate, guarded but polite.

Meg was in PR, Kate remembered. She must be used to putting a good face on things.

"You're welcome," Kate said.

Okay, this was awkward. Everyone was still staring, including a tall, handsome teen with a sandy mop of hair, and two adults Kate had never laid eyes on before, a pretty blonde next to Matt and a dark-haired man with Meg. Also tall, tanned, and beautiful, dressed with a casual ease that spoke of money and privilege.

With an effort, Kate restrained herself from fingering the scar on her cheek.

Taylor curled in a chair between her uncle Matt and the blonde.

Kate smiled. "Hi, Taylor."

She didn't expect a response. She was just "Mommy's boss" to Taylor, just another grown-up on the periphery of her life. The last time they'd met, outside the courthouse, had hardly been a pleasant occasion.

But Taylor smiled, cautiously. "Hi."

The table in front of her was littered with bottles of beer and half-full glasses, bowls of chips and dip, platters of cheese and meat and olives.

A real family party.

Kate's stomach sank. Coming here had been a mistake. She should have waited. Should have called again.

Never get personally involved.

The teenager reached over Taylor's shoulder for a handful of chips, knocking her camouflage cap askew. She made a grab for the hat, twisting in her chair to make a face at him. He grinned. Kate watched Taylor's smile melt into unguarded adoration.

"My son, Josh," Matt said.

The boy flashed the grin in Kate's direction. "Hey."

She smiled helplessly back, as charmed as the child.

"Miss Dolan." Matt's voice was deep and cool. His arm rested protectively along the back of Taylor's chair. "What can we do for you?"

Meaning, *What are you doing here?*

Good question, Kate thought.

The blonde laid her hand on his arm in a silent gesture of support. The fiancée, Kate thought. She'd heard Luke's brother was recently engaged. They looked like a couple, like a unit, with the child between them. Kate wondered if that would change now that Luke was home.

"Sam Grady." The guy with Meg introduced himself with a smile. His bottle green eyes held a hint of sympathy. "Can I get you something? A drink?"

Kate pulled herself together. She didn't need his drink or his sympathy. "I'm fine, thanks. I didn't mean to interrupt your dinner," she said to Tess.

The teenager laughed. "This isn't dinner. This is a snack."

"But . . ."

"We're cooking ribs tonight," Tess said.

Kate glanced at Matt, the fisherman. *Not seafood?*

Luke's eyes gleamed in unexpected understanding. "No pork in Muslim countries," he explained. "Or beer." He raised his bottle in salute. "Want one?"

"Or there's tea," Tess offered.

Sweet tea, the wine of the South.

Their hospitality, after she'd shown up like ants at a picnic, made Kate feel more like an intruder than ever. She shouldn't have come. She didn't belong here. She never belonged. But she had to get through her errand.

Next to her uncle, Taylor snuck a chicken wing off her plate to give to the dog and then reached for the chips. Kate grimaced. Shouldn't she wash her hands? But the child was obviously happy, smiling, one of the family. After her mother's death, Taylor needed love, warmth, and support. It was clear the Fletchers gave her all that in abundance.

"No. Thank you." She cleared her throat, meeting Luke's gaze. "I was hoping to speak with you alone."

His blue eyes narrowed. He nodded slowly. "Sure. Out on the deck."

"Anything you can say to him you can say to us," Meg said. "We're family."

"What's wrong?" Tess asked.

The question hung in the air like a whiff of something burning, spoiling the mouth-watering scent of ribs in the oven.

Taylor sat very still, her eyes dark as bruises in her thin face.

Kate's gaze went from face to face, a knot tightening in her stomach. The Fletchers didn't dislike her. But they had clearly closed ranks in the face of bad news.

And there was no way to pretend this was anything but bad news.

Matt pushed back his chair, the sound scraping against the sudden silence.

"It's okay." Tom spoke from his position at the head of the table. "Luke'll handle it."

Meg scowled. But no one spoke, no one interfered as Luke tugged open the back door and gestured for Kate to precede him outside.

She walked around the table and through the silent kitchen, feeling the Fletchers' collected attention like a knife between her shoulder blades.

THE EVENING SKY looked warm, all fluffy pink clouds and golden haze, but a cool, damp breeze blew off the sea and rose from the sound, carrying the tang of water. The smell of home.

Luke held on to his beer. Not because he needed the alcohol, but because he wanted the prop. Something to do with his hands, some action to combat the adrenaline surge in his blood. In spite of the peaceful setting, he felt jazzed, his palms damp, all his senses on alert. *Outside the wire, facing the enemy.*

Luke'll handle it, his father had said.

So he would.

Even if he didn't have a fricking clue what to say or do next.

He watched Kate Dolan's butt as she walked past him in her neat navy suit, her sensible heels clacking on the wood deck like gunfire. He'd handle her, too, given a little encouragement.

He shook his head. Obviously, he'd spent too long in Burqa Land. He was not hitting on his dead ex-girlfriend's lawyer. Even if she did have great legs. And—despite the stick up her butt—a really nice ass. Hard not to notice that.

She hugged her arms across her body, as if the chill had penetrated the blue jacket she wore like body armor. "It's nice out here."

He breathed in the smells of salt, sea grass, and pine. Took a pull of his beer, as if he could permanently wash away the dust of Afghanistan. "Yeah."

She turned to face him, the sun behind her firing her curly coppery hair to gold. "Quiet," she offered.

"No snipers," he said.

She looked at him, startled.

Ah, shit. "You didn't come here to talk about the weather," he said, covering. "Or the view."

"Are you all right?" she asked.

He was jet-lagged and exhausted. But at least he was all here. Ten fingers, ten toes. No right to complain. "Fine."

Her gaze searched his face, uncomfortably perceptive. What color were her eyes? Blue? Green? With the light behind her, it was hard to tell. "Because we can do this another time."

"You must have thought it was urgent," he pointed out. "Or you wouldn't have driven out here."

She took a deep breath that expanded her chest, parting the lapels of her jacket. She wore some kind of lace thing under it, and a thin gold chain that dipped between her breasts and caught the light. *Nice.* "I had the evening free."

"Lucky for me," he drawled.

Under her makeup, she flushed to the roots of her hair like only a true redhead could. Which set off another line of speculation he had no business pursuing.

"I received an e-mail today from a colleague. A friend, Alisha Douglas," she said, still picking her words like each one cost a hundred bucks. He forced himself to focus on what she was saying instead of the fine glint of metal on her skin or the color of her hair. "She works for the county department of social services."

The short hairs raised on the back of Luke's neck. "Okay," he said cautiously.

"She wanted to know how to reach you. I told her you were expected home soon."

"Not expected. Home." Luke leaned against the deck rail, affecting a casualness he did not feel. "What does she want?"

Her brows twitched together. "She's sending you a letter that will explain. Basically, she wants to meet with you, with all of you, to assess Taylor's situation."

She sounded like a medic, wrapping bad news in big words and a soft tone to lessen the blow. "Her situation is her mother's dead. She lives with me."

"Pending her permanent placement. Unfortunately, Alisha's office received a complaint about your ability to care for Taylor."

His tired brain struggled to keep up. "What do you mean, a complaint? Who complained?"

"Alisha couldn't tell me. Reports to social services are confidential." She hesitated. Moistened her lips. "However, Child Protective Services is often called in custody cases."

"Wait." His tired brain struggled to keep up. "You're saying the *Simpsons* called social services?"

"Sadly, not everyone makes reports due to real concerns for the well-being of a child. Ernie and Jolene may be retaliating because their motion for temporary custody failed in court. Or they may believe that accusing you of neglect will help them get permanent custody."

It took a moment for him to process what she was saying. For outrage to ignite. "Are you fucking kidding me?"

She didn't flinch. "It's a common legal strategy."

"It's bullshit."

"Yes." That one word, short and uncompromising, made him feel better than any amount of soothing. "Alisha is certainly prepared to keep an open mind. But she's concerned because your family hasn't let Taylor have any contact with the Simpsons."

Instant denial seized him. He shook his head. "My parents wouldn't do that."

"The Simpsons kept a log. Unreturned phone calls, times Taylor was 'unavailable' to speak with them."

He struggled to make sense of the unthinkable over the rising buzz of anger in his head. "They want to see the kid more often, let them call me." Right now he'd rather tell them to pound sand, but . . . "They don't need to get a damn social worker involved."

"Unfortunately, once an allegation is made, social services is required to respond."

"What allegation, for Christ's sake?"

She shrugged. The angrier he got, the cooler and calmer she became. "I haven't seen the intake report. Alisha only contacted me because she knew Dawn worked in my office."

"Did you tell her Dawn wanted the kid to be with me?"

Kate gave a little nod. "I did. I also reminded her that the Simpsons had already challenged custody after your mother's accident and that the judge at the temporary hearing ruled it was in Taylor's best interests to remain with your family."

"Right. Thanks," he said belatedly.

She was not the enemy, he told himself. She'd come here tonight as an ally to warn him. To help. He'd worked with allies before in Iraq and Afghanistan. He could trust her . . . at least until her own self-interest was threatened. "So now what?"

"Alisha will contact you to set up a time for a home visit. She'll want to talk to Taylor. To everyone. There's another minor child in the household?"

His blood went from hot to cold faster than the desert at night. "You mean, Josh?"

"That's your nephew? He lives with you?"

"Out back," Luke said reluctantly. "My brother has a cottage."

"She'll need to speak with them as well."

"*Fuck*." He set down his bottle, reached for his cigarettes. He needed time. He needed . . . "Mind if I smoke?"

Her nostrils pinched together. "Not at all."

He lit up, releasing a long white plume into the cool December air. Met her eyes over the curl of smoke. "I'm quitting," he said. He quit after every deployment.

"That would be wise," she said.

"You worried about my health? Or Taylor's?"

"I'm concerned about your home assessment. Your hearing date is already set. Alisha is motivated to resolve this complaint as quickly as possible. It's important that she likes you. There's no reason she *won't* like you. But you have to be absolutely cooperative. You need to answer everything she asks, even questions you think are none of her business."

He stared at her, appalled. Speechless.

Kate met his gaze, her expression softening. "I'm sorry. I know this is a lot to hit you with your first night home. I'm just trying to prepare you."

"Yeah." He closed his eyes a moment, willing away the headache throbbing against his temples. "Thanks a lot."

HE LOOKED TIRED, Kate thought with a liquid tug of sympathy. His Captain America face was drawn, his jaw roughened by stubble, his eyes bruised with exhaustion.

Thirty hours from Kandahar to Lejeune, he'd told her when she first called to inform him of Dawn's death.

But he came.

Even when Kate had given him reasons not to, he'd come home for Taylor. She still didn't know why Dawn never told him he was a father. But he was no deadbeat dad.

She risked a touch on his forearm. His skin, bronzed by the desert sun, felt very warm under her fingertips. He opened his eyes, startlingly blue, and her nerves jumped, low and quick in her stomach.

Kate swallowed. She was *not* going to be flustered, damn it. This was about Taylor. She would not be distracted from her duty by an inconvenient hormone surge. "Look, the Simpsons' challenge to the temporary custody order failed. It's obvious that you provided appropriate care for Taylor while you were overseas."

"My family did."

"And they did a wonderful job. Taylor's clearly adjusting. In most circumstances, absent a finding of unfitness, you would be entitled to the care and custody of your child. But the Simpsons will argue that you haven't established a parental relationship with Taylor."

"I'm her father."

Kate suppressed a sigh. "A continuous, meaningful relationship," she said. "You need to prove that you maintained contact."

"I called." His tone was defensive. "Skyped."

"That's good," she said encouragingly. She hesitated. "I don't suppose you kept a phone log?"

"Hell, no."

"No." *Of course not.* She'd learned that good families, normal people, didn't obsess over documenting every interaction, no matter how small. "Well, if you have anything else—doctors' bills, receipts for clothing purchases . . ."

"I don't keep track of every dime I spend on the kid. She's my daughter, not a tax deduction."

Kate sympathized with his frustration. But she worked with these cases every day. Good intentions weren't enough. They needed proof to back them up in court. Her job was to explain the law, to guide her bewildered and defensive clients through the seemingly senseless system.

"I'm simply saying a judge will look for evidence that you can provide for Taylor. Her physical needs. Her medical care. Her emotional well-being."

"I can take care of her."

"Now," she said. "What happens when you're deployed again?"

He glared. "What do you want from me?"

She wanted him to understand. She was trying to *help*. "This isn't about what I want. It's about what Taylor needs. What are your plans for the future?"

"Well," he drawled, "I was going to have another beer. And then I thought I'd take a whole night off to visit with my family. Get to know my daughter. Do I need to write that down for the judge?"

Her cheeks burned.

This is what came of getting personally involved. Of reacting emotionally, impulsively, instead of thinking things through. Naturally, he resented her interference.

"I'm sorry," she apologized stiffly. "Sometimes I get a little . . ."

Judgmental, one ex-boyfriend had accused.

Controlling, her therapist had said.

"Focused on the mission," Luke supplied.

She blinked in surprised gratitude. "That's a nice way of putting it."

Anyway, it beat Will Brown's *Interfering bitch*.

Luke rolled his bottle between his hands. "Look, I get that you're trying to help. I appreciate you driving out here to give us the heads-up on this social services thing. I'll make the appointment with your friend, I'll cooperate my ass off with her questions. But the rest of it . . . We'll make it work. You said yourself that Taylor's adjusting. You just don't understand how it is in a military family."

"I understand very well."

"You think you do. But you only see the ones that don't make it. It's different from the inside."

"Not in my experience."

"Let me guess." Those sharp blue eyes narrowed on her face. "Your ex-husband's a Marine."

Kate tugged on her jacket, pulling it around her like armor. "My father."

Oh, hell. She hadn't meant to say that. She didn't talk about her family. Habit and shame kept her silent. She'd grown up, moved out, moved on. But her father still loomed in her memory, a shadow figure between them.

"Would I know him?"

God, she hoped not.

"Colonel Roger Dolan," she said. Square-jawed, close-shaved, meticulously pressed and polished. "He died two years ago."

Luke shook his head. "Nope. Sorry."

"Don't be."

Their relationship was over long before he died.

A midlevel bureaucrat, Colonel Dolan had never received the respect or recognition he felt he deserved. But he'd commanded fear from his men and wife and daughter. *Obedience is required in a war zone*, he insisted. And he'd made home a war zone.

His discipline was absolute and arbitrary. His professional frustration found relief in drinking and outlet in a senseless, ceaseless battery of orders, inspections, and foam-flecked, screaming rages on the parade ground and at home.

As a child, Kate had tried desperately to please him. But no matter how clean she kept the house or how well she did in school, nothing was good enough. *She* was not good enough. She could not make up for her father's career disappointments. She could not fix his drinking.

She could not wait to get away.

And she never went back.

She fought a shiver.

Luke watched her, his blue eyes unreadable in the twilight. What did he see? How much had she betrayed?

"You want to reconsider that drink now?" he asked.

She laughed, relieved because he was kidding. Not that she would ever, under any circumstances, drink as a response to stress. But he was dropping the subject, and that was good. "No, thanks. I really should get going."

"You're welcome to stay. There's plenty of food."

For a moment, she was tempted. Not just by the tantalizing aroma of slow-cooked ribs, but by the warmth of a real family. By the simmering heat in Luke's eyes.

She shook her head. She wasn't good in personal, social interactions. She had no guide for normal behavior. And she hated to guess. "I shouldn't intrude."

"Bit late for that," he said. "For both of us."

Four

LUKE SAW THE light under Taylor's door as he went up the stairs.

She has nightmares, his mother said.

Poor kid. Luke could sympathize. He couldn't remember the last time he'd had a good night's sleep. Two A.M., four A.M., regular as clockwork, he woke with a racing heart and gritty eyes and a stale taste on his tongue. The Corps trained you to kill, but nobody trained you how to deal with it. In your dreams, you never remembered the ones you saved, only the ones who died.

He wondered what Taylor dreamed about. Her mother, probably.

Hell.

He hesitated outside her door, tension knotting his muscles. Should he knock? It didn't seem right that there were at least three adults downstairs who knew more about putting his daughter to bed than he did. Kate's words popped into mind. *Now that you're back, the Simpsons will argue that you don't have a relationship with Taylor. A continuous, meaningful relationship.*

In the short time he'd been home before, they hadn't had the chance to establish a routine. Taylor hadn't seemed to need anything from him then except to be left alone.

He didn't have a clue what she needed from him now.

He took a deep breath and rapped softly on the door before opening it.

A flurry of movement exploded from the bed before Taylor flopped back against her pillows, clutching her covers to her chest like she was hiding something. *What?* Christ, she was only ten. What did she have to hide?

Her face was all red, her blond hair sticking up all over her head like corn silk. His desert-colored utility cap rested on the pillow by her head. Luke's heart turned over helplessly in his chest.

Tucking his hands into his pockets, he wandered into the room. Fezzik looked up with a doggy grin, thumping his tail against the braided rug. So that explained the sudden movement from the bed. The dog probably slept with her. Must take up half the mattress.

He rubbed Fezzik's head and then straightened. "Hey."

Taylor watched him with wary, narrowed blue eyes. "Hi."

This close, he could see the cords trailing from her ears. An iPod. He hadn't given her an iPod, he thought with a twinge of guilt. He wondered who had.

"What are you listening to?"

She pulled out one ear bud. "Music."

He waited, but apparently her answer had exhausted that topic. He glanced around the room. "You all settled in here?"

She nodded.

The room, his mom's old sewing room, was as neat as a soldier's tent. No posters on the walls. No stuffed animals. No dolls. Maybe she was too old for dolls, he didn't know. No family pictures. Luke frowned. Every guy he served with carried a photo of somebody. His mom had pictures of the three of them—Matt, Meg, Luke—scattered around the house. Taylor ought to have a picture of her mother. Still, there was a stack of school books on the desk, a rocking chair in the corner, a collection of shells spaced out along the windowsill. Signs, he hoped, that the kid was making herself at home.

A judge will look for evidence that you can provide for Taylor, Kate Dolan reminded him earnestly. *Her physical needs. Her medical care. Her emotional well-being.*

"Do you need anything?" he asked, and he wasn't just talking about a drink of water.

Taylor shook her head.

"Okay." He took his hands out of his pockets. Nothing else he could do tonight.

She looked so little against the pillows of the bed. Was he supposed to tuck her in or something? Matt would know. He should have asked Matt.

"Well . . ." Luke cleared his throat. "Good night."

She slumped deeper under the covers. "'Night."

Dismissed. Relieved, he shoved his hands back into his pockets and turned toward the door.

"Do I have to move now?" a small voice asked behind him.

He froze. Shit, oh, shit. He did *not* want to get into this conversation on his first night home.

We'll make it work, he'd told Kate. *You don't understand how it is in a military family.*

He did. He'd moved four times before he was eight years old. Somehow his mom had held them all together, making each reassignment seem like an adventure. With Matt watching out for him, with Meg charging ahead, Luke had never felt lost or alone. *Back to back to back.* The rallying cry of his childhood.

And then Dad retired, and his parents bought the Pirates' Rest, and the island became home. For most of his childhood, Luke had run as wild as the island ponies, protected and free.

He'd figured it would be the same for Taylor.

But maybe he'd taken too much for granted. Maybe the Simpsons were right. In four short months, the kid had lost her mom and relocated twice. Maybe she wanted it all back—her old friends, her old school. Her old life.

Wouldn't that be a kick in the teeth.

Slowly, he turned. "Do you want to move?"

He watched—shocked, terrified—as tears sprang to her eyes. "Uncle Matt said I could stay."

"Okay. Jesus. Don't cry."

Her tears panicked him. Marines did not cry. And if they heard her downstairs, his family would never let him hear the end of it. Major Fatherhood Fail, his first night home.

She sniffed mightily. "You're not supposed to swear."

Shaken, he groped for his bandanna. "Yeah, you're right. You don't have to . . . You're not going anywhere, okay? We'll figure this out." *Together. Somehow.*

She knuckled her eyes in a gesture that tore his heart.

"Here." He thrust the bandanna at her and dropped into the rocker while Taylor mopped her eyes and blew her nose. His own throat constricted. Burned. He cleared it noisily. "You okay?"

Her head wobbled up and down.

"Good. That's, uh . . . good." *Okay, dumbass, make this right.* He leaned forward, elbows on knees, thinking fast, going with his gut. "Here's the deal. I've got thirty days' leave coming before I have to go anywhere." After that, he probably had another three months, training, before he deployed again. But that was a discussion for another day. "I want to be with you. You could stay in your room here, but a month's too long for me to be bunking in a guest room. So I figure I'll talk to Grandma and Grandpa about renting the other cottage out back. For the two of us."

Taylor nodded, more decisively this time. "Like Matt and Josh."

He released his breath in relief. "Yeah." His parents would probably be glad to have the rent in the off-season. "Everybody will still be around, to take care of you and stuff, but we'll have our own space."

And maybe having a place of their own would be enough to convince social services that he and Taylor were a family.

Maybe it would even convince them.

His daughter was regarding him with the abused expression of a dog who's learned *Want to go for a ride?* was code for a trip to the vet. "What if we have to leave? Like, if the cottage is rented to guests or something?"

Man, she didn't trust anybody. That seemed like an advanced worry for a ten-year-old, but what did he know about kids?

"Then I'll shift for a couple of nights, sleep on the boat or your uncle Matt's couch, and you can have your old room here."

Taylor's face scrunched as she considered. "Could Fezzik come, too?" she asked at last.

At the sound of his name, the big shepherd mix raised his head from his big paws, his dark eyes fixing on her face.

"We'll see." Luke gave the dog another quick, careless rub, thinking of his surprise. "Fezzik is Uncle Matt's dog."

"Uncle Matt says Fezzik is the family dog."

For a guy who didn't say much, Luke thought, Matt sure had been running his mouth a lot. "Sure. Yeah. But it could be cool to have your own dog."

"Or a cat," Taylor said, with a look through her eyelashes.

No. Hell, no. His plans did not include a cat. "A dog," Luke said. If everything worked out the way it was supposed to. "Maybe a puppy."

He'd hoped—maybe he'd counted on—her being delighted. Everybody said she loved the dog, slept with him every night. Luke had figured he had this one chance to be a hero, to get this one thing right.

Her face took on the mulish expression he saw sometimes in his own mirror. "A cat would be better."

"No cat," Luke said. He couldn't take care of her and the dog and a cat, too.

She nodded, not delighted, not disappointed, just . . . resigned. Like she was used to not getting what she wanted. Shit.

"Sorry," he said, meaning it.

She jerked one shoulder. "'S okay," she said, when it was obvious things were not okay, that something was wrong.

Luke frowned. "It's not that I don't like cats. It's just . . ."

"You're allergic," Taylor said in a tone of voice that suggested she'd heard that excuse before.

"No," Luke said, surprised. *Let it go. Go to bed. Get out of the kill zone.* But what came out of his mouth was, "Why would you say I was allergic?"

Another shrug. "That's what Grandma Jolene always said. Before. When I asked her."

"You asked your grandmother for a cat," Luke said, feeling his way.

"I told her I wanted *my* cat. Snowball. But Grandma Jo said we couldn't keep her because of her allergies."

"You have a cat." First he'd heard about it. He wondered if Matt knew.

Her head jerked. *Yes.*

He was groping, trying not to blunder in the dark. He needed twelve hours' sleep and maybe one less beer. "So, where is it?"

Her shoulders hunched. "I don't know."

"Well, who's taking care of it?"

"I don't *know.* Grandma Jo said I couldn't bring her with me. She said Snowball could take care of herself. But Snowball is an inside cat. She doesn't know how to climb trees." Taylor's voice rose, the trickle of words churning into a flood. He was drowning here. "She could be run over by a car. Or eaten by a dog." Fezzik lurched to all fours, responding to the word or her tears. "She's proba- bly . . ." Taylor broke off.

Dead, Luke thought bleakly. Like her mother. This was the burden his daughter had been carrying alone.

"Hunting," he said. "She's probably hunting for food."

Fezzik nudged Taylor's hand as it lay on the covers. She stroked the dog's big head.

Even the dog was better at comfort than he was. Luke cleared his throat. "Cats are tough. Hell, we had cats in Afghanistan could take down . . ." *Rats three times their size.* Not a comforting thought to send with her into sleep. "Cats are good at surviving," he said instead.

Taylor blinked. "But she's all alone."

Ah, Jesus. "It's okay," Luke said. "Everything's going to be fine. I'll take care of it."

Those blue, tear-sheened eyes fixed on him. "How?"

He had no idea.

"I'll figure it out," he said.

LUKE WAS USED to going door-to-door in hostile territory. He couldn't let a little thing like the Simpsons reporting him to Child Protective Services discourage him from his current mission. At least they weren't going to shoot him through the door.

Probably.

He'd been to their house before, when he came to collect Taylor three months ago. Forty years ago, in his parents' day, this town had a textile plant and a sign out on the highway: THE KKK WELCOMES YOU TO TWISTED CREEK. But the town had died along with the factory. Here and there the residents had tried to get into the Christmas spirit with plastic Santas and strings of Christmas lights, but the streets were pocked with barred and empty storefronts, and the sidewalks were cracked.

Ernie and Jolene lived in a cinderblock bungalow with a detached shed near the end of a block. Luke parked his Jeep, collected from the storage lot that morning, and climbed the steps. The sound of the TV inside almost covered his knock. The sagging porch held a mildewed couch, a broken fan, and a black plastic trash bag, but he could smell ammonia, as if someone had recently tried to clean something.

The limp curtains in the front window fluttered.

Dawn's mother, Jolene, opened the door, a big woman built like a biscuit with large, white arms and a doughy face and pale, protruding eyes. "You. What are you doing here?"

Be professional, be polite. "Hi, Mrs. Simpson. I want to talk to you about Taylor."

"Unless you're bringing Taylor back, I got nothing to say to you. You can talk to our lawyer." She started to close the door. Luke stuck his foot in the way.

"Jolly, who is it?" Ernie Simpson called from inside.

Jolly?

Luke raised his voice over the noise from the TV. "It's Luke Fletcher, Mr. Simpson. I was hoping you could tell me what happened to Taylor's cat after Taylor came to live with you."

Jolene crossed her pillowy arms across her massive bosom, blocking his view inside. "I don't know. We couldn't have it here. I have allergies."

"So you took the cat to a shelter?"

"And have them put it down?" She looked genuinely shocked by the suggestion. "I couldn't do that. It would have broke poor Taylor's heart."

So they'd abandoned the cat instead. Thinking of the strays he'd known, Luke thought it was probably the cruelest thing they could have done, both for the pet and Taylor.

Ernie came up behind his wife, as brown and thin as she was pale and round, with dark wisps of hair on his head and chin. His look of bleary suspicion hadn't changed in ten years, as if Luke was still a high school boy up to no good with his daughter.

Luke suppressed a twinge of guilt. Ernie Simpson had been right about him back then. But times had changed. *He* had changed. "Hi, Mr. Simpson."

"What do you want?"

"Do you have a minute? I wanted to talk to you about Taylor."

"I'll tell you what about Taylor," Jolene said, her round face set. "That little girl don't belong to you. She belongs with us. She knows us. It's not right for you to come here and take her away from her own family."

"I'm her family, too. I'm her father."

"So you say."

Luke gritted his teeth. "It's what Dawn said. And I had a paternity test."

"Then how come Dawn never told you she had a little girl?" Jolene's watery eyes glittered with tears or anger. "How come you never sent a dime while she was alive? It's only now she's gone that you show up, looking for what you can get."

"All I want is a picture," Luke said.

He felt a tickle on the back of his neck like the crawl of sweat or a spider and turned.

Kevin, the Simpsons' son, sauntered up the walk from the shed. Dawn's brother was Meg's age—five years older than Luke—tall and rake-thin like his father, with his mother's pale eyes and a couple of tattoos that would earn him a reprimand in the Corps—a pair of SS bolts on his neck, a messy half sleeve on one arm. A real badass wannabe. When the other island kids had been drinking their daddies' beer under the pier, Kevin had been into the hard stuff. For an extra couple bucks, he'd buy the younger kids a bottle or some weed and drink or smoke it with them. Luke had bought some Old Crow off him once, but he'd had no desire to repeat the experience. Especially not after Matt caught him puking in the bushes.

"What the fuck is he doing here?" Kevin asked.

"I'm here to see your parents," Luke said.

"Well, they don't want to see you."

"That's fine," Luke said. "I just came to get a picture of Dawn."

"You fucked my sister. You're not getting fuck from us."

Luke stepped back (*Move away from your attacker. Distance is your friend.*), angling his body so he could talk to the elder Simpsons and still keep Kevin in sight. "I just want a photo."

Jolene fixed him with her pale, watery eyes. "You never

came around to see her while she was alive. What do you care what she looked like now she's dead?"

Luke winced. Hard to argue with that. "It's not for me. It's for Taylor."

Ernie scratched his beard. "I guess that would be—"

"Taylor wants to see pictures of her mama, she can come here," Kevin said.

"That's not up to you," Luke said.

"I'm her uncle."

That spider sense crawled again on the back of Luke's neck. "You don't live here," Luke said.

Kevin smiled. Not a good look for him, since his teeth were stained from years of tobacco use or meth. "Nah. I just come by."

Yeah. When his utilities were cut off, Luke guessed. Or when he needed groceries.

But who was Luke to judge? He was living in his parents' back yard.

"All I want is a picture of her mother to give to Taylor."

"I *said*, we got nothing for you," Kevin said. "Get out."

Luke's jaw bunched in frustration. "Look, I don't want any trouble." Getting in a brawl with a civilian wasn't going to help him. Not with the social services investigation pending.

"Then you'd best leave," Ernie said. "Sorry, boy."

"Mrs. Simpson." Luke appealed to Dawn's mother. "Jolene—"

She stuck out her round, quivering chin, siding with her son. "You heard Kevin. You've taken everything else from us. We're not giving you a damn thing."

KATE HAD BEEN at her desk since early morning, answering phone calls, responding to e-mails, putting out small, domestic fires.

One of these days, she would make an effort at having some kind of personal life. Go out for drinks after work with Alisha or join an online dating site. Something that didn't include batteries. No remote, no vibrator.

A memory whispered through her mind of Luke, solid in the twilight, with his wide shoulders and dark blue eyes.

I had the evening free, she'd said. *Most evenings free.*

Lucky for me, he'd drawled.

What had he meant by that?

She shook the thought away, tucking her phone under her ear, jotting notes on the legal pad in front of her.

"I understand," she murmured soothingly to thirty-nine-year-old Tammy Blakemore.

Tammy's husband, a prominent dentist, had just informed her during their counseling appointment that he intended to go on banging his twenty-six-year-old hygienist, and he expected his wife to be okay with that. After all, Tammy explained tearfully, she lived in his house, she carried his name and his children, he gave her a car and a generous allowance. He deserved something in return.

Yeah, like slow castration with a butter knife.

But of course Kate didn't say that. She rarely told clients how she really felt. Her therapist's voice played in the back of her head. *Children of alcoholics are taught to perceive their own emotions as being wrong and bad. Which is why you frequently minimize and ignore your feelings.*

Whatever. Kate wasn't paid for her feelings. Only her legal advice.

"Why don't you come in tomorrow," she suggested. "I can answer all your questions then. No obligation."

Tammy's voice quavered on the other end of the line, offering a familiar litany of excuses.

"I know he doesn't want a divorce," Kate said. "The question is, what do *you* want?"

The problem, Kate thought as Tammy talked and wept, was that the other woman didn't really want a solution. She wanted sympathy.

Kate felt for her predicament. She did. Chad Blakemore was scum. But there was a small, hurt, childlike part of

Kate that found it difficult to empathize with women like Tammy, wives more worried about protecting their status than their children, more determined to preserve their privileged existence than their self-respect.

Women like her mother.

Kate rubbed absently at the scar on her cheek, fingering the edges over and over like braille.

Every case was different, she reminded herself. She shouldn't take any of them so damn personally.

You're welcome to stay, Luke had said to her last night. But she knew better. She was more effective when she kept her distance.

"Eleven o'clock," she told Tammy firmly. "Let me explain your options before we discuss your next move."

And maybe Tammy would even keep her appointment, Kate thought hopefully after she hung up. The Blakemores had children. Daughters. Surely Tammy would consider what kind of example she was setting for them?

Kate stood to stretch the kinks from her spine, ignoring the five e-mails that had popped up while she was on the phone. She circled her head on her shoulders, listening to her neck snap and pop. She needed . . . something, she decided. Caffeine. A break. She went to grab a Diet Mountain Dew from the refrigerator in the kitchen.

The carpet squished underfoot.

Kate yelped.

A puddle spread from beneath the powder room door into the hall.

She lunged forward, ignoring the ringing of her office phone. "Shit. Damn it."

She splashed through an inch of water toward the tiny half bath, trying frantically to remember the last time she'd used it.

The front door buzzed. *What now?*

"Coming!" she yelled. But first . . .

Not a toilet overflow, she saw with relief as she opened the powder room door. The water flooding the floor was clear. She gasped. And *cold*. Her toes curled inside her soaking shoes. Water rattled through the pipes, hissed in the bowl. She sloshed forward, bending down to turn the shutoff valve behind the toilet.

"Spud washer," a male voice said behind her.

Kate jumped, narrowly missing smacking her head on the underside of the sink. She turned, her heart pounding.

Luke Fletcher stood on her sopping hall carpet, tall and lean with his straight, bleached hair and hunky arms, appealingly male and annoyingly dry.

She was immediately conscious of her frizzing hair and wet shoes. Embarrassment made her stiffen. "I beg your pardon?"

He raised one blond eyebrow. "You said to come in." He nodded toward her flooded bathroom. "Your tank's leaking. You need a new spud washer. Maybe bolt gaskets. And some plumber's putty."

"Are you a plumber?"

"My parents own a bed-and-breakfast. There's not a lot I can't fix."

How about my life?

Kate's mouth went dry. *Not a good thought*. She stared at him, her heart thumping in her chest.

His mouth curved, hardly smirking at all. "Want me to have a look?"

She liked that he offered. Liked more that he asked, instead of shouldering her aside. "Thanks, but I can handle it."

Her whole life, if there was a problem, she was the one to handle it. She did everything herself, because that was easier—*safer*—than counting on anybody else. If you didn't rely on other people, you couldn't be disappointed.

She smiled to soften her refusal. "You don't want to get your fatigues all wet."

"Doesn't matter to me. I'm on my way home."

"Oh. Well . . ." She supposed Beaufort *was* on the way from Camp Lejeune to Dare Island. But that didn't explain why he'd stopped. She didn't trust impulsive gestures. It wasn't like they were buddies. Like he was interested in her *that* way. Or any way. Obviously. "Have you heard from Alisha?"

"Yeah. Got the letter from social services this morning asking to set up a home visit like you said. That's not why I came, though."

"Oh." Her imagination ran wild.

"I had some questions about Taylor." He smiled slightly. "I would have called first, but I figured you wouldn't mind. After last night."

"Of course." She flushed. This was what happened when you let your barriers down, when you let things become personal. People—men—took advantage. "Naturally I'll help any way I can." She glanced at the puddle spreading through the hall. They would have to wade to reach her office.

"Great." He unbuttoned his cuffs. Rolled back his sleeves. Uncovered, his forearms were even more impressive, hard with muscle and dusted with fine, dark hair. "Get some towels, would you?"

"Towels."

"To dry out the tank."

Kate narrowed her eyes. She did not take orders. On the other hand, it was really nice of him to offer to fix her toilet. And he knew what he was doing. Competence was always attractive.

Not that she was attracted.

Exactly.

He crouched beside the leaking tank, making the muscles of his thighs swell against the confines of his fatigue pants. Lots of muscles.

She cleared her throat. "Anything else?"

"Yeah." He looked up, a glint in his eyes, and her breath stuttered. "A mop would be good."

Five

LUKE HADN'T FIGURED on spending his first full day state-side playing plumber for a woman he barely knew. But after his abortive mission to the Simpsons', there was something almost relaxing about getting his hands dirty. Getting something done. Nobody was taking shots at him or sneering or—*Jesus*—crying.

He shoved away the memory of his daughter's drowned eyes, shutting it in the closet of Things He Wasn't Going to Think About, focusing instead on the task at hand. The heightened awareness he'd brought home from Afghanistan made everything clearer, sharper. The pale December sunlight slanting through the front door. The smell of fluffy blue towels, fresh from the dryer. Kate's curling coppery hair, bright against the soothing colors of the hall. The shape of her really excellent ass as she bent with the mop.

No panty lines.

He took a breath and stared back at the bolt in his hand. Yeah, okay, so maybe he *had* dropped by as an excuse to see her. Why not? She was a smart, attractive woman. Conscientious. She'd driven all the way out to the island last night to give him the heads-up on the social worker's visit. Plus, there was that ass.

He wasn't looking to find love at first sight, the way his parents had. But he'd learned to trust his instincts. And his instincts said, *Go for it*.

Or maybe that was his dick talking.

Ninety minutes and one trip to the hardware store later, he'd replaced the old washer and gaskets and lifted the tank back onto the bowl. Kate, after mopping the floor and blotting the carpet, had retreated to her office. He could hear her occasionally on the phone, using hundred-dollar words and a don't-mess-with-me voice, laying down the law to somebody. He grinned. She made a good ally. Too bad he didn't have her along this morning to deal with Dawn's folks.

Now she picked her way toward him over the still-damp carpet, fastidious as a cat walking through wet grass. "Do you want anything?" she asked.

Like a waitress at a restaurant. He wondered if Kate was on the menu. What she'd say if he nuzzled her cheek. If he licked her neck. How she'd taste.

He shook his head, wiping his hands on one of her pretty blue towels. "Almost done."

"Then . . . a beer?"

He was tempted.

Before he came home to an instant family, to a kid who *needed* things from him, iPods and kittens and time, he'd spend at least a couple evenings with his buddies, drinking beer, telling lies, and picking up women.

He had other responsibilities now.

"Can't," he said briefly, regretfully. "I'm driving."

Her smile was warm enough to make him blink. "Diet Mountain Dew? Diet Pepsi?"

Girl drinks. He wondered if she had a man in her life, somebody to keep her refrigerator stocked with cold cuts and nondiet soda. Of course, she'd offered him beer . . . "Got anything with sugar?"

Her expression turned apologetic. "Sorry, no."

He didn't want to be the cause of that fading smile. "Water will be fine."

She brought it to him in a glass, with ice and a little slice of lemon floating on top. For a moment, he could only stare.

Her brows twitched together. "Is something wrong?"

He thought of the water he'd drunk in Afghanistan, as hot as tea from a vending machine, with the same pale brown color and metallic tang. "No, this is great. Thanks."

Her fingers were cool from the glass as he took it from her. He imagined them on his skin as she watched him drink, still with that tiny pleat between her eyebrows. "Now that you've fixed my toilet, what can I do for you, Staff Sergeant?"

Back to business, he thought. "Now that I've fixed your toilet, I figure you should call me Luke."

"All right. Luke." She hesitated over the name, like it didn't taste quite right in her mouth. "What can I do for you?"

He sighed. "I need a picture of Dawn."

"A picture."

"Yeah. For Taylor. Mom found one in my old yearbook." He shook away the memory of her smiling face, so young, so alive, *Jesus, we were both so young, don't think about that.* "But I was hoping you maybe had something more recent."

"That's an excellent idea." Her voice warmed. "The pictures in the office—the pictures on Dawn's desk—are all of Taylor. But the Simpsons must have pictures of Dawn."

"Yeah." He kept his face, his voice neutral. "I asked them already."

"You did." Her tone invited him to say more.

"Before I came here."

She tilted her head. "I take it they were not responsive."

You've taken everything else from us. We're not giving you a damn thing.

"Not really," he said.

Kate studied him, like she could see inside his head to

read the things he would not say. "In that case, I had everything of Dawn's put in storage after I cleaned out her house. I know there are pictures. Whole scrapbooks of them, actually."

"In storage?" He'd never thought about storage. Never thought about much of anything except getting the kid settled with his parents so he could get back to his unit. "That's kind of expensive."

"I didn't take the cost from the estate, if that's what you're concerned about."

Man, she was prickly. Or maybe she thought he was questioning her decision. He'd served under officers like that, guys who wouldn't back up their NCOs, who had to micromanage and interfere and pick at every little thing. If her old man had been one of them, that would be enough to drive anybody on the defensive. "I meant . . . I figured Dawn's stuff would be with her parents."

"Oh." She turned pink. "No. The contents of the house are part of the estate. As long as Taylor's guardianship was still unsettled . . . Dawn's brother kept asking me how much I thought everything was worth. I didn't want Dawn's things to wind up in a garage sale before Taylor had a chance to go through them."

You've taken everything else from us . . .

He could sympathize with the Simpsons' desire to hold on to their memories of Dawn. Hell, he could even understand their wanting custody of Taylor. Given the size of their house, the furniture on the porch, it figured they might not have room for all of Dawn's stuff.

But he hadn't considered that they might want to get their hands on it for the money.

To preserve Taylor's memories, her inheritance, Kate had jumped in to store Dawn's things. Out of her own pocket, apparently.

Yeah, he was glad to have her on his side. "I'll pay you back."

"You don't have to. Dawn was my friend." Kate glanced

away, as if even that small personal admission embarrassed her. "Anyway, it was only for a couple of months."

She didn't want to take credit, but Luke appreciated what she'd done. Not only the cost, but the effort involved. He should show his gratitude. Buy her dinner. Buy her flowers. Strip her out of that tight little lawyer suit and do whatever she wanted.

Strictly to show his appreciation.

It wasn't like she was the first woman he'd seen in eleven months. Only one of the first who wasn't wearing a burqa or cammies. Who wasn't looking at him like she hated him or feared him or wanted him the fuck out of her way. She hadn't thanked him for his service, but she wasn't looking at him to save her, either. Or treating him like a soulless baby-killer.

Given some of the things he'd seen and done, that might have been enough. But on top of all that, he liked her. The compassion she cloaked in professional interest. Her face.

"You box everything up, too?" he asked.

"I didn't have a choice. Her rent was paid only through the end of the month."

She could have hired someone else to do the job, Luke thought. "So the house is empty."

She nodded. "I can take you to the storage unit if you want to look for that picture of Dawn. Or anything else."

"What about the cat?"

"Dawn's cat? Snowball?"

"Yeah. You know what happened to it?"

"No, I'm sorry. It wasn't at the house when I was there. Did you ask the Simpsons?"

"Yeah. Jolene told me how they couldn't take the cat because of her allergies. So I asked her what they did with it."

"And?"

"Nothing," he said, disgusted. "I called the animal shelter, but they don't have a record of a white cat being turned in. I thought I might have a look around her old place."

"I don't see what good that will do. Someone else is probably living there now."

"I hope so."

Her brow pleated. He watched her work it out. "You think if someone moved in, they could have seen it."

"Or are feeding it. Yeah." He shrugged. "It's worth a shot."

"I think that's very admirable." She hesitated.

"Do I hear a 'but' coming?"

She laughed, but her eyes were serious. "Are you ready to take on the responsibility for another living being right now?"

He wasn't used to having his judgment questioned. Maybe he wasn't an experienced dad like Matt. But he was a squad leader, responsible for the lives of his men and the success of their mission. He kept them equipped, conditioned, trained, and alive. He did not have to explain or defend himself. So he joked instead. "I guess this is a bad time to tell you about the dog."

"What dog?"

Definitely a bad time.

"Listen, we're talking about a kid's pet here." *Weren't they?* "Taylor just lost her mom. I can't tell her it's too much trouble to look for her damn cat."

"And when you're gone?" Kate asked quietly.

Yeah, okay, she wasn't just talking about the cat anymore.

"We'll work it out," he said, not sure how, but it sounded good. "My family will help."

"You have a good family."

He grinned, amused by her precise pattern of speaking. "Is that your professional opinion?"

She straightened her shoulders, which did nice things for her very pretty breasts. "My professional opinion is the only one that matters."

"Not to me," he said, and was fascinated when she blushed under her makeup, the little ridge on her cheek standing out white against the pink. A scar.

"I just meant . . . The court gives more weight to considered analysis than to emotional appeals."

"Sure. But emotion enters into their decisions, right?
You said yourself that this social worker has to like us. Like
me. So, what do you think?" He stood closer, enjoying the
way her eyes dilated, the color running under her skin. His
own blood heated in response. "Do I have a shot?"

"I guess we won't know until we get there." Deliberately, she took a step back. "We can stop by on our way to
the storage center."

He was momentarily confused. "Stop by?"

"Dawn's house." Her lips twitched. "That is what you
were asking, wasn't it?"

His grin mirrored hers. "You're going with me."

"It's on our way. We might as well check things out."
There it was again, that glint of humor, like a shell tumbling at the water's edge, gone almost before it could be
identified. "Anything's possible."

Ooh-rah.

And maybe, he thought as he got in his Jeep and followed her to the outskirts of town, the new tenants had
adopted the cat already. Maybe Taylor would be satisfied
with that, honor would be satisfied with that.

He wasn't satisfied yet.

He wondered if he would ever be satisfied where Kate
was concerned. *Anything's possible.*

The houses got smaller and farther apart. White picket
borders gave way to chain link fence, boats in the driveway
replaced with rusting propane tanks and swing sets. Kate
parked on the soft shoulder of the road in front of a brick
bungalow. Luke pulled in behind her and got out.

It wasn't the greatest neighborhood. But it was a step
up from her parents' place. His respect for Dawn, for what
she had accomplished on her own, for the life she had made
for their daughter, grew.

Jolene's accusing voice played in his head. *You never
sent a dime . . .*

Scattered toys and weeds had overtaken the yard next door, but the grass around the bungalow was recently mowed, the yard empty except for a red-and-white FOR RENT sign.

No cat lurking in the bushes.

No helpful tenants, either. *Damn*.

"Here, kitty, kitty."

"Try the back," Kate suggested.

He walked and whistled, poked under bushes and peered under the porch, feeling like an idiot. "Here, Snowball."

No answer. He tromped around front again.

"We should have brought a can of tuna," Kate said.

"Are you looking for Dawn?"

A young woman leaned against the chain link fence, pretty, sharp featured, with a butterfly tattoo on one side of her throat and a baby on her hip.

"Her cat," Luke said. "Have you seen it?"

"Sure. A couple of times. After . . . you know. Dawn died." The baby grabbed a fistful of his mother's shirt and tugged, exposing a lot of smooth, young skin and another tattoo. A fairy.

"Recently?" Kate asked.

"Four months ago."

"No, I meant, when was the last time you saw the cat?"

"You're not animal control." The girl's gaze slid back over Luke, taking in his olive T-shirt and fatigue pants. "Marines?"

He smiled reassuringly. "Yes, ma'am."

"Thought so." She fixed him with wide brown eyes that reminded him of the dog in Afghanistan. Hopeful. Needy. "How did you say you knew Dawn again?"

I didn't know her. We dated in high school and I knocked her up. "I'm Taylor's father."

"Really? What's your name?"

"Luke. Do you remember the last time—"

"I'm Sierra. I've never seen you around here before."

His jaw tightened. *No excuses.* "No."

"He's been overseas a lot," Kate said.

"Funny, Dawn never mentioned you," the girl said.

Luke exhaled hard. Dawn had never mentioned Taylor, either, not to him, which was something else he couldn't understand and was finding hard to forgive her for. Forgive himself for.

Not that he spent a lot of time thinking about his *feelings*, for fuck's sake.

"How well did you know them?" he asked.

She shrugged, making her top slide farther. "Oh, you know. Pretty well. Us single moms have to stick together. Taylor used to come over sometimes and watch the baby. Not that I ever go anywhere. But she'd play with her, read to her, while I did stuff around the house." She shifted the baby on her hip. "How's she doing? Taylor?"

"She's fine," Luke said. Wasn't she? He had a hard time picturing the silent, suspicious daughter he knew playing and reading with a baby.

"Must have been awful for her, losing her mom like that."

Luke's jaw tightened. "Yeah."

Kate took a business card out of her purse and handed it to Sierra. "This is my number. If you see the cat again, will you call me?"

Sierra took the card, still looking at Luke. *Help me. Save me. Love me.* "You got a card, too?"

He shook his head.

She sighed. "Well, let me have your phone. I'll type in my number. In case you want to ask about Snowball. You can call anytime," she said, handing the phone back. "I'm all alone here. Just me and the baby."

"Uh, thanks." He threw Kate a desperate look. No way was he calling. The girl looked fresh out of high school, for Christ's sake. With a kid.

Just like Dawn at that age. He winced.

Kate coughed. Or maybe she was covering a laugh. "I'm sure the staff sergeant appreciates your offer," she said smoothly. "We'll be in touch."

He walked Kate back to her car and opened her door.

He was glad Meg wasn't with him. His sister would never let him hear the end of it, her tough-guy brother fleeing in terror from a barely-legal teenager. But Kate didn't bust his balls. She didn't take offense, either.

"Thanks for having my six."

Kate slid behind the wheel, smiling up at him. "All in a day's work."

"Right." He frowned. After listening to Kate on the phone, he could tell she cared about her clients. He appreciated the way she went above and beyond in the line of duty. But he didn't want to be just another part of her job.

He watched her pull out ahead of him, signaling her turns carefully, giving him a little wave once in her rearview mirror, two fingers and a smile.

It was enough to make him think . . . Hell, he didn't know what to think.

He was used to sizing things up, acting swiftly to secure a situation or an advantage. Kate Dolan was too guarded to be read. Too careful to be rushed. Too complicated to resist. A challenge, in fact.

He'd never been any damn good at all at backing away from a challenge.

Six

KATE UNLOCKED THE numbered storage unit door, acutely aware of Luke behind her. Not crowding, but she felt him anyway, a subtle pressure, a prickling awareness on the back of her neck.

She shivered and yanked on the locking bar, sliding it out of the way.

All in a day's work, she'd said, her voice cheery, but this errand felt deeply personal.

There weren't enough pieces of her own past left to fill a cardboard box, let alone a storage unit. Her kindergarten artwork, a dollhouse from her aunt, a blue candy dish, a stuffed monkey she'd clung to in the hospital when she got her tonsils out at six . . . Gone, all gone. *Useless junk*, her father had barked when it came time to move again. *Get rid of it*. And her mother had always acquiesced.

Some memories weren't worth holding on to.

But Kate had done her best to preserve Taylor's. To save the bits and pieces of her childhood, her legacy from Dawn.

Everybody should have a picture somewhere, even if the happy family it depicted was a lie.

It was hard for Kate to imagine her mother smiling. But she would love to believe there was a photo of her somewhere, of the two of them together, tucked in the attic or the bottom of a drawer, something that had escaped her father's notice and control.

Luke bent and grabbed the metal handle, arms bunching, all those lovely muscles sliding under his shirt.

Kate looked away, a little out of breath. The overhead door rattled up, releasing a draft of stale air. She breathed in the smell of mothballs. She was out of her comfort zone here, uneasily aware of overstepping her own boundaries into uncharted territory.

"I have to get back," she muttered.

He looked surprised. And then he shrugged. "Sure. Leave the key. I'll lock up."

"No, I meant . . ." Her face heated. *Get a grip, Dolan.* "Never mind."

She fumbled for the light. Flipped it on. The contents of the storage unit jumped into stark relief, stacked cartons and shrouded furniture looming out of the shadows.

Luke inhaled sharply. She glanced over as he moved inside the unit, turning his back to the wall.

Oh. She bit her lip in sudden comprehension. She'd seen cops stand like that at the courthouse, protecting their rear, watching the entrance, guarding against attack.

Luke was just back from a war zone. It would take him time to adjust to civilian life.

If he ever did.

Compassion squeezed her chest. She dug in her purse, giving them both a moment to recover. "I boxed all the framed photos and albums together," she said, her tone deliberately matter-of-fact. "I have a list . . ."

"Of course you do."

She narrowed her eyes, suspecting some kind of dig. But he was smiling, watching her with lazy blue eyes. A little rush of pleasure ran over her skin.

"My mom makes lists," he explained. "Military family, remember?"

She hadn't thought of it that way, as a habit she'd learned from her father's frequent deployments. As something they could have in common.

She didn't want anything to do with that life anymore.

Blindly, she looked down. "Here we go." She smoothed the pages. "'Living room—Pictures.' It should be near the front."

He nodded and turned away to scan the sides of the cartons.

Kate followed suit down the other side, trying to dismiss that inconvenient spark of attraction. Everything was jumbled together, the boxes sorted by size rather than content. KITCHEN, CHRISTMAS, SUMMER CLOTHES . . . Even without opening the boxes, Kate could see Dawn's pink sweaters, her big hair, her bright smile. She'd been so young. Three years younger than Kate. *Her whole life ahead of her*, the minister had droned at her funeral.

Her throat ached. What was she doing here? Luke was perfectly capable of searching the storage unit on his own. What was she hoping to accomplish?

Kate blinked fiercely, forcing the swimming letters on the boxes into focus: TAYLOR—BOOKS, TAYLOR—BEDROOM. Maybe . . . Had there been a picture of Dawn on Taylor's dresser? She couldn't remember. She tugged that box toward her. She could hear Luke shifting cartons on the other side of the unit, stacking them to get to the ones farther down in the pile. Tape ripped.

And then . . . It was awfully quiet all of a sudden.

She dropped the folds of comforter she'd used to pad the box and turned. Luke stood motionless by an open carton, staring down at the frame in his hands.

Kate couldn't see the picture. She didn't need to. His expression told her all she needed to know. He was doing that stone-faced Marine thing again, jaw bunched, thick blond lashes veiling his eyes.

She swallowed the lump in her throat, struggling for a

brisk tone, trying to protect them both from an excess of emotion. "Did you find what you need?"

WAR TAUGHT YOU to shut up about your feelings. To shut off your memories. Which was a good thing, because at that moment Luke had more feelings and memories churning around than he wanted to deal with.

"Did you find what you need?" Kate chirped.

Dumb question. But he was grateful for her voice, pulling him back to the dim storage unit.

"Yeah."

The Dawn in the photo was a year or two years older and maybe fifteen pounds heavier than the girl he remembered, her face rounder, fuller, more grown-up. But despite the changes and the baby on her lap, she still looked the same, like the girl he knew in high school. The girl he'd loved, or at least loved having sex with.

He could see a bit of birthday cake, a pink party hat perched like a crooked horn on Taylor's smooth blond head. He wanted to build some fantasy where he belonged in that picture, his hand on Dawn's shoulder or his arm around the baby. Or out of the frame, taking the shot. But he couldn't. There was no room in that photo for anybody else. Mother and child looked like a unit. Happy. Complete.

Dawn sure never looked at him the way she looked at that baby.

Gently, he laid her picture back in the box.

He'd been pretty broken up when she dumped him.

I'm not waiting for you, she'd cried when he told her he'd enlisted. *I want to get out of here. I want a real home. A real family.*

Luke hadn't cared so much about getting out. The island was home to him. But he had been determined to prove himself. Matt was the responsible one in their family, Meg was the smart one. He was the afterthought, the baby, their brother. Until he became a Marine, like their father.

Maybe nobody knew anymore if the war had been a

good thing, but nobody had questioned his choice back then. Not in the wake of 9/11. Oh, his mother had cried a little before she did that mom thing with her face, smiling through her fear, telling him she was proud.

Dad . . . Well, Dad never said much. But Luke thought he was proud.

What if Dawn had come to him then and told him she was pregnant?

What would he have done?

"Taylor's first birthday," Kate observed softly beside him.

He twitched, but he didn't react the way he would to, say, a Taliban insurgent popping up at his elbow. So that was good. He looked down again at the picture in the box, a funny pressure in his chest.

"Were you there?" he asked Kate.

For some reason, she flushed. "No, I . . . She wasn't working for me then. Not that we saw a lot of each other outside the office. But—"

"Hey, you don't need to apologize." He managed a smile. "I wasn't there, either."

She bit her lip. "I'm sorry. That wasn't an apology," she added hurriedly. "I just meant . . . It can't be easy for you, missing out on so much of your daughter's life."

So many milestones, he thought. First birthday. First step. First day of school.

But he didn't want Kate's pity. Anyway, she was wrong.

"That's not the hard part," Luke said.

She was close enough that her curls brushed his shoulder. Despite all the makeup she wore, she smelled fresh and clean, like shampoo.

His chest felt tight. He exhaled. "The hard part is what she's going to miss going forward, what they'll both miss. All the other birthdays for the rest of Taylor's life. Her high school prom. Her graduation. Christ, her wedding day. Her mom should be there. She needs her mom."

Kate's hand squeezed his arm. He turned his head. Her gaze met his, soft and compassionate. "She has you."

"That's not enough."

"It's quite a lot. Daughters need their fathers to develop a positive self-image and healthy relationships with the opposite sex."

He raised his brows. "Are you speaking from experience?"

"No, I'm speaking from years of therapy."

Her frankness made him laugh. He admired her honesty. "So where does that leave me and Taylor? I wasn't around for the first ten years of her life."

"You're making her feel wanted. You're making her feel secure. Children, particularly children like Taylor who are recovering from a loss, need four things: routine, security, honesty, and love. As long as you can give her those, she'll be fine."

"How do you know?"

"I see a lot of parents and children in my office. Most of them are recovering from some sort of trauma. A lot of them are in counseling. And from what I see of you and Taylor, I believe you can do this."

She sounded so sure, when everything around him was uncertain. So determined, like she would *make* him be up to the job through sheer force of will. Without really thinking about it, he leaned forward, and she was there, her eyes wide and startled, her lips pink and parted, he was glad she was there, he was grateful she was with him, and then he was kissing her, which was better than thinking and a hell of a lot better than talking.

The taste of her was a surprise, the heat under the sweet, like cinnamon candy. He went abruptly hard, the blood rushing in his head, pounding in his veins, as she kissed him back, as her fingers brushed his shoulders, touched the back of his neck. He licked deeper, eating into the sweetness and softness of her. She tasted good, better than good, and she made this little sound in her throat that shot straight to his groin. His mind blanked. His hands slid down, found her hips and pulled her close. Oh, God, yes, like that.

She jolted as their bodies came into hot, tight contact.

"It's okay," he whispered. He moved his hands back to

her waist. Safe territory. *Just let me kiss you. Let me hold you. Let me . . .*

She pushed at his shoulders. He raised his head. Her eyes, more brown than green, were dark and dazed. "What's this about?"

He wasn't sure. But he wanted it again. "How about 'thank you'?"

She blinked. "What?"

"Thanks for being here. For everything you're doing for me and Taylor."

"Oh. You're welcome." She swallowed, easing away from him. His body protested the loss of her softness. "Maybe next time, you can write me a note."

He grinned, going with his gut. "How about I take you to dinner instead?"

Her fugitive smile flickered before she shook her head. "I don't think that would be a good idea."

He cocked his head. "Why not? Unless you're seeing somebody."

She licked her lips, which made him want to kiss her again. "That's really none of your business."

"So, no," he said with satisfaction.

Her breath escaped in a huff of laughter before she caught it back. "You can't know that."

"Calculated guess," he informed her. "I figure you'd come straight out and tell me to get lost if there was somebody else. Plus, you kissed me back."

"All right, fine. I won't deny that I'm attracted. And flattered. But—" She held him off with one hand. "You just got home. You're understandably feeling unsettled. This is hardly the right time for you to be . . . for us to be doing . . ." She waggled her fingers in the air between them. *"This."*

His grin broadened. "I'm not sure I recognize your hand sign. You mean dinner?"

She rolled her eyes. "You know what I mean. Any sort of personal contact—relationship—between us would be terribly complicated."

"Only because you're thinking like a lawyer."

"I *am* a lawyer."

"Right. You're used to complicating things. Marines keep it simple. Identify your long-term objective, execute the steps to achieve your objective."

Her eyes narrowed. "Do you honestly expect me to believe your objective is to have dinner with me?"

"No," he admitted. "Dinner would be more like the short-term strategy."

"I thought so."

"Getting to know you would be the objective," he explained.

Her lips quivered in a smile. But then she shook her head. "Whatever. The fact is, you've been gone a long time. You've returned to a new and stressful family situation. Under the circumstances, it's natural for your emotions to be heightened. *All* your emotions."

He looked at her in amused disbelief. "You think I asked you out because of my 'heightened emotional state'?"

"I didn't mean to insult you."

"I'm not insulted." *Much*. "But if you think I'm only hitting on you because I'm at loose ends or looking to get laid, you're selling yourself short."

Her face turned red. "I only meant . . . When most people come into my office, they're in crisis. It's my job to guide them through some of the most difficult personal decisions they'll ever face, decisions with lasting consequences, at a time when their lives are a mess and their emotions are making things worse. I can't help them, I can't do my *job*, if I let my personal feelings get in the way."

"I'm not your client."

"No, you're Taylor's father." She waited a beat, to underscore her point. "And I'm the executor of Dawn's estate. You're in the middle of a social services investigation, facing a permanent custody hearing in two weeks. Taylor has to be your top priority."

"She is." He shoved his hands into his pockets, battling frustration. "I'm here, aren't I?"

"Yes, you are. I appreciate everything you're trying to do for Taylor. I want to help. Which is why . . ." She drew a deep breath. He thought maybe she found it harder to ignore her personal feelings than she let on. Anyway, that's what he wanted to think. "We should focus on identifying what Taylor needs."

He regarded her wryly. "You're not just talking about a picture of her mother, are you?"

"No." Another smile, another hint of the humor that lurked beneath her buttoned-up attitude. He liked both sides, he decided, the warm woman and the cool lawyer. "But that's a good start."

KATE'S HEART HAMMERED.

She'd told Luke to back off, and he'd backed off.

Situation dealt with, she told herself. Problem solved.

Except . . . He turned, his hard, lean body in boots and fatigues, his blue eyes level under straight, thick lashes, and everything inside her purred and yearned. Her hormones were still in an uproar because he'd kissed her.

Yikes. She did not trust him. Or rather, she didn't trust her own breathless attraction to him. *Daughters need their fathers to develop a positive self-image and healthy relationships with the opposite sex*, she had said.

And if you never had that . . .

She was on her own here. Making things up as she went along. Not a good place for her. Especially not with a man like this.

Luke glanced at her face and gestured towards the open carton marked TAYLOR—BEDROOM. "Okay to take this?"

"Of course." Hastily, she rearranged her features in a smile. "'Travel light' is fine if you're a Marine. It sucks if you're in a Marine's family." She was the survivor of too many moves, of too many things broken, abandoned, and left behind, books, bikes, neighborhoods, friendships.

"I guess it never bothered me. My mom used to say . . . Well." He picked up the box.

Kate raised her brows. Apparently he was the strong, silent type. She was taking a hiatus from dating at the moment—okay, maybe longer than a moment, a couple of years, at least—but she preferred men who gave you some clue to what they were thinking. Writers, academics, other lawyers, men who discussed their feelings instead of letting them build behind a wall of macho silence until they erupted in alcoholic fury. Men as different from her father as she could imagine.

"What did your mother say?" she asked before she could stop herself.

"Mom used to tell us that as long as we had each other we had everything. *Back to back to back*. That was kind of our motto, Matt and Meg and me. Only in Afghanistan . . ." He hesitated, shifting the weight of the carton in his arms.

She really wasn't interested in his personal life, she told herself.

Except she was.

"In Afghanistan," she prompted softly.

He shrugged. "You start to appreciate things. Like care packages. You're grateful for the eye drops and drink mix and socks, but it's the other stuff everybody keeps. Letters. Pictures. Stuff to remind you of home."

Something turned over in Kate's chest, like a key in a lock, like her heart. "So you decided Taylor needed stuff." That was so sweet. What a decent guy.

"Her own stuff." He nodded. "Yeah. Especially when we move into our own place."

"I thought you were staying with your parents."

He carried the box to the Jeep. "I'm renting one of the guest cottages out back, at least for now. That way Taylor won't have to switch schools again this year."

So he'd thought of that, too. That was pretty sensitive of him.

Darn it. Here she was, priding herself on her ability to listen and assess, to consider the facts dispassionately and offer her clients objective counsel. And yet with Luke, she'd allowed herself to make the kind of snap judgment she normally scorned. Why? Because he was a Marine, like her father? Because her own hello-there-sailor response to him made her uncomfortable?

That wasn't fair.

Guilt burned in her chest, her face. She could not offer him her apology without explaining just how badly she'd misjudged him. But she wanted to make it up to him. To help him somehow.

She trailed him to his vehicle. "What about furniture?"

He slid the box in back, muscles flexing. He really had great arms. And shoulders. Great everything, really. "What about it?"

"You'll need some if you're moving." She glanced away—*oh, God, had he caught her staring?*—toward the open storage unit. "And there's plenty here."

"Thanks, we're good," he said. "The cottage is furnished."

"Maybe a bookcase for Taylor?"

"Maybe."

She didn't understand his reluctance. She was trying to help. "You could come back with a truck if you don't have room right now."

His gaze met hers briefly. His jaw set. "I don't need . . . It doesn't feel right taking Dawn's things, okay?"

A guy with scruples. How attractive. She didn't see a lot of those in her line of work.

"They're Taylor's things now," Kate reminded him. "It's no different from using her trust."

He didn't say anything.

She gnawed her lip, a suspicion growing in her mind. Since Dawn's life insurance company would not pay out directly to a minor child, Kate had set up a trust for Taylor, managed by the bank. Dawn's death benefit was paid into the trust so that Taylor's guardian—Luke—could draw on the money to pay for her expenses.

"You're not having any trouble accessing her funds, are you?"

"I don't think so." He met her gaze and shrugged. "I haven't tried."

"What about Taylor's Social Security benefits?"

"It's all there. In her college fund. Her account," he corrected. "Maybe she'll decide college isn't her thing when she gets older. But the money will be there for her. She won't have to bust her butt like Meg did or take out loans."

"You shouldn't have to bust your butt, either. Dawn paid into that policy so that you would have that money for Taylor's expenses."

He rolled those impressive shoulders in another shrug. "She bought the policy for Taylor. If there's something Taylor needs that I can't afford, fine. Otherwise, the money will be there for her when she grows up."

"Wow. That's very . . ." *Principled? Impractical?*

"Fair," he said. "Dawn carried all the costs of the first ten years of Taylor's life. Now that I'm finally in the picture, seems she should be my responsibility."

It was more than fair, she thought. It was decent. He was a decent guy. Not a lot of that going around. Plus, there were those arms. Those eyes.

She tried to take a normal breath. "Well. If there's nothing else you need . . ."

"I didn't say that," he interrupted, that intense blue gaze on her face.

She could pretend she didn't know what he was talking about. She stuck out her chin instead. "You know, I don't normally go around kissing men in storage lockers."

Or at all. There was that whole dating hiatus thing she had going on. Not to mention the do-not-leap-before-you-look thing. The tired-of-disappointment thing. The I-don't-want-to-loan-you-money, talk-about-your-ex, listen-to-you-hedge-about-our-relationship thing. She was not jumping into something just because the man had nice arms and seemed to want to do the right thing by his daughter.

He smiled. "You got something against kissing?"

"Not against kissing. Per se. But . . ."

"Latin." He moved in, still smiling. "Very hot."

Her heart raced. It was just a kiss, she rationalized. She'd kissed men before. Not recently, true, but she didn't need to invest this kiss, this man, with any special significance.

To prove it, she stood on tiptoe, twined her arms around his neck and pressed her lips to his.

See? she told herself. Not a prob—Oh, God, the man could kiss.

In no time at all, he'd opened her lips with his, his tongue in her mouth and his hands in her hair. Her brain fogged as he kissed her, progressively slower, deeper, wetter kisses. Her skin steamed with lust.

She had to . . . She couldn't. They shouldn't.

Shaking, she pulled back. "I told you . . . The timing . . . This is a bad idea."

He kissed her hot cheek. She tried not to melt. "Yeah, I heard you."

She swallowed. "Then, why—"

His eyes were bright and impossibly blue against his desert tan. "I didn't say I agreed with you."

"Then we have a problem."

His mouth quirked. "Maybe we can talk about it later. I want to be there when Taylor gets home from school."

He gave her another hard, brief kiss before he tugged down the overhead door and left, taking the boxes with him.

She watched his Jeep drive away, her lips tingling and her heart in turmoil.

Oh, yes, they definitely had a problem. Not because he wasn't listening. Because she wasn't sure she wanted him to.

Seven

PLANNING HAD SEEN Tess Fletcher through countless moves as a military wife. As long as she stayed organized, as long as she kept busy, everything would be all right.

She ran down the list on the kitchen counter, crossing off items as she removed them from the refrigerator. Milk, butter, orange juice, *check, check, check,* loaded into the box.

The back door creaked as Tom returned from carrying the last carton from Taylor's room upstairs. Not that there was much up there to pack.

Tess sighed. When Taylor first came to live with them three months ago, Tess hadn't planned on raising another ten-year-old. But all her doubts had melted away the first time Taylor looked at her with Luke's blue eyes. She'd been full of hopes and plans for this surprise granddaughter, this unexpected blessing in their lives. It hadn't always been easy. It had taken Taylor a while to learn to trust them. Tess's own accident had derailed so many of her plans. And now . . .

The list blurred. Tess blinked fiercely and refocused on the shelves. *Eggs, apples . . .*

"What are you doing?" Tom asked.

Tess kept her head turned toward the refrigerator. Nothing terrified poor Tom like the threat of tears. "Stocking the cottage fridge for Luke and Taylor. The home visit's tomorrow."

"Babe, social worker's not going to look in the fridge to see if Luke's feeding her properly."

He was probably right. Still . . . "She might."

"Then he should buy his own groceries. The boy can guide a Marine patrol in enemy territory; he can probably find a grocery store."

Tom was right. Of course he was right. But Tess needed to do something. To feel useful somehow. "It's just some basic supplies to get them started."

"Fine. Maybe it will keep him from mooching your cooking all the time."

Tess sniffed.

Tom eyed her in alarm. "What?"

"I'm going to miss him."

"Luke?"

She eyed him with exasperated affection. "Of course Luke. And Taylor."

"They're moving across the backyard, not overseas."

Tess swallowed. "I know."

It was different for Tom, she acknowledged. All those years he was the one who went away while she stayed home and made sure the children had what they needed, new shoes, vaccinations, dinner on the table every night, signed permission slips. In their division of duty, the family was her billet.

She felt her usefulness slipping away, her children slipping away, even as their needs grew.

"You need a break anyway," he said, trying to help.

"I'm fine. It's the kids I'm worried about."

Tom raised his heavy eyebrows. "All the kids?"

"Well, not Matt," she admitted.

Matt was busy organizing the new watermen's association, deeply in love with his Allison, and happier than she'd seen him in years. The young, idealistic teacher was exactly what her son—and the island—needed.

Of course, once they married, the two-bedroom cottage Matt had shared with Josh for the past sixteen years would be too small for all three of them. They would move to a larger house, and Tess would no longer have her grandson growing up practically on her doorstep.

Which was a good thing, she told herself. But in her heart she felt it as another change. Another loss.

"Nothing wrong with Meg," Tom said, his gruff tone failing to hide his pride in their only daughter.

Bright, ambitious Meg had had a rough couple of months, getting fired from her well-paying job in New York, selling her condo with its view of Central Park, breaking up with her long-term boyfriend. But now . . .

"She does love being her own boss," Tess agreed, adding wickedly, "and Sam would make any woman happy."

"He can make Meg happy. You're a married woman."

She smiled. "With three grown children. And two grandchildren. If only Luke—"

"Don't worry about Luke. He's home, Tess. First Christmas in two years," Tom said.

"He is. I'm so glad. I just wish," she said, and shut her mouth.

I wish I knew what was going to happen with Taylor. I wish I could fix things.

When their children were little, when Tess was younger and strong, they had believed she could make anything better. Maybe for a while, seeing herself in their eyes, she had believed it, too. It hurt, recognizing there were bruises she could not soothe, problems she could not solve, issues they had to work out for themselves.

"I just want them all to be happy," she said.

"They're fine." If he was upset at all about tomorrow's visit, about a stranger coming into their house to question their care of their granddaughter, he didn't let on. His stoic acceptance was deeply reassuring.

And the tiniest bit annoying, Tess admitted to herself.

"You worry too much," he said. "And you do too much."

"Not as much as I used to. When Matt came home with Josh—" He was only twenty, Tess remembered. Her first son, her firstborn, so determined to meet his responsibilities, reeling from his wife's desertion and lack of sleep . . .

"Sixteen years ago, babe. We're not that young anymore."

Tess narrowed her eyes in amusement. "Is that supposed to make me feel better?"

"I'm sure as hell not trying to make you feel worse. You've been knocking yourself out taking care of everybody else as long as I can remember. I didn't say anything back then because you wouldn't have it any other way." Tom linked his long arms around her waist to nudge her closer. "But you've got to take care of yourself now. Let the kids handle things for a while."

She let her head rest against his lean chest, breathing in the familiar scents of salt and shaving cream. She'd just graduated from her walker to a cane. His support felt good in more ways than one. "Matt did everything while I was in the hospital. Ran his charter business and the inn, took care of Josh and Taylor. And when I got out of rehab, Meg came home to help. But I'm better now." Tess lifted her head to meet her husband's eyes. "I should be able to do more."

"Doctor said you need to take things slow. You do too much, you're going to wipe yourself out."

"I did close the inn for the holidays," she reminded him. "We don't have any guests until Sam's sister's wedding at New Year's. We'll just be family for Christmas."

"So you'll only be stuck with running around for, what? Seven people?"

"Nine," Tess said. "With Allison and Sam."

She was delighted to welcome Matt's new love into their home and their hearts. And Meg's Sam, bless him, had been part of the family since before they were in high school.

"Anyway, Meg is taking over the baking this year. Allison wants to help with decorating," Tess said.

Tom grunted, clearly unimpressed.

Tess couldn't help herself. Straight-faced, she added, "And I thought you could buy everybody's gifts this Christmas."

His jaw slackened. "You want me to . . ."

"I can write you a list," she offered helpfully, tongue planted firmly in cheek.

He braced like a man going into battle. "Sure. Whatever you . . ." He bent down to study her face. "You're kidding," he said in relief.

She smiled and patted his cheek. "I finished all the shopping online two weeks ago."

Tom chuckled. "Good one, babe."

"Thanks." Her grin spread. "Let me know if you want to help with the wrapping."

His hands slid to her butt and gave an affectionate squeeze. "Why don't I take you out to dinner instead?"

"Oh, Tom, I'd love to. But it's Taylor and Luke's first night in their new house."

"So they can get their own dinner."

"Or they could come with us," Tess suggested.

Tom met her gaze straight on. She was reminded suddenly of the first time she saw him, forty years ago, striding into her family's restaurant in Little Italy, straight as a rifle and cocky as hell. Two weeks later, they were married.

Maybe he didn't want to go out with the kids.

After months of her being in the hospital, in rehab, in pain, they had recently, carefully, begun to make love again. In some ways, her accident had brought them closer together than ever before. But the balance between them had shifted. Like old partners learning a new dance, they had yet to find their rhythm.

"Whatever you want," Tom said.

Tess flushed. What did she want?

I want everything to go back to normal. I want to be my old self again.

* * *

LUKE DUMPED A stack of folded T-shirts into an empty drawer. Compared to his sandbagged, mice-infested plywood hooch, this two-bedroom cottage was a palace. He had heat and hot water, a real toilet, and meals that didn't come out of a box.

He hoped the social worker was impressed.

He tossed some socks in after the shirts, chafing as if he hadn't changed his clothes or scrubbed under a hose in weeks.

He didn't mind a little boredom. He was used to long stretches of mind-numbing waiting punctuated by minutes of adrenaline-fueled terror.

He could handle the busy work. That's how he spent his downtime—repacking gear, recleaning weapons, linking machine gun rounds into his belt. You trained and prepared so that when the moment came, you were ready. You could react without thinking. And without mistakes.

But in Afghanistan, Luke knew exactly what he had to accomplish at all times. Everything was a matter of survival, of life or death. His men trusted him. And when he gave an order, they obeyed.

With Taylor . . . He didn't know what the hell he was doing. How something as simple as checking his daughter's homework or packing her lunch for school could blow up in his face. Or why he was fighting with a ten-year-old over which television shows she could watch or whether or not she ate her leafy vegetables. He could lead men into battle, but he couldn't get his daughter to eat a fucking salad.

And this home visit with the social worker threatened to expose all his weaknesses.

God only knows what she suspected him of already, what kind of talk was going around the island. Kate said the complaint was anonymous, the report confidential. But that wouldn't stop their neighbors from talking when Child Protective Services showed up at the door. Most of the talk would be kind. The Fletchers were well liked. But Luke felt terrible for bringing this trouble down on his family. His parents. Matt. Josh.

As long as you cooperate, Kate had said, *you have nothing to worry about.*

Which was the sort of thing the brass told you before they sent you without backup into a situation that was already FUBAR—Fucked-Up Beyond All Recognition.

Luke slid the drawer shut. His reflection glowered back at him from the mirror, frustration tightening his eyes and mouth.

You can do this, Kate had said.

He wanted to believe her.

He wanted to see her. Naked would be good.

He liked her, her humor and compassion and hot, sweet mouth, liked the laughter that lurked beneath her lawyer's mask and that little sound she made in her throat. He respected the way she battled for her clients, the way she'd had his six, her fierce focus on doing the right thing.

Taylor has to be your top priority, she'd said, and the hell of it was, she was right.

He was Taylor's father. He had to act like one for as long as he was around. His family expected it of him. He expected it of himself.

He didn't know what Taylor expected. She barely spoke to him.

Give her time, Matt had advised.

Easy for Matt to say. She talked to Matt. Matt had been there for her when the real shit went down, when Luke went back to Afghanistan, when some asshole drunk in an SUV plowed into their mother's car. Matt had handled the nightmares, the homework, the visits to the vice principal's office and to family court. Providing that stuff Kate talked about, things like routine, security, honesty, love.

Thank God for Matt.

Luke only heard about his daughter's life, his mother's accident, secondhand and after the fact, with all the gory details edited out. They all followed the unwritten contract of a deployed military family, dating from Tom's years in the Corps: *I won't tell you what it's really like here if you don't tell me what you're going through there.* There were things he'd seen and done he had no intention of talking about ever. Not even to his dad, who had done two tours in Nam.

Maybe especially not to Dad.

You need to answer everything she asks, even questions you think are none of her business, Kate had said about the visit from the social worker.

The thought made Luke break into a sweat.

He wished Taylor would talk more, though. Enough to let him know how she was doing. Or give him a clue to what he was doing wrong.

He looked up and there she was in the door of his room, silent as a ghost in her new athletic shoes, watching him from under the brim of his utility cap. Her face was blank, her eyes guarded.

He recognized the look and sighed. *At least she wasn't throwing rocks.* "How's your room?"

"It's fine."

In the Fletcher family, "fine" could mean anything from *It's all good* to *It's just a flesh wound.*

He tried again. "All unpacked?"

She nodded.

"You got your old stuff?" There hadn't been as much in that single carton as he'd hoped. A blue comforter and some pillows, Mardi Gras beads and a couple of stuffed animals. That picture of her mom from the box of photos.

Taylor gave another nod.

Luke's jaw clenched. He had hoped she'd show a little . . . He wasn't looking for gratitude. But some acknowledgment that he was here, that he was trying, that they were a unit now, would be good. He wanted his daughter to feel like they were a family. Like this was home. They had their own house now. She had her own room. She needed . . .

"One more thing," he said. He waited until her gaze

met his. "It came in yesterday. A buddy of mine was holding it until this weekend, but I was thinking we could pick it up today. If you want to ride along."

It was a safe bet she'd say no. She had yet to show any real desire for his company.

"Okay." Taylor tilted her head. "Where are we going?"

With her head cocked, she looked like Bibi, the dog his squad had adopted back in Afghanistan. Hopeful. Doubtful.

The knot in his jaw eased. "It's a surprise."

"I don't like surprises."

"You'll like this one," he said.

He hoped.

They stopped by the main house. At almost thirty years old, he didn't need to tell his parents every time he went out. But he didn't want them to worry about the kid.

"I've got Taylor," he called. "We'll be gone for a while."

"Good," Tom said.

Luke raised his brows. His parents were standing close together—*very* close together—by the kitchen counter. His mother's face was pink. Her eyes were bright.

"Where are you going?" she asked.

"It's a surprise," Taylor piped up.

"Heading to the base," Luke said. "Pick up that package I told you about."

"Is that a good idea? With, well, everything else going on?"

Because of everything else going on. "We'll be fine," Luke said.

"I thought you were going Saturday."

Luke met his dad's eyes. "Change of plans."

"Semper Gumby," Tom said.

"What?" Taylor asked.

Luke glanced down. "It's a saying. Like . . . be flexible. Like Gumby."

"Oh."

Maybe she was too young to remember the cartoon.

His mother smoothed her hair. "Will you be home for dinner?"

"Thanks," Luke said. "We're good."

Time to get out of the old people's hair and let them get back to . . . Well, Jesus, he didn't want to think about what they were getting back to. They were his parents, for Christ's sake. But it was pretty cool that they were still into each other after all these years. One of these days . . .

Okay, no. He wasn't looking for a house and a ring and the next forty years waking up next to the same woman. Any woman, he told himself as he went outside to the Jeep, and shook Kate Dolan from his mind. He would be gone in three months. He could be dead. He didn't think about the future. He had responsibilities, he thought with a touch of desperation. To his men. To the Corps. He had *commitments*.

Taylor climbed into the Jeep in front of him, wiggling around to reach for her seat belt, all bony angles and soft blond hair, and the solid ground beneath him shook and shifted like a road in the wake of an explosion.

His hand clenched on the door of the Jeep as he struggled for balance.

He had a responsibility here, too. A commitment. What was he going to do about that in three months? What was he going to do about Taylor?

He took a deep breath and started the ignition. Nothing, he decided.

They'd get through this home visit and then they'd figure something out. Taylor would be fine. The family would pull together, the way they always did. He would do his duty, the way he always had. Nobody could ask, nobody could expect, more of him than that.

They never had.

TAYLOR ROLLED HER head against the back of her seat, sneaking a look at her dad . . . at Luke under her eyelashes as they drove along. He had a good face, thin and tan and strong, with little wrinkles at the corners of his eyes like he smiled or squinted a lot.

He wasn't smiling now. Maybe he was sorry he invited her along.

My mom thinks your dad is hot, her best friend Madison Lodge had whispered in class this morning when they were supposed to be working on their group science project.

Taylor had resisted the urge to roll her eyes. Madison's mom thought Uncle Matt was hot, too.

Wouldn't it be cool if he asked her out? Madison had continued. *What if they got married? Then we would be sisters.*

Taylor really liked Madison and her little sister, Hannah. It would be cool to have a sister. Or sisters. But she wasn't ready for another mom. She wasn't even used to having a dad yet.

She snuck another look at his profile, feeling a little glow of pride at the way he looked in his uniform, all tall and serious. He had big boots that laced halfway up his legs and made a loud sound when he walked. Like his boots meant business.

When he came to pick her up that first day at Grandma Jo's, she'd never been so glad to see anybody in all her life.

She'd felt safe. No more sleeping on the couch. No more creepy Uncle Kevin.

Her dad was there to protect her.

But then he'd gone away again.

Maybe she shouldn't get used to having a dad. Because what if she did and then something happened to him?

Taylor swallowed and stared out the window, a funny feeling in her stomach.

She tried to make up some story, where her dad got injured in the war and she nursed him back to health and he loved her and stayed home with her forever. But she couldn't make the story work, even in her head. She was just a kid. She couldn't take care of anybody. Anyway, she wasn't even sure her dad liked her very much.

I want to be with you, he'd said, like he meant it.

Maybe.

But he was still going away.

Sometimes she wished her mom had told her about Luke when she was alive. Maybe, if Luke had known about her before, he would have wanted to see her sometimes.

Maybe she would have grown up visiting with the Fletchers, Uncle Matt and Aunt Meg, Grandma Tess and Grandpa Tom. And Josh. She loved Josh.

And then she felt bad. It wasn't like she had needed a dad back then. She had Mom. She missed her mom. *We don't need anybody*, Mom would say as they snuggled together on the couch, staying up late, watching movies. Or going into Kinston to watch a baseball game, eating hotdogs under the lights.

But then Mom died. What if her dad died, too?

Taylor couldn't stand it.

A rush of air battered her ears. She looked over. Luke had rolled down his window and was reaching into his shirt pocket for a pack of cigarettes.

She scowled. "You're not supposed to smoke in front of me."

"Sorry." He tapped the pack back into his pocket. Rolled the window back up.

"You're setting a bad example," she said, taking a certain satisfaction in being a brat.

Luke looked at her, a smile tugging at the corner of his mouth. "You don't sound like you're about to light up just because you watched me smoke a cigarette."

Taylor sniffed, resisting the urge to smile back. "I might. Anyway, smoking's bad for you. You could get cancer." *You could die.* Her heart clutched. "You should quit."

"You're right." He nodded. "I will. I only smoke on deployment anyway."

She eyed him sideways, wanting to believe. "Seriously?"

"Yeah. The smoke's not good for you, either. This way we'll both stay healthy."

Okay. That sounded like he planned to be around a while. "Promise?" she said, not sure exactly what she was asking. *Please quit? Don't die? Don't leave me?*

"Promise," he said.

Taylor sighed and let her head rest against the back of her seat, only partially reassured.

THE ENTRYWAY OF the small brown house smelled of diapers and dogs.

"Sorry, Staff Sergeant." Corporal Danny Hill led the way through the narrow hall to the kitchen. "It's been crazy around here. Beer?"

"No, I'm good, thanks." Luke edged a stroller out of their path. Behind him, Taylor stepped over the bright plastic rings scattered on the floor. "Appreciate you doing this. How's the new mama?"

"Stephanie's out with the baby." Danny grimaced. "All this is a little much for her."

"Yeah, I bet." Luke cleared his throat, embarrassed. "I meant the dog."

"Oh, right. See for yourself. She's right here. Bibi!" he called.

The tan hound scrambled from under the kitchen table, her thin tail whipping back and forth, her dark-ringed eyes on Luke.

Luke dropped to a crouch, gladness flooding him. "Hey, Bibi. Hey, girl. How's it going?"

In answer, the dog flopped on to her back, exposing her belly for a rub.

Luke obliged, noting as he did so that her stomach was almost back to normal. "Taylor, meet Bibi."

"Hi, Bibi." Taylor got down on the floor beside him, offering her hand to the dog. Bibi sniffed and took a polite swipe at her palm with a soft, pink tongue. "She's nice. Is she yours?" Taylor asked Danny.

"Yeah." Danny thrust out his jaw. "You save a life, it belongs to you."

Taylor's eyes widened. "You saved her life?"

Some of the defensiveness went out of Danny's pose.

"Not me. Your dad did. Rescued her when we were out on patrol. Bibi saved *my* life, chasing off some bad guys."

"Good dog." Taylor rubbed the flat, scarred head. "Good Bibi."

Above her head, Luke met Danny's eyes. "Is Stephanie okay with this? With the dog?"

"Yeah, sure. She bought Bibi a steak the first night, like a thank-you present. She likes dogs. It's just . . . You know." Danny shrugged.

Luke didn't know, exactly. Hell, he wasn't married. But the emotional well-being of his men was his responsibility. And he'd watched his parents long enough to guess where the trouble could be.

"Sure," he said casually. "Coming home. New baby. New pet. It's an adjustment."

"It's a lot of work. I try to help out," Danny said. "But she just gets mad if I do things my way."

Oh, yeah, he knew this one. Tom and Tess had always done their best to present a united front to their children. But after every deployment, Tom would spend a couple of weeks barking orders, and Chicago-born Italian Tess would make it clear that whatever tactics had worked with his Marines wouldn't fly in her house.

"Stephanie's been handling everything on her own for eleven months," Luke said. "You've got to respect that."

"I do. She's terrific."

"Have you told her how proud you are of her?"

"I . . ." Danny stopped. Grinned sheepishly. "Shit."

"You can tell her when she gets home." Luke rose with a final pat, satisfied he'd made his point. "And you tell her we took one of your problems off your hands today."

"Thanks, Staff Sergeant. They're out back," Danny said.

"Where are we going?" Taylor asked Luke.

"This way."

She trailed him to the door. "Is it my surprise?"

He gestured to her to go ahead.

"What is . . ."

Yip yip. An eddy of movement in the yard, a swirl of black, tan, white.

"*Puppies!*" Her voice rose with delight.

Luke grinned, victory and relief loosening his shoulders. So he'd done okay. It felt good, like getting his Expert badge in marksmanship.

A wave raced across the browning grass and flung itself at the steps. Taylor waded in and was engulfed in a whirlpool of small, solid, furry bodies—Bibi's three pups, tumbling over each other in competition for her attention. Taylor giggled—a pure, happy sound he'd never heard from her before—and sank down, her arms outstretched as she tried to touch, pat, hug them all. The little girl, the joyful dogs and sunlit yard combined into a picture so bright it stung his eyes. His chest tightened.

He cleared his throat. "So what do you think?"

She turned her head to face him, catching a lick on the chin from the sandy-colored pup. She snorted with laughter, putting her arms around the wriggly body in her lap. "They're so cute. They're so little."

"They'll get bigger. And they're old enough."

"Old enough for what?"

"To find homes. New homes. Which one do you like?"

"I love them all. I . . ." Her head jerked around again. "What? Why?"

He swallowed, trying to keep things from getting sloppy. Kate's words replayed in his head. *Are you ready to take on the responsibility for another living being right now?*

The puppy needed a home, he told himself.

Taylor needed a home.

"Well, Danny can't keep them all here," he said matter-of-factly. "Cody Burrows—he's another buddy—he's taking two to his family's farm in Texas. That leaves one for you."

"For . . ." Her voice trailed off. Her eyes met his, wide, shining. "*Me?* It would be my dog? Mine?"

Her desperate hope, her stunned disbelief, humbled and

scared him. He nodded, tucking his hands in his back pockets. "Seems only fair. Since you'll be the one doing all the work. Feeding it and stuff."

"I would. I will. I'll take really good care of it. I'll walk it and feed it and . . ."

"Relax," he said. "You'll be fine. He'll be fine."

"Are we getting a boy dog or a girl dog?"

Did it matter? Maybe to a ten-year-old, he thought. "Whatever you want. Bojangles there, with the patches, is a girl. Popeyes and Ronald—that's Ronald—are boys."

Taylor looked at the cream-colored fluff ball squirming in her lap, enthusiastically covering every inch of exposed skin with puppy spit. "Ronald is a terrible name for a dog," she said with disapproval.

"He's kind of a clown," Luke explained.

Her nose scrunched. She didn't get it.

"You can change his name," he added. "If you want."

Doubt warred with naked longing in her face. "Won't Fezzik mind?" she asked earnestly. "If we get another dog?"

"Nah. He needs somebody to boss around."

She looked unconvinced.

"He needs somebody to play with," Luke amended. "To take care of."

And so, he thought, do you.

Her squinched little face relaxed. She nodded, her arms tightening possessively around the puppy. The gesture gripped at his heart, clenched his gut.

So do I, he thought, before he caught himself and brushed the feeling away.

Eight

KATE STOOD PARALYZED in the Morehead City pet super store. *This* was what came of making impulsive decisions. Of getting emotionally involved. Of falling victim to the appeal in a little girl's eyes, the temptation of her daddy's kiss. You wound up stalking the cat food aisle, trying to decide between chicken-n-gravy or seafood medley.

Children of alcoholics are frequently afraid of making the wrong choices, came the lecturing voice of her therapist, Judith Frum. *You need to learn to trust your instincts.*

Easy for Judith to say. Her instincts had obviously never landed her in Cat Food Hell.

Kate fought down panic, surveying the bright rows as if careful study would yield the desired answer. She was almost certain that yesterday she'd seen a dirty white shadow slinking under Dawn's bushes. It had to be Snowball. Anyway, *something* had been eating the canned tuna she'd left on Dawn's back porch.

Raccoons, supplied the lawyerly side of her brain. *Possums. Rats . . .*

Kate shuddered. She'd already plunked down fifty dollars for a humane cat rescue kit. All she had to do was bait her trap.

"The hell with it," she muttered.

She grabbed an armload of cans at random from the nearest shelf and marched toward the registers.

"Ronald! *Ronald!*" a child called.

"Damn it, dog." A man's voice, more amused than annoyed.

Kate froze. *Was that . . . ?*

"There he is!"

She caught a blur at the corner of her eye, moving fast and low to the ground, and checked herself just in time to avoid the puppy scampering up the main aisle. His leash whipped across the floor. Kate tripped, slipped and flung out her arms, executing a clumsy shuffle-change step as a little girl—*Taylor*—dashed by in pursuit. Cans of cat food scattered and rolled.

A hard, warm arm wrapped her waist. A lean, muscled body took her weight.

"Nice moves," Luke said in her ear. "You okay?"

Her breathing hitched, lifting her breasts against his chest. His face was close and smiling.

Heat swept from her throat to her hairline. "Fine," she said stiffly. "I—"

Taylor reappeared, the puppy tugging on a leash behind her. "Sorry," she said. To which one of them, Kate wasn't sure.

The child's anxious gaze tugged at Kate. She'd always liked Dawn's daughter, who was bright and confident and funny, if Dawn's stories were true. But the sad truth was Kate wasn't very good with children outside her office. What did she have to offer them besides her jar of candy, her box of tissues?

"Hi, Taylor," Kate said.

"Hi."

Kate looked down at the puppy, tan and wobbly, with huge paws and a kink in its tail. Its short face was marked with black patches in place of eyebrows, giving it a permanently quizzical expression. Kind of like Taylor's. "Who's this?"

Taylor beamed. "That's my dog." Her gaze switched to Luke, her big eyes suddenly anxious. Kate tensed in instinctive sympathy. "I was watching him, honest. He just pulled all of a sudden, and I—"

"It's okay," Luke interrupted.

Kate cleared her throat. "I'm sure she was trying—"

"I said it's okay."

"I didn't mean to let go," Taylor said.

"I know. Try holding on like this." Releasing Kate, Luke dropped to his heels and slid the loop of the leash over Taylor's wrist. "You were right about that name," he added.

The girl regarded him warily from under the brim of her hat. "Yeah?"

Kate held her breath.

"Yeah. We should change it." His smile crinkled the corners of his eyes. "Dog sure as hell isn't answering to 'Ronald.'"

Taylor's laugh sputtered out. Luke grinned back.

A void opened in Kate's chest. So much love there, she thought. In his eyes, in his smile. She wondered if either of them recognized it yet.

His hand hovered, as if he might pat Taylor's shoulder, and then he tugged her cap instead. "Why don't you go find the mutt here something to chew on besides my boots while I talk with Kate, okay?"

"Okay. Come on, puppy." She pulled the leash. The dog caught it in his mouth and danced alongside her up the nearby aisle, his black-tipped tail moving in frantic circles, his whole body quivering with pleasure.

Kate watched them dive into a bin of rubber bones and Santas. She glanced at Luke, wondering how to tell him what his carefully casual reassurance had meant to her. To Taylor, she corrected. She could only imagine her own father's reaction if she'd been careless enough to cause a disturbance in a public space.

"Nice move," she said, using his words.

Luke rose, tall and substantial in his olive green shirt and fatigues. "It doesn't take Einstein to figure out that kids like dogs."

That wasn't what she meant, but she let it pass for now. "So you bought her a puppy," she said dryly. *A man of action.*

"Not 'buy.' He's a rescue."

"You got your daughter a shelter dog?" That was kind, she thought.

"Sort of. My squad adopted the mother dog a couple months back. Or she adopted us."

"I thought there were rules against pets in a war zone." Roger Dolan had been big on rules. The problem was he never informed his family when those rules changed, and behavior that was acceptable one day could earn a slap or a sneer the next.

Luke shrugged. "Most bases have cats and dogs. They keep the mice down and morale up. Usually they stick around when the unit's rotated out and get adopted by the next guys. But we were turning the base over to the Afghans. The mama dog used to patrol with us. I couldn't leave her there."

She looked at his daughter, squatting on the floor with the puppy, and back at Luke. A warm, liquid rush flooded her chest. Maybe, in some small corner of her heart, she'd still doubted him. Not his intentions—she knew he was trying his best—but his commitment. What did she know about him, after all, except that he'd knocked up his high school girlfriend and moved on? He hadn't known about Taylor. He hadn't cared enough to know.

But she'd been wrong. This was a man who couldn't leave a dog behind. Who must have gone to considerable trouble to rescue this one.

I couldn't leave her.

"So you brought her with you."

"Not with. The shelter in Kabul shipped them out. There's a thirty-day waiting period after they got their shots."

They? *The mama dog*, he'd said. Kate glanced again at the puppy. "That must have been expensive, flying . . . How many dogs?"

"Four. Bibi and three puppies."

"Four dogs from Afghanistan."

He jammed his hands in his pockets. "We all chipped in. Hell, Ortega was ready to organize a bake sale to get them home. And the shelter helped with donations."

"Well." A smile tugged her lips. "I guess it was cheaper than buying Taylor a pony for Christmas."

He met her gaze. "You said she needed love," he reminded her. "Nothing loves you like a dog."

She had said that. But she hadn't expected him to listen, let alone take her advice. She glanced away, unaccountably breathless. The puppy was crawling in and over Taylor's lap, lunging at the toy in her hand, licking everything within reach.

That couldn't be hygienic. "It certainly seems affectionate," she said uncertainly.

"You don't like dogs?"

Was that some kind of test question? Had she failed already? "I'm not used to them."

"No pets growing up?"

"No." Too blunt. She tried again. "My father didn't like animals in the house. They shed, they smell, they cry, they don't listen . . ."

Luke was watching her, that too perceptive, too sympathetic gleam in his eyes. "Like kids."

She winced. "Yes." Her father didn't like her, either.

Luke nodded toward the scattered cans. "So now you have a cat."

Kate bit her lip. She wasn't ready to confess that she'd been back to Dawn's house four times already searching for Snowball. What if the trap didn't work? What if Snowball was lost? Or dead? "Um, no." *Not yet.*

Luke crouched again and began to pick up cans. "So what is all this? You eating cat food while you pay off your student loans?"

A laugh bubbled up. She knelt to help him, awkward in her skirt and heels. "I'm thinking I might get a cat. I want to be prepared."

He shook his head. "Lawyers."

She arched her eyebrows, instantly on the defensive. "You have a problem with the law?"

"I don't have any outstanding warrants, if that's what you mean. I just think it would be better, easier, if people settled their disputes without going to court."

"Or to war."

He smiled, acknowledging her point. "That, too."

He wasn't offended. She stood with an armload of cans, her heart pattering with relief and lust. "So is it lawyers in general you have an issue with or has something happened to upset you?"

"No, we're good." He hesitated, then added, "I talked to your friend in social services. Alisha Douglas? She's coming out to the island tomorrow."

She dragged her mind off her stupid heart and focused on his case. "Well, that's good," she said heartily.

"Our lawyer said an investigation could take weeks. But the social worker acted like it was no big deal."

"It shouldn't be," Kate said, confident now that they were on safer, legal ground. Here, at least, she knew what she was talking about. She could offer him something, encouragement or reassurance. "No one in your family has a criminal record. There's no history of the police getting called or unexplained trips to the emergency room. No substance abuse. Nothing to substantiate the allegations in the report."

He stuck his thumbs in his front pockets. "How do you know?"

She opened her mouth. Shut it. "I may have . . . discussed your case with Alisha. Sometimes a simple home visit is all that's needed to resolve a complaint."

"Appreciate it," he said quietly.

Kate felt herself flushing under that bright blue gaze.

"I was merely sharing my professional judgment as someone familiar with the parties involved. I would never interfere where the safety of a child was at stake. I believe in the system."

"Systems can screw up."

"Yes, they can." She looked at Taylor playing with the puppy and thought of all the children who fell between the cracks. The runaways, the lost, children on the streets or in unsafe homes, battered, scared, abused. "That's why there are safeguards," she said. "Social Services is required by law to respond to every report. That doesn't mean they have to waste precious time and resources on every crackpot who complains about a neighbor who lets her child run into the street. Or a grandparent calls," she added deliberately, "with an axe to grind."

He studied her thoughtfully. "Why are you taking my side?"

"I don't know," she admitted. Somehow, without meaning to, she'd aligned herself with Luke and his daughter. Acting from her gut, choosing with her heart.

And that terrified her.

In Kate's experience, emotional decisions were bad decisions.

Look at her mother, who'd married her father out of love and stayed with him out of fear. Look at ninety percent of her clients, who were willing to sacrifice money, dignity, even the safety of their kids because they could not separate their emotions from their judgment.

"I'm on Taylor's side," she said, choosing her words carefully. "And the law's. Taylor wants to stay with you. And the law says that unless you act in some way that abrogates your rights as a parent, you and Taylor are a family."

His gaze never left her face. "The Simpsons are her family, too. First time we talked, you thought she should be with them."

Her flush deepened as she recalled that first, awkward phone conversation. "That was before I knew . . ." *You.*

"The full situation," she said. "If you hadn't been willing or able to care for her, it would have made sense for Taylor to stay with Dawn's family."

"Uh-huh." He moved in, threatening her personal space, a wicked gleam in his eyes. "And now that you know . . . the situation better, how do you feel?"

She felt hot, overwhelmed by his nearness, mesmerized by that touch of stubble under his jaw where he'd missed shaving. She was excruciatingly aware of him, of his body, close and honed and dangerous as a knife. So close, he must see everything, too. The blush she struggled to suppress. Her scar.

She drew a shaky breath, fighting to regain her emotional footing. "I feel you and Taylor deserve a chance. It's what Dawn wanted. And that's what I told Jolene."

"Wait." He pulled back. "*You* told Jolene? You talked to Dawn's parents?"

She nodded, swallowing her regret over the loss of his heat. "After your mother's accident, the Simpsons asked if I would file the motion to amend the custody agreement."

"But you didn't."

"No."

"Why not?"

She glared. "Conflict of interest."

Except it hadn't been, not really, she admitted to herself. The truth was, she hadn't *wanted* to take their case.

"Because of Dawn," he said.

Because of you, she thought. *And Taylor.*

Because by the time Dawn's parents asked Kate to represent them, she'd already met Luke. The contrast between his tight-lipped determination to do the right thing and Ernie and Jolene's teary-eyed, grasping affection had forever tipped the balance in his favor.

"The reasons don't matter," Kate said, wanting desperately to believe it. Because lust was not a good reason, and trust was too often misplaced. "The point is, I told them to get another lawyer."

Luke crossed his arms, making the hard curve of his biceps bulge. Really, it ought to be illegal for a man to have muscles like that. "You told my brother and sister the same thing."

"I recommended Vernon to them, yes." The recommendation had been her gift to Taylor and the Fletchers. Old-school lawyer Vernon Long had over twenty years in the North Carolina courts. He was as wily and aggressive as a bull shark, perfectly suited to surviving in his environment, his bow ties and folksy charm hiding a tenacious intelligence and a crushing bite. Kate admired him tremendously. "He's good," she said.

"I'll take your word for it." Luke looked at his daughter, currently engaged in a tug-of-war with the puppy over a red rubber ball. "He says Taylor doesn't need to come to court this time."

Was that a request for reassurance, under the tough guy tone?

She yearned to comfort him. But she didn't know how. It had taken her years to learn to accept, to respect, her own feelings. But she was still uncomfortable talking about them. And she was no good at all at offering emotional support.

So she gave him legal advice instead. "Not unless she's subpoenaed. Which she won't be. Not after she told the judge last time that she wanted to stay with you. The Simpsons are probably counting on the social services investigation to support their case."

"Great." Luke's jaw bunched in a way she was beginning to recognize.

"It *is* great." She risked a touch on his arm. "Their strategy could easily backfire. Assuming Alisha concludes her investigation before your hearing date—which she will—this could all go away by Christmas."

"Right." He met her eyes. He didn't smile, but the warmth in his eyes was as good as a kiss. Almost. "Thanks."

Her heart thrummed. "You're welcome."

Squeak squeak squeak went the ball.

Luke thrust his hands into his back pockets. "What about you?"

Kate blinked. "What about me?"

"Any special plans for the holiday?"

"Oh. No." She pulled herself together. "I have to work."

He raised one blond eyebrow. "At Christmas?"

"Holidays are a stressful time even for families that don't have problems." Even to her own ears, she sounded dull. Stiff. "When people are depressed or angry, they make bad decisions."

"And you try to stop them."

She tried to *save* them. She tried to fix them. The way she'd never been able to fix her own family.

"I try to keep them focused on a positive outcome, yes," she said lightly.

"Like you just did with me."

"I . . ." She met his gaze. His blue eyes were aware. Appreciative. Something inside her softened and deflated, like a child's punch clown when the air was let out. "Maybe."

"Must make it tough on your family, you working over Christmas."

She didn't want to talk about her family. "Not really. There's just my mother. She spends the holidays with her sister in Virginia." Aunt Sharon, who didn't judge, who had children and grandchildren to satisfy her mother's desire for the appearance of family.

"So you'll be here. Alone?"

She put her chin up at the suggestion of sympathy. She didn't need his pity. "Working."

"We'll see you around, then."

Just for a moment, she allowed herself to picture it, Luke and Taylor, the puppy and a Christmas tree, bright and shiny as a family on TV or a window display at Nordstrom.

And about as far removed from her real life, she reminded herself. Like the child she had been, watching the Huxtables for clues to normal behavior, like a homeless woman staring in the shop windows, she could look, but not touch.

"Not exactly around," she felt compelled to point out. "You live forty minutes away."

"I'll see you," he repeated, his gaze steady on hers, and she felt a little thrill run up and down her arms, as if the words were a threat.

Or a promise.

Nine

"LIGHTS OUT NOW. I mean it," Luke said.

Taylor and the puppy looked at him from their separate beds with the same huge, abused eyes. "But I always sleep with a light on."

He dragged his hand over his face, resisting the urge to bang his head against the door. "Yeah, I know. That's fine. I meant . . . No more noise. It's time to go to sleep now, okay?"

Five more minutes and he'd be begging. How did his mother put up with this? How did Matt?

"O-*kay*," Taylor said in a put-upon voice.

Luke sighed. "Good night," he said for the twelfth or maybe the twentieth time that night. Gently, he closed the door. He knew damn well that the brand new dog bed in the corner would be empty as soon as he left the room.

Sure enough, he was halfway down the hall when he heard a whine from the dog and then a whisper from Taylor. He caught himself grinning, listening to the scratch of puppy paws across the hardwood floor.

But maybe this time they understood he meant business.

Or maybe all that jumping up and down was tiring them, too. Because this time after the initial scrambling there weren't any sounds he couldn't pretend to ignore.

He paced through the empty cottage, as jumpy, as restless in his own way as the dog. He opened the refrigerator and shut it, turned the TV on and off, slipped on to the front porch to grab some air.

A quarter moon was rising above the roof of the Pirates' Rest. The chill struck through his long-sleeved shirt. The sky was clear and cold and pulsing with stars, the breeze edged with salt.

God, he'd missed this. Not the cold. There were nights in Afghanistan, shivering beneath two layers of everything he owned, when he thought he'd never be warm again. But he'd missed the scent and the sound of the sea. The sense of home.

He tipped back his head. It was a night made for howling at the moon. All he needed was . . . Something.

Or someone.

His mind jumped to Kate Dolan, his body springing to attention like Fezzik spotting a squirrel. *Instinct.*

A lot of Marines returning from war sought to replace the adrenaline buzz of combat with some other form of high-risk behavior, booze or brawls or motorcycle racing. Maybe he simply felt more alive when he was with her, his senses heightened, his overactive memories drowned out in the rush of her presence.

Maybe Kate was his motorcycle. His jockey rocket.

He grinned. He could just picture her face if he told her that.

Whatever it was, she did things to him. Stirred him up or settled him down. She was so beautiful, with her bright hair and darkening eyes. He liked her big words and little smile and quick lawyer's brain. The way she moved quietly behind the scenes to get things done. The fact that she cared so much and tried so damn hard.

He liked *her*, the warmth and humor that snuck out from

behind the stiffness and polish. He wondered what she looked like without all that makeup. Without all her clothes.

He exhaled. There was a time not so long ago when Matt would be the one home with the baby, he thought. When Meg would be studying up in her room, busting her ass to get into Harvard, while Luke went joyriding with his friends and drinking under the pier. Now Matt was over at Allison's, and Meg was out with Sam. Both of them getting lucky, Luke figured.

He shifted, restless in his own skin. His body felt heavy. Hot.

But he needed more than a woman. He wanted . . . Kate.

A creak carried on the evening breeze.

His senses went on alert.

The old inn was never completely quiet. Added to the noise of family and guests were the pops and cracks of any century-old house, the rattle of windows and shutters, the sighing and tapping of trees.

But this was different, Luke thought. A hushed whisper. A muffled scrape. Like somebody trying not to be heard.

Or seen.

Luke's pulse quickened as he scanned the area. Matt's cottage was dark except for a light on the porch and another in Josh's window. Anyway, the sound didn't come from there.

Across the yard, the glow of the television and the twinkle of Christmas lights reflected against the inn's back windows. Their work done, his parents sat at the end of the day in the family room off the kitchen, taking comfort in each other and some old movie. The deep eaves at the side of the house shadowed the wraparound porch and the guest patio, sheltered by a trellis.

Another furtive sound scraped against his straining ears. *There.*

His heart pumped, all his pent up energy pouring out

in suspicion and sweat. He was overreacting, he told himself. Edgy from lack of sex and a ten-month tour. The noise would only be caused by a guest or a cat or the wind.

But . . . It was too late and much too cold for guests to sit out and admire the empty garden.

It couldn't hurt to check things out.

He glanced over his shoulder at Taylor's window. The glow of her night-light edged the blind. She wouldn't miss him. He'd only be gone a minute. Silently, he made his way across the back yard and along the side of the inn.

Shrubs screened the patio. A few camellias still bloomed, white saucers in the dark. Deep in the shadows, something moved. Luke tensed, his gaze sweeping the bare tables and empty chairs, the shrouded lounger in the corner.

The shroud billowed.

Luke inhaled sharply.

And his nephew Josh sat up in the lounger, dragging the blanket with him. "Who . . . Uncle Luke?"

"Yeah." Luke released his breath, suppressing a grin. He must have given the kid a heart attack. *Fair's fair.* His own pulse still raced. He strolled forward, hands in his pocket. "What are you doing out here?"

"I, uh . . ."

The blanket undulated again, revealing the other occupant of the lounger. The young, female occupant, a fresh-faced girl with a tumble of dark red hair and an impressive rack.

Luke stopped.

She struggled upright, tugging at her sweater. "Hi," she said with remarkable self-possession. "We haven't met. I'm Thalia."

"Nice to meet you. Luke," he introduced himself, working to keep his expression neutral. "Josh's uncle."

"Yes, I know. You just got back from Afghanistan." She fumbled on a side table for dark-framed glasses and put them on. "Thank you for your service," she added politely.

He never knew what to say to that. *Ooh-rah? You're welcome?* "Thanks."

Luke looked from Josh to the lounger. Hell. The kid was sixteen, only a couple years younger than some of the boots under Luke's command. He did not want to police his nephew's sex life. But now that he'd walked in on the boy practically having sex under a blanket, he couldn't just walk away. "Kind of cold to be outside," he observed.

Probably not cold under the blanket, though. Especially not if you were doing what they were doing.

Josh stood, yanking his untucked shirt down to cover what was undoubtedly an erection. "I'm not supposed to have friends in the house when Dad's out," he said.

Which Luke translated to mean *No girls.* Obviously Matt was trying to save his son from making the same kind of mistake they'd both made at that age.

"But the porch is okay," Luke said.

Josh grinned sheepishly and refused to meet his gaze.

"Actually, I was just leaving," the girl said brightly, rescuing him and the situation. "It's getting kind of late. See you tomorrow," she said to Josh.

"I've got that thing after school."

That thing. Luke tensed. The social worker's visit.

"Then I'll see you in class," the girl said equably.

"Thanks. I mean, yeah. See you."

"He can walk you home," Luke said. Maybe the cold air would do them both some good. Maybe Josh would make out with the girl on *her* porch, and her father would come out and beat some sense into him. He wouldn't be Luke's responsibility then.

"No, it's all right. I drove my parents' car," she explained. "So I'll be fine. Good night."

"Good night," they both echoed.

Luke watched as she slipped down the long side of the inn to the front, negotiating easily in the dark. Like she'd done this before. Like she knew where she was going. The car was parked by the curb, out of sight of the house and the inn's back windows.

Shit. He was going to have to say something.

He thrust his hands into his pockets. "Nice girl."

"Thalia?" Josh asked, elaborately casual, like there were other girls.

Maybe there were.

Jesus, he felt old. Luke dropped into a chair—*See? Nonthreatening*—while he figured out his next move. He cleared his throat. What would Matt say? "Do we need to have a talk?"

"No," Josh said.

Luke kept silent, a trick he'd learned worked with the Marines under his command.

Apparently it worked with Josh, too, because he swallowed and volunteered, "It's not like that, honest, Uncle Luke. We're just friends."

Luke raised his brows. "So you were shaking hands under that blanket?"

"Yeah. No. I mean . . ." Josh flopped onto another chair, set at an angle so he could avoid eye contact. "We were fooling around, that's all." A pause. "Thalia's really smart."

Smart enough to avoid getting knocked up at sixteen?

"So are you," Luke said. "Even smart kids can screw up."

"She wants to go to Chapel Hill," Josh said.

The University of North Carolina at Chapel Hill. Luke didn't get the connection. "And you don't," he said, testing.

"Hell, no," Josh said. "Mom's there. She teaches in the psych department."

Josh's mother left him and Matt when Josh was three months old. As best as Luke could recall, Josh hadn't spent any real time with her since. Maybe a week, eight years ago, after she'd remarried? Luke had been in Fallujah at the time. But he seemed to remember the visit had not gone well.

"You don't get along?"

Josh grinned. "Sure, we do. Every once in a while she reads something about parent-child attachment and calls me. Or sends a really nice check in the next birthday card."

Luke didn't know what to say. "Sorry. That sucks."

"No, it's okay," Josh said. "We're good. I've got Dad. I'm glad she leaves us alone."

Like stones in a well, the words sent up echoes inside

Luke. What had Dawn written? *We've never needed any-body, Taylor and me.*

"What about now?" Luke asked.

Josh's forehead wrinkled.

"Allison," Luke said. "Your dad's getting married again."

"Allison's cool. For a teacher."

"You taking any shit at school?" It had been ten years, but Luke remembered that the island was like a military post, with everybody into everybody's business. And the smaller high school grapevine fed on and intensified the gossip.

"You mean, because Dad's marrying my English teacher?" Josh shook his head. "Well, I had to pound some on Ethan Wilson for calling her a MILF."

"A MILF." Luke laughed. Winced. "Jesus. She's what, my age?"

"Younger." Josh grinned. "You're getting old, Unc Luke."

"I can still take you, wiseass."

"Because you're a Ninja."

A Marine. Close enough.

"When Grandma was in the hospital," Josh said and stopped.

Luke waited.

"It was right after the accident. Dad, everybody was at the hospital except for me and Taylor. And Allison came. To be with us, you know?" Josh looked up from his sneakers, his face young and raw. "She was there."

Luke nodded to show his understanding. "She shows up."

Josh met his gaze. "She sticks," he said simply. His mother had not stuck. "And she's good for Dad."

Pride and affection closed Luke's throat. Whatever Josh's mother had or hadn't done, Matt had done a great job raising the boy on his own. He was a good kid. Kind. Responsible. And almost a man.

He cleared his throat. "You sound awfully well adjusted. For a punk."

"Yeah." Josh shot him a sly, bright look. "Wait til you hear me charm the social worker."

"Has your dad talked to you?"

"About the visit tomorrow? Yeah."

Luke gritted his teeth. "About taking responsibility."

Josh looked at him blankly.

Oh, crap. Did he have to spell it out? "About birth control. Condoms."

Josh grinned. "Come on, Uncle Luke. We're talking about *Dad*. Mr. Responsibility. He sat me down for the big sex talk the second I started sprouting hair. He's kept an open box of condoms in the bathroom since I was, like, fourteen."

Relief roughened Luke's voice. "Make sure you use them."

"Will do." Another grin. "Just because I'm, like, the poster child for unprotected sex doesn't mean I'm stupid."

"You turned out all right." They sat a moment in companionable silence, staring out at the darkened garden. "You know your dad never regretted having you, right?" Luke said gruffly.

Josh ducked his head, embarrassed. "Jeez, Uncle Luke. I know."

"Okay."

"Thanks, though." A sidelong look. "Are you sorry you had Taylor?"

The question caught Luke like an undertow, dragging him in too deep. *Was he sorry*?

When he'd first heard from Kate that he was a father, he'd thought the whole thing was a horrible joke. But then there was Taylor, waiting for him to get off the bus, braced like a Marine for battle, his cover jammed over her cornsilk hair. Or dissolving into giggles, playing with the puppies in the sunlit yard.

"No," he said slowly. "I'm not sorry. I'm sorry I didn't know about her for so long, though."

Wasn't he?

If he'd known Dawn was pregnant with his child, he might never have enlisted, might never have left Dare Island. He wouldn't have kept the peace in Kosovo or distributed water in Haiti or brought his platoon safe through hostile countryside.

He was proud to be Tom and Tess's son, grateful to be Matt and Meg's younger brother. But it would not have been enough.

As much as his family loved him, they did not need him the way his men did. The way his country did.

For Taylor's sake, he could put the life he had chosen on hold for a little while. But being a Marine was all he knew. The best thing he'd ever done.

He didn't know what else he could be.

THE COTTAGE WAS quiet. A lamp cast a pool of yellow light on the table by the couch.

Luke glanced at the sliver of light under Taylor's door. He should check on her. Maybe it was better to let sleeping dogs—and children—lie, but he couldn't shut off the habits of patrol. Couldn't shake the feelings Josh's question had churned up inside him.

Are you sorry you had Taylor?

No. Yes.

No.

He'd come home out of duty and, yeah, remembered affection for Dawn. A guy didn't forget his first serious girlfriend, even when she dumped him. Maybe especially if she dumped him.

Without even thinking, Luke had accepted that he would live up to his parents' standards, to his big brother's example, to his father's model of what it meant to be a man.

Taylor was his daughter. His responsibility. Over and out.

Funny, though, he hadn't really considered her as a person in her own right. A brave, suspicious, ten-year-old person who fought with her teachers and played video games with Josh and wore a USMC utility cover everywhere.

He heard a whimper and eased open the door.

His daughter slept curled in a tight little ball under the

covers, cocooned in her old blue comforter. Another whimper escaped. Not from the puppy, wedged in the crook of her knees. From Taylor.

Luke frowned. In Afghanistan, he and his men had squeezed in, bunk to bunk, less than an arm's length between them. Even with earplugs, he could hear everything, all the noises men made when they were sleeping. Or trying to. Coughs, snores, moans, the sounds of jerking off.

Taylor muttered.

She has nightmares, his mother had said.

Probably having one now. He winced in sympathy.

It had been an eventful day. New house, new bed, new puppy. Plus the strain of the social worker's visit tomorrow. He probably shouldn't have done drive-thru for dinner, either, he thought guiltily. There was no fast food on Dare Island. Certainly not in Tess's kitchen. Stopping on their way home had seemed like a harmless indulgence, a kid-friendly celebration to mark their new status as an independent family unit.

Taylor twitched and moaned.

Luke hesitated. He'd learned the hard way that waking somebody from a nightmare wasn't always the best idea. At least his daughter wasn't likely to wake up swinging. Not like Eric Cordero, who relived an IED explosion every night. Or Aaron Short, who was haunted by the dead.

Anyway, the kid was only ten. No danger there.

"Taylor, hey," he said softly.

Her head thrashed against the pillow. The puppy snuffled and nestled closer.

"Taylor. Hey, baby," Luke said, and smoothed a hand down her arm.

Her muscles went rigid. Her eyes dragged open, glazed with sleep. She saw him standing over her bed with the light behind him.

And screamed.

"Shit," Luke said, startled, and dropped her arm.

She screamed again, flailing, striking out. The puppy whined, scrambling through the covers.

Luke's heart revved. He took a deep breath, imposing calm on his body. On his voice. "It's okay," he said—to the dog, to the girl. "Taylor, it's Luke." *Not enough. Not nearly enough, in the face of her terror.* He tried again. "It's Dad. You were dreaming. It was just a dream."

Her eyes, dark and dilated, stared into his. Her mouth hung open. Her lower lip trembled.

"You're safe," he said, the way he would to Eric. To Aaron, before the poor bastard blew his brains out. "You're home. You're safe."

Understanding bloomed in her eyes. She whispered, "Daddy?"

The blood left his head in a rush, flooding his heart, making him giddy. *Congratulations, it's a girl. You have a daughter.* He had to sit down. "Yeah."

He didn't want to grab her. Didn't want to spook her. He lowered himself to the end of her bed, putting his hand on her foot through the covers, and gave her toes a little squeeze. "You okay?"

Stupid question. He could see she was not okay. But she nodded anyway, looking small and forlorn against the heaped up pillows of the bed.

Since he couldn't hug her, he rubbed the puppy's head. "You kind of scared us there." *You scared the shit out of me.*

She held out her arms. The puppy crawled into her lap, and she lowered her face to its fur, holding the warm, squiggly body tight.

Luke watched as she lost her fear in comforting the dog. "So." He cleared his throat. "You want to talk about it?"

She shook her head wordlessly.

Maybe that was best. Sometimes talking made it easier to let the images go. And sometimes talking just fixed them in your head.

He gave her foot another pat. "Okay." Matt, he remembered, stayed with her the first few times she had a nightmare. "You, uh, want me to sit awhile?"

"I'm fine," she said, the words muffled.

Okay, he was no Matt. And she had the puppy.

"Well, I'm here," he said. "Right across the hall. If you need anything."

Another head wobble. A nod.

A child recovering from a trauma needs four things, Kate said in his head. *Routine, security, honesty, and love.*

Today had hardly been routine. Security and honesty? He was here. He had offered to talk.

He felt a twinge of . . . something in his chest. He could do better. Taylor deserved more.

Daddy? she'd whispered.

Yeah. From now on and forever.

Slowly, he stood. Carefully, he leaned over her and kissed the top of her head. She smelled of sunshine and shampoo and faintly of dog.

He straightened. "'Night."

Her smile blinded him. "Good night," she said and snuggled back down with the puppy.

Ten

THE LADY FROM social services (*Call me Alisha*, she'd said, like they were friends. Like Taylor *would*.) had smooth brown skin and warm dark eyes and a briefcase.

"Is there someplace Taylor and I can go to talk?" she asked Taylor's dad.

They were all sitting around the kitchen table in the Pirates' Rest, her dad and Uncle Matt and Allison, Aunt Meg in her New York clothes sitting next to Sam, Grandma and Grandpa and Josh. Grandma had put a plate of cookies on the table, but nobody was eating. Taylor felt slightly sick to her stomach.

It made her feel better, though, to have them all there. *Back to back to back*, Uncle Matt would say.

"Anywhere you want," her dad said. "We're staying in the cottage, if you want to see it."

"That would be excellent." The social worker stood and smiled at Taylor. "Maybe you could show me where you sleep."

A hard knot of panic rose in Taylor's throat. She threw an agonized glance at her dad.

He leaned down, bending forward so he could look her in the eyes. "It's okay," he said, flat and firm, almost making her believe him. "She's just going to ask you some questions. All you have to do is tell her how you feel."

"Like you did with the judge," Aunt Meg put in.

Taylor swallowed and nodded.

"'And remember, this is for posterity, so be honest,'" Josh said.

Uncle Matt smacked him lightly on the arm. The social worker looked confused.

But Taylor recognized the quote, Count Rugen in the torture chamber from *The Princess Bride*, and smiled gratefully at Josh. He winked.

After that, it wasn't quite so scary to cross the yard and talk to the social worker alone.

"This is a pretty house," she said when they were inside the cottage. "How do you feel about living here?"

She was safe here. *I'm here*, Dad had said last night. *Right across the hall.*

"It's okay," Taylor said. *Please, please don't take me away.*

The sound of their voices woke the puppy snoozing in the corner of the kitchen. He scrambled to the baby gate in the doorway, pressing his small, furry body to the rails, whining a little in excitement.

"Can I let him out?" Taylor asked.

The social worker smiled. "Why not?"

So that was better, too. Taylor freed the puppy and then sat with him on the floor, holding his warm, wriggly body for comfort.

"What's his name?" the social worker asked.

"It was Ronald," Taylor said, not bothering to hide the scorn in her voice. "But we mostly call him just dog. Or JD."

"Is he your puppy?" the social worker asked, which was kind of a dumb question, since JD was in Taylor's house and in her lap, but Taylor nodded politely.

The social worker opened her briefcase. She had a low, smooth voice and a way of talking that reminded Taylor a little of Allison, and she asked the same sort of questions, the kind you couldn't answer with just yes or no. *What are the things you like best about school? Do you go every day? What kinds of things do you like to do with your friends? What are some things you don't like about school?*

The last question made Taylor squirm. But Luke—Dad—had said they needed to cooperate, so she told the truth. "Mrs. Williams tried to take my hat."

The social worker glanced up from the papers in her lap to the USMC utility cap on Taylor's head. "Yes, I heard about that. Can you tell me what happened?"

If she already heard about it, why did she have to ask?

"Uncle Matt came to school." Just thinking about it, the way he'd shown up on his motorcycle and yelled at the vice principal, made her feel good inside. "And now I get to keep the hat at my desk."

"Is that the hat you're wearing?"

Taylor nodded proudly. "My dad gave it to me. Before he left for Afghanistan."

"How do you feel about having your father home?"

"I like it." The social worker didn't say anything, so Taylor added, "I'm glad he's not getting shot at."

"Do you miss your grandparents?"

"No," Taylor said, surprised. "I see them all the time. They're just across the yard."

"I meant your other grandparents. Do you miss seeing them?"

The knot reformed in Taylor's stomach. She *did* miss Grandma Jo sometimes, who bought Krispy Kreme donuts every Sunday morning and let Taylor watch anything she wanted on TV. And Grandpa Ernie's slow smile and familiar smell of cigarettes. Until four months ago, they were the only grandparents she'd ever known.

You can't tell, Uncle Kevin had said. *Your grandma just lost your mom. She's really sad. You don't want to make her feel worse.*

Taylor didn't want Grandma Jo to feel bad. But she didn't

want to go back, ever. She would rather die than go back to Uncle Kevin and the dark. She hugged JD tighter. "Not really."

"What was it like living with them?"

Her heart thumped. Her palms sweat. What should she say? What could she say?

She put her head down in JD's fur so she wouldn't have to meet the social worker's eyes. "All right, I guess," she said, her voice muffled.

The social worker's pen scratched as she wrote something down.

Taylor felt like throwing up. What if that was the wrong thing to say? What if . . . ?

Tell her how you feel, Dad had said.

Like you did with the judge, said Aunt Meg.

Taylor had a sudden memory of Miss Kate kneeling on the sidewalk in front of the courthouse, looking her right in the eyes, gripping her shoulders. *Feelings are never wrong, they're just feelings. As long as you're honest, everything else will work out.*

Taylor raised her head. "I'm not going back." Her voice was loud and thin. "I don't care what you say. I want to stay with my dad."

The pen stopped moving.

Taylor's blood pounded in her ears. Her fingers tightened in JD's fur until the puppy whimpered. She dropped her eyes, patting him in apology.

"Good to know," the social worker said gently. "Is there something else? Anything else you want to tell me?"

Taylor's heart threatened to choke her. She couldn't tell. She couldn't ever tell. It would *kill* Grandma Jolene. "No," she mumbled.

The social worker sighed. "All right. Well, if you change your mind—" she reached into her briefcase and took out a business card "—this is my number. You can call me anytime, okay?"

Taylor took the card, even though she knew she would never call.

And maybe the social worker knew it, too, because she said, "Is there somebody else you can talk to? Like, when you get hurt or if you feel sad?"

Taylor didn't even have to think. "Lots of people."

"Like . . . ?"

"Uncle Matt. And Allison. Grandma Tess. Aunt Meg." Just saying their names, seeing their faces in her head, made Taylor feel better. "Josh."

"Do you talk to your dad?"

"Sometimes," Taylor said cautiously.

The social worker smiled and closed her briefcase. "Why don't we go talk to him now?"

"Are we done?" Hope cracked Taylor's voice. She almost didn't care.

"I think so." Another smile. "Why don't you show me where you sleep, and then I'm going to chat with your family a little while."

KATE SWITCHED ON the speakers in her car so she could listen to Alisha's call and drive at the same time.

"It's a shame about her mama," Alisha said. "Taylor's still dealing with something there. But you were right about the Fletchers."

Kate felt an absurd, almost proprietary pride. "They're a nice family," she said, and heard an echo of Luke's teasing. *Is that your professional opinion?*

"Good looking, too," Alisha said wickedly. "That Luke? And his brother. And the sister's man, Sam? What a hunk. Even that boy, Josh, is probably breaking hearts in high school."

"So you liked them," Kate said, testing. Anxious.

"Hard not to. They obviously care about Taylor. And she flat-out told me she wants to stay with them."

"Then you're closing the investigation," Kate said. *Please.*

"Yep. I'm writing up my report now. I'm going to recommend counseling for Taylor, but that will be up to the

Fletchers. You didn't hear this from me, but I don't see any reason at this time for social services to be involved. They should get the letter Monday."

"That's wonderful." Relief lightened her voice. "Thanks so much for letting me know."

"My pleasure. I'm surprised he didn't tell you."

"'He'?"

"Luke."

Kate felt her face heat. She was grateful Alisha couldn't see. "There's no reason . . . I didn't really expect him to. I'm not his lawyer."

But she'd been hurt all the same that Luke hadn't reached out. Hurt and disappointed.

"I got the impression there was something between you two," Alisha said.

I did, too, Kate almost said.

I'll see you, he'd said, his eyes hot on hers, and just for a moment she'd let herself believe.

But that was three days ago. She hadn't heard a word since.

Of course he'd been busy. She made excuses for him in her head. Obviously, he couldn't drop everything to make time for her. She was glad he was making Taylor his top priority.

But if he were interested, wouldn't he have at least called?

"Obviously not," she said. "Which makes things a little awkward."

"Awkward, how?"

Kate hesitated, tempted to let down her guard. She and Alisha had always been friendly in a professional sort of way. But their relationship had never gone any deeper.

And whose fault was that? Kate wasn't six anymore. Or even sixteen. She didn't need to protect her family's secrets from her friends or her friends from her father's rages.

She didn't have to lie.

The freedom made her almost giddy.

"I, um, have something that belongs to him," she confessed. "I need to find a way to give it to him."

Alisha made an interested hum in her throat. "Are we talking something small, like boxers? Or something big, like a car?"

Kate laughed. "Something alive. Like a cat."

"Excuse me?"

"It's really Taylor's cat. Or it used to be. It got left behind at her old house when Dawn's parents took her to live with them."

"And you found it?"

"I trapped it," Kate said with a little rush of pride. "I'm taking it to the vet now. But then I don't know what to do with it."

"Well, that's easy. You call him."

"You think?" Kate worried her lip with her teeth. "He just got his daughter a puppy."

"So what? It's the perfect excuse."

"I did not rescue this cat so that I would have an excuse to call Luke Fletcher." Kate's flush deepened. At least, that wasn't the only reason.

"Maybe not," Alisha said. "But it sure is convenient."

"CONVENIENT IS *NOT* the word I'd use," Kate muttered two hours later.

She popped the hatch of the Mini Cooper. The white cat flinched, huddling deeper toward the back of the humane trap she was still using to carry it around.

It hated her.

She didn't blame it. "Sorry about the vet's."

A baleful glare from yellow eyes.

Kate hauled out the cage and the bag of veterinary supplies. The cat yowled once, piteously, as she lugged it up the walk, malnourished, dehydrated, and covered in parasites. *I can sell you some topical medication*, the vet had said. *But she'll need a flea bath before you introduce her into a household with other animals.*

Screw it, Kate thought. This wasn't her cat. She didn't want fleas in her house. She should call Luke right now. If he didn't want to talk to her, he could let her call go to voice mail.

She set the cage in a patch of sunshine, sat on the stoop and dug for her phone.

Luke answered on the second ring. "Kate?" His deep voice, surprised and glad, plucked a chord inside her.

Her whole body thrummed.

"I've got your cat," she announced without preamble.

"My cat," he repeated. "Snowball? Are you sure?"

"I think so. It's white. Long haired." Kate regarded the dirty feline on her porch. Well, it *had* been white. Once upon a time. It would be white again.

"That's great," Luke said.

Some of her defensiveness melted away at the warmth in his voice. "I trapped it on Dawn's porch. The vet says cats rarely venture more than half a mile from home, so . . ."

"Wait. You took it to the vet already?"

Her gaze dropped to the scratches covering her arms. "I had to make sure it was healthy." *Not rabid.*

"And?"

The cat settled closer to the wire, its shoulders sticking up sharply through its coarse, dry fur. Pathetic, really.

"It's okay," Kate said. "Mostly scared."

She poked a cautious fingertip through the bars of the cage. The cat regarded her with disdain.

"Great," Luke said. "I can be there in an hour."

He was coming? Here?

Tonight.

Her knees turned to butter. She sank onto the front stoop. "You don't have to do that," she protested automatically.

"What? You going to keep it?"

"No, but—"

"I want to see you," Luke said. Not demanding, just putting it out there. Honest. Direct.

So why didn't you call? Or text. Something.

Her heart thumped erratically. Snowball—*Are you Snowball? Please, please be Snowball*—sniffed at her finger, its whiskers tickling. "And the cat," Kate said, testing.

"Sure." She could hear the smile in his voice. "The cat, too."

She swallowed. She had to be practical. She had to . . . She couldn't think. "What about Taylor?" she managed.

There. That sounded logical. Adult.

"It's Friday night. No school tomorrow. She can stay up and play video games with Josh til I get home. Seven o'clock," he said. "I'll bring dinner."

Oh. Sudden longing speared her.

When was the last time she'd had someone to eat with, to talk to at the end of the day? Her friendships were mostly confined to the courthouse. It had been months— seven? eight?—since she'd accepted a date.

She wasn't anti-men, whatever her mother said. She definitely wasn't anti-sex.

If she accepted Luke's offer, tonight there would be no picking through the wilting spring mix in her produce drawer to make a salad. No hunting in her empty freezer for a desiccated chicken breast. No sitting alone with only the flickering families on TV for company.

And the cat. Don't forget the cat. She looked down at Snowball. *Oh, God*, she thought. *I'm turning into a cliché.*

"Seven," she said crisply. "Thanks for picking up dinner."

"No problem," Luke said.

No problem for him, Kate thought after they disconnected. Mr. Man of Action. He didn't worry and second-guess every decision the way that she did. He was so sure of himself, so confident of his welcome. He must have been very well loved as a child.

She thought of her own frightened and confused upbringing. Her mother, who alternately blamed or ignored her. Her father, who could be distant or a monster.

Every time Kate looked at Luke she was reminded that

she was not normal. Her attempts to pretend that her child-hood was like everybody else's had only made her more isolated.

She'd been in therapy. She knew that the normal response to trauma was to shut down emotionally.

And the only way to heal was to stop avoiding the things that made you shut down.

Kate let out a shuddering sigh. *No problem.*

Luke would bring burgers or pizza or barbecue—manly food, she decided, he was a manly guy—and they'd talk. Nothing serious. Nothing complicated. Just a casual dinner between two adults who had the evening free and found each other attractive. Surely she could manage that much.

She lugged the cat and the bag of supplies upstairs to her apartment. It's not like this was a date. Luke was com-ing over for Snowball. Kate didn't need to tidy her apart-ment or change her sheets or even shave her legs before he got here.

She set the cage on the floor of her bathroom.

No, all she had to do was give his wretched cat a flea bath.

She turned on the water in the tub.

He bought Chinese.

And flowers.

Luke stood on Kate's front porch with his takeout bag and a cellophane-wrapped bouquet, white roses with red berries and sprigs of pine. Standing in the supermarket, he'd thought they looked pretty. Happy. But maybe flowers were too much.

His soon-to-be brother-in-law Sam brought Meg flowers all the time. The guy was like a fricking magician, con-stantly pulling bouquets out of a hat or his ass. But it had been a long time since Luke had bought any woman other than his mom flowers. He felt less like a magician and more like a pimply kid at prom trying to impress his date. Hop-ing to get lucky.

Maybe he *was* trying. Hoping, too. But that wasn't why he'd bought Kate flowers. He'd been caught up these past few days in the aftermath of the social worker's visit and Taylor's nightmare. After a ten-month tour, his social skills were rusty. But he wanted to do something to show Kate how much he appreciated all she'd done for him and Taylor. Give her something to tease that fugitive smile out of hiding.

He frowned up at the porch light. She sure was taking a long time to answer the door. He was about to ring again when it jerked open.

And there she was. Her bright, wild hair. Her face, pink and animated. Her soft, shadowed eyes. Under her lawyer skirt, her legs and feet were bare. The sight of her punched him in the chest.

When he could breathe, he said, "Hey. You look nice."

The flush deepened. "I was about to change."

Once he got past her face and her pale, bare legs, he could see dark water splotches on her blouse, making the fabric cling to her very nice breasts. "More toilet problems?"

"No." She stood back to admit him. "I was giving the cat a bath."

"Then you earned these." He offered the flowers.

There was the smile, he thought, satisfied. He grinned back.

"Thanks." She touched a rose with one fingertip. "They're beautiful. But I don't need flowers."

"I wanted you to have them. They reminded me of you."

Her brows arched.

"Prickly," he explained. "And they smell good."

This time she actually laughed. "I . . . Well, thank you." She reached for the bouquet. Beneath the rolled-up sleeves of her blouse, angry red scratches marked her inner forearms.

Luke caught her wrist, holding her arm in the light of the hall. "Did the cat do this?"

Kate tugged away and slid down her sleeve, casually

hiding her wounds from view. "She doesn't like the vet's. Or baths, apparently."

He felt terrible. "Can I do anything?"

"Nope. She's flea free and all wrapped in a towel."

"I meant for you."

"Oh." She blinked those big eyes, like nobody had ever offered to do anything for her before. *Hazel*, he thought suddenly. That was the word for that changing color. "No, I'm fine. Let me just get these flowers in water and we can eat."

"Let's take care of this first," he said and closed the gap between them, catching her mouth with his.

She made this little sound, surprise or protest, but she didn't move away. So he kissed her again, brushing his lips over hers, coaxing, urging her to open. He couldn't take her in his arms. He had the bag of Chinese food in one hand, and she held the flowers between them. But he cupped her jaw with his free hand, running his thumb over her cheek. Her skin was so smooth. She opened her mouth, her lips soft, her tongue sliding against his. Her kiss sucked the air from his lungs, the thoughts from his brain.

Cellophane crinkled. The scent of pine and roses swam in his head as he kissed her, deeper, slower. As she kissed him back.

He felt . . . connected. Accepted. Alive. And so damn relieved that he could do this, feel this, now, with her, his body responding, his mind fully in the moment, his emotions engaged. Not every guy who came back was so lucky.

She drew back, her eyes dark. "We should go upstairs."

Yes. He stared at her, his blood a hot, primitive beat, unable to believe his ears or his luck. *Thank you, God.*

She cleared her throat. "The downstairs is all office and conference rooms. And storage. I actually live upstairs."

Some of the blood returned to his head. She was not inviting him into her bed. Just to her apartment.

"Whatever you want," he said. *Dinner. Sex. Anything.*

He followed her up, noticing again her pretty bare feet and the round, smooth shape of her ass and that whole no-visible-panty-line thing she had going on under her skirt. His brain still wasn't working properly, but his legs functioned fine, climbing the stairs.

Her living quarters were designed on a modified open floor plan—a couple of doors he figured must lead to bedrooms, bathroom, closets, and the rest all one big room. He set the bag with the food on the heart pine table and looked around. Cream walls, white woodwork, beige carpet. Except for one fat red candle on top of the TV, practically everything was beige and impersonal. Like her office. Like the desert. Hell, he'd seen military tents with more personality.

But Kate was standing in the middle of the room, her pink cheeks and coppery hair all the color he needed.

She crossed one naked foot over the other, as if she was cold. Or uncertain. Or nervous about having him invade her space. Like he was conducting a house-to-house search for bomb-making materials.

"Nice. How long have you lived here?" he asked, to put her at ease.

"Five years."

More than enough time to decorate, if she'd wanted to. He didn't say anything.

But she must have picked up on some vibe, because her chin rose defensively. "It's practical. Of course, not everybody wants to live where they work."

"I always have. So I'm okay with it."

"You have." Her tone made it not quite a question.

"Sure. Especially on patrol." Sleeping in a tent surrounded by four sand berms topped with concertina wire. "At least when you step outside to take a leak, nobody's going to shoot at you."

"No." She blinked. "I'm sorry."

He hadn't told her that to upset her. He tried to find a better memory to share. "Before that, too. My parents run a bed-and-breakfast, remember."

"Was that difficult?" she asked. "Having outsiders in your house all the time?"

"No," he said, surprised. He'd never really thought

about it before. Which meant his parents had done a better job than he'd ever realized. "We had our own rooms. Our own space in the back. Family dinners and a basketball hoop in the driveway. They gave us chores around the inn—Meg swore she'd never make another bed or clean another toilet—but it always felt like home to me."

"You were lucky." Her voice was wistful.

"Yeah, I guess I was. Am."

Not everybody joined the Marines from a sense of duty or tradition or the desire to serve. Some were desperately seeking a place to belong. And some were looking to escape—a dead-end job, a dead-end relationship, a shitty home life.

For no reason at all, he thought of Kevin, Dawn's brother, always seeking an escape or an excuse for the disappointment his life had become.

Way to kill the mood, dumbass. He hadn't come over tonight to talk about his childhood. Or to make her sad.

"Go get something on those scratches," he said. "I'll dish up."

She looked down at the flowers in her arms, slightly the worse for wear. "I should put these in water."

Colonel's daughter, he thought. She had trouble taking orders.

But no hesitation stepping up. She had the drive, the education, the smarts to be practicing law in some big-city firm, overbilling clients and overworking her staff. Instead she'd spent the afternoon on a vet visit and flea bath for a stray cat. For Taylor.

The least he could do was relieve her of some of that responsibility she assumed so readily.

"I'll take care of it." He took the bouquet from her. Gave her a little push in the direction of the row of doors.

"Plates are in the—"

He shook his head. "I told you, I've got this."

Still, she hesitated.

"Afraid of what I'll find in your junk drawer?" he teased.

That won him another smile. "Maybe."

"Go," he said. "I promise not to rearrange the cabinets while you're gone."

"I'm sorry. I didn't mean to imply that you wouldn't respect my space."

He grinned. "Babe, I'm all over your space. I just don't give a damn how you organize your cabinets."

Instant humor leaped to her eyes. "I'll go change now."

"You do that."

He waited until the door had closed behind her before he put a kettle on to boil for tea.

And tried not to think of her peeling her damp blouse from all that pale, smooth skin on the other side of the door.

•

Eleven

KATE STRIPPED OFF her blouse with quick, jerky movements. This wasn't a date, she cautioned herself. But he'd brought her dinner. And flowers. *They reminded me of you.* The sentiment should have been cheesy. Instead, he'd made her laugh.

And yearn.

Still . . . Not a date. Maybe a booty call? Simple, basic. Oh, God, she should have shaved after all.

She could hear him through her bedroom door, opening cabinets, rattling flatware. It made her edgy, having a man in her space, moving among her possessions, touching her things when she wasn't there.

Afraid of what I'll find in your junk drawer?

Maybe.

She had too much clutter in her past, too many ugly memories stashed away. It was hard to overcome the habits of a lifetime, the fear of inviting someone in, physically or emotionally.

No one came over when Kate was a child. No friends

from school, not even Aunt Sharon, her mother's sister. Kate had understood without ever being told that nobody could know about Daddy's drinking.

The secret was her father's.

But the scars and the shame were Kate's.

She took a sweater from a drawer. She wasn't a child anymore. She knew what it meant when a guy showed up with takeout and flowers, when you met him with a tongue-tangling, breath-stealing kiss at the door. He wanted sex. And she wanted . . . Oh, God, she wanted him.

And that was the danger. Because as soon as you wanted something, it could be taken away. Especially if you let yourself want someone like Luke, with a family who loved him, a little girl who needed him, and a job that guaranteed he wouldn't stick around. She could not possibly be anything more than an adjunct to his life.

But did that mean he couldn't be part of hers?

She clutched her sweater to her breasts, grasping at the possibility. Maybe Luke could be a special treat she allowed herself. Like a candy bar. You couldn't live on a constant diet of candy bars. Eventually you'd either starve from lack of real nutrition or get sick from a surfeit of sweetness.

But Luke was decent. He made her laugh. She craved his company, was so hungry for his attention. Surely she could have . . . a taste?

She cracked open the door to the bathroom where she'd left the cat. Snowball was in the corner on a pile of towels. At Kate's entrance, the cat froze with one leg in the air.

"It's okay. It's just us girls. I need to do a little grooming myself."

Kate smiled. Maybe the cat was a ruse for both of them. Luke hadn't even asked to see Snowball yet.

She turned to the medicine cabinet over the sink. And nearly shrieked at her reflection in the mirror. The humidity of the bath had frizzed her hair, creating a mess of wild curls. Her makeup had migrated under her lower lashes. She looked like a Mardi Gras mask.

She scrubbed hastily at her face, dabbed antibiotic

ointment on her scratches and—still clinging to some concealment—patted tinted moisturizer over her scar. She yanked her sweater over her head before taking another glance in the mirror. Her appearance would have to do. Maybe it was just as well she didn't have time to fuss.

Or to change her mind.

She turned to the cat in the corner. "Ready?"

Snowball regarded her with wary yellow eyes. Kate wasn't at all sure how the cat would react to being picked up. But carrying the cat with her would remind Luke— would remind *Kate*—that she had a life, too. She was not only a booty call.

"You and me, cat. Showtime."

Somewhat to her surprise, Snowball tolerated her touch. Hesitantly, Kate scooped the cat into her arms. It was all bones and fur, its heart beating frantically against her palm. But it made no move to get away.

Encouraged, Kate walked into the other room.

And stopped, feeling as though she'd stepped into a foreign country. Her little table was set with white dishes and her fat red Christmas candle. There were flowers jammed in a pitcher on the counter and sweet, spicy, garlicky smells in the air. *Babe, I am all over your space.*

Her heart took a hard, quick extra thump. "I wasn't expecting . . ." *Candlelight and roses. Romance.*

"The all-you-can-eat Chinese buffet?" Luke offered dryly.

She laughed, subtly reassured. "There does seem to be a lot of food."

He shrugged. "I don't know what you like, so I got some of everything."

"That was . . ." *Unprecedented.* "Thoughtful. It looks great." She shifted Snowball awkwardly in her arms. "I brought the cat."

"Not as a menu item, I hope."

A smile tugged her lips. "Definitely not. I thought you should get to know each other."

"Hey, Snowball." He extended his fingers. The cat didn't

hiss. But when he scratched its head, its ears flattened and it shrank closer to Kate.

"Guess I shouldn't have made that crack about the menu," Luke said.

"She'll come around. She's not feral," Kate said, cuddling Snowball almost protectively. "She's a stray."

Luke ran a finger around the cat's ear and under its chin. He had long fingers. Broad, square nails and knuckles. "There's a difference?"

Kate nodded, trying to ignore that strong, masculine hand just under her jaw, so close to her face. "The vet explained it to me. A feral that has never had positive human contact rarely makes a good pet. But a stray like Snowball, an animal who comes from a normal, loving home, is already socialized. You shouldn't have any problems with her."

The cat turned its head into Kate's sweater, ignoring Luke entirely.

He withdrew his hand. A corner of his mouth kicked up. "I'll take your word for it."

"She's standoffish now because she's scared," Kate said. *You and me both, Snowball.* "All she needs to be part of a family again is love and patience."

Luke's gaze rested on her thoughtfully.

Kate's pulse thudded. What did he see?

"I can be patient," he said at last. "Why don't you put the cat down while we eat? Maybe she'll get used to me."

Kate stooped to release the cat, grateful for the chance to hide her face. She watched as Snowball slunk over the carpet, pausing now and then to sniff at her new surroundings.

"Thanks for rescuing my kid's cat."

The look in his eyes made her face warm. "No problem," she lied breathlessly. "I hope it gets along with the new puppy. Um, Ronald?"

"Not anymore. Taylor changed its name."

"To what?" Their other dog, the big one, was Fezzik, she remembered. "Inigo? Humperdinck?"

"You know *The Princess Bride*?" He sounded surprised.

"I love *The Princess Bride*." It was one of her comfort movies as a child, as much for the deep affection between grandfather and grandson as for the romance of Princess Buttercup and her farm boy. Both fairy tales, both as far removed from her own experience as the moon.

"Inigo would be good," Luke said. "Mostly we've been using Dog. Or JD."

"Just Dog?" Kate guessed and was absurdly pleased when he nodded. "This looks amazing," she said as they sat down. "Is that sesame beef?"

"Sesame beef, General Tso's chicken, pork fried rice, shrimp with garlic."

"It's too much."

"So you'll have leftovers."

"No, I meant . . ." Her gesture encompassed the flowers, the candle, the gently steaming tea. "All of it. I didn't figure you'd be so . . ."

"Housebroken," he suggested, a gleam in his eyes.

"Into table settings."

He spooned rice onto his plate. "Mom insisted we all pull our weight around the house. Meg's a better cook, but I can set and clear the table. Do dishes. Make hospital corners."

"Was that your mother's doing or the Marines?"

He grinned. "Let's say Mom would have made a good DI." He gestured toward her place. "No chopsticks for you?"

She shook her head. "I never got the hang of them. Too messy." And she didn't like to do things she wasn't good at.

He shrugged and dug into the carton of sesame beef, wielding his own chopsticks expertly. "So I guess your parents trained you, too."

She swallowed. This was one of those topics that normal people probably talked about all the time. One of those things that marked her as different. One of those memories too painful to share. "Oh . . . Yes. My father liked to live on base. But he wouldn't pay a cleaning crew, and my mother could never get the house clean enough to please him or pass inspection. So I learned to clean."

Scrubbing the bottom of the oven and the rubber seal of the refrigerator door with a toothbrush. Staying on her knees after midnight, wiping down cabinets and baseboards with white vinegar and water. Praying her efforts would be good enough to avoid triggering her father's deep dissatisfaction with his life.

"Moving was the worst," Luke agreed. "You did that all yourself?"

She set down her fork. "You can't really be interested in my housekeeping skills."

"Exchange of basic information, babe. Part of getting to know you."

"All right. Tell me about your home visit," she said.

He raised his brows. "Changing the subject?"

"I am. Also I'm interested." Which was easier to admit than *I care.* "Exchange of basic information," she reminded him.

He grinned, acknowledging her point. "It was fine."

She released her breath in relief and disappointment. "Just 'fine'?"

"What do you want me to say? Your friend came. She talked to Taylor. She seemed . . ." He paused as if searching for a word.

"Friendly?" Kate suggested dryly.

"That. And competent. Anyway, she didn't ask any leading questions. No 'when did you stop beating your daughter' stuff."

"She liked you. All of you," Kate said.

"Good to know. Dad may have flirted with her some. Sam, too."

"And you? Did you flirt?" *Kate* was flirting. She liked it. Like another taste of candy bar, unfamiliar and delicious.

He leaned back in his chair, his eyes full of cocky humor. "I cooperated. Like you told me to."

"Well, it worked. Alisha thinks you all are providing an excellent environment for Taylor."

"Does that mean she's going to tell the Simpsons they're full of shit?"

Kate shook her head. "It doesn't work that way. The most she can say is that the report was not substantiated and they're closing their investigation."

"So the Simpsons could still bring up the allegation in court."

"They can bring up anything they want. But now, Alisha can just as easily testify in your favor."

"She can do that?"

Kate smiled brilliantly. "If your lawyer subpoenas her. And if I know Vernon, he's already filed the paperwork."

Luke held her gaze. "You're really something, you know that?"

She flushed. "I'm going to take that as a compliment."

"I meant it as one."

She hesitated. She was pretty sure this was not the moment to critique his parenting techniques. But the subject had to be broached. "Alisha mentioned she was recommending counseling for Taylor."

He picked up his chopsticks. "Yeah, she said something about that."

"And?"

"I told her I'd look into it."

That sounded noncommittal. Kate frowned. "It might really help Taylor to talk to somebody."

"You're probably right. She sure isn't talking to me. But it's only been a week and a half."

"I meant a professional. Maybe someone on base . . ." She broke off as he shook his head. Her stomach sank. She should have expected this resistance. He was a Marine. In the military, there was still a stigma attached to seeking counseling. But if there was anywhere they had experience helping children cope with loss and grief, it would be there. "If you're worried about how it would look—"

"I'm not."

She tried again. "Ignoring Taylor's issues won't make them go away."

"I didn't say I was ignoring them."

"No, but I know how it is." The memories crowded, thick and painful. "You can't admit you have a problem because you're afraid you'll look weak. Or it will hurt your career."

"You don't know anything about it."

"I know what my father—" she said and stopped.

Luke waited.

She didn't say anything.

"Your father," he prodded.

She closed her eyes briefly. She was trained not to open the door to a line of questioning. And she'd thrown that door open with Luke. She'd let him in. Dangerous for Kate the lawyer. Disastrous for Kate the woman. Her throat swelled. She couldn't speak.

He leaned forward and took her hand across the table. "Look, I get that you want what's best for Taylor. So do I. I've lost too many buddies because they wouldn't get the help they needed. I just don't think Taylor needs to drive an hour and a half each way to talk to somebody on base. I thought maybe you could give me some names."

"Me."

"Yeah. Before, you said you saw a lot of psychologists in your line of work. I figure you might know somebody local who would be good for Taylor."

"I . . ." Once again, he'd surprised her. "Of course. I'd be happy to make some recommendations."

"Great."

"But she might not be able to get an appointment until January," Kate felt compelled to say. "The holidays are a busy time."

"That's fine. It's still probably faster than she'd be seen on base. I appreciate the help." He released her hand and sat back easily in his chair. "So, what made you want to go around rescuing things?"

Her hand felt cold without his. She clasped it around her tea mug. "It's my job."

"It's *a* job," he corrected, those brilliant blue eyes on her face. "It didn't have to be yours."

"There's always a need for family attorneys."

"I get that. The country needs Marines, too. But not everybody joins up. Was it, like, a family thing?"

"What?"

"Being a lawyer. Did your parents encourage you?"

"Not exactly."

"But they're proud of you. I mean, you help people."

He would see it that way, in terms of service rather than salary. "I guess." She shrugged. "We don't really discuss my job much."

"Too confidential?"

Too close to home. Alcoholic husbands who beat their wives were not an acceptable topic of conversation in her mother's world.

Kate pushed her food around her plate. "They were pleased when I was accepted into law school. I suppose it gave my mother some bragging rights with the other officers' wives. Not as good as getting a son into the Naval Academy or having her daughter marry a doctor, but—"

"Wait. Why shouldn't you go to Naval Academy? Or be a doctor, if that's what you wanted?"

"Oh, please. Like I have to explain military culture to you. You're a Marine."

"So that automatically makes me a sexist?"

"In my experience, yes. Women are harassed and discriminated against in the Marine Corps every day."

"Not on my watch."

"So you believe women should have equal rights with men," she said, testing.

"Yeah. And equal pay and opportunities. I'm not saying that bad shit doesn't go down, I'm just saying I've served with some outstanding female Marines." He held her gaze. "So maybe I've learned not to generalize."

"Wow." She sat back, surprised and impressed. "Did you just smack me down for making generalizations about the Marines?"

He grinned at her and served himself out of a carton. "Why would I do that?"

"Oh, I don't know," she said dryly. "Maybe because I've been making unfair judgments about you since before we met?"

"Or maybe," he said, "I want you to know that Taylor is safe with me. That I'm not going to put limits on her because she's a girl. That I will support her and encourage her to grow up to be whatever she wants to be."

She stared at him, stricken. *This* was what talking led to. This painful honesty, this horrible yearning, this awful desire for the kind of family, the love and support she'd never had.

Luke's eyes narrowed. God only knew what he saw in her face. "Kate . . ."

"Take me to bed," she blurted.

He went very still. "Now?"

She'd surprised him. Good. It restored the balance between them a little. "Why not?"

Sex would be less dangerous, less revealing, than this terrible emotional intimacy.

"Because you're upset. What did I say to upset you?"

"Nothing. I just . . ." She closed her eyes, embarrassed. "Isn't that what you came for?"

"One of the things. I also said I wanted to get to know you."

"Please. The whole getting-to-know-you deal is just a polite way to get everything out there before you have sex with a total stranger. Herpes. Birth control. You might as well ask about my health history. Or prior partners."

"Okay," he said so promptly she wondered if that had been his object all along. "No STDs, I practice safe sex, and you know about my only significant ex. Your turn."

She stared. "You're serious."

He smiled. "You started it."

Like they were playing a game. She hadn't had many opportunities to play as a child. But she did like to win. "Um. Okay. No diseases."

"Ever married?"

She shook her head. "That would require that I actually date first. Which I don't anymore."

"No time or no interest?"

At least he didn't assume she had no opportunities. She supposed she should be flattered. "No energy."

"Yeah, all that going out to eat can really take it out of you," he said, straight-faced.

A reluctant smile broke across her face. She tended to take things—herself—too seriously. She liked that he could make her laugh. But, still . . .

"It's different for guys. Look around next time you're at a bar or a restaurant or even at the movies. The men are in jeans and T-shirts. Maybe they've shaved. And their dates are all made up and dressed up, like they have to knock themselves out just to be with these guys." She stabbed her fork into a shrimp. "I have to dress for court. I don't need to waste my weekends tweezing, waxing, and worrying about my underwear in return for ordinary food and mediocre sex."

He was looking at her with the warm, slightly unfocused look men got when they were thinking about sex.

Point to me for mentioning the waxing thing, Kate thought smugly.

"You could try doing something about that," he suggested.

What? Oh. "I suppose I could hold out for better restaurants."

"Or better sex." A low note of laughter underscored his voice.

Kate lifted her chin. "I can handle the sex part fine on my own. I don't need a man to have an orgasm."

"Then maybe you should try a better man."

Their gazes met. Held.

Kate's mouth went dry. Her heart beat in the quick, staccato rhythm of a court reporter's keys. What would sex with Luke be like? *Better than mediocre*, that look promised.

She licked sweet sauce from her lips. His gaze dropped to her mouth, and her pulse went wild. Something twisted deep inside her, tension coiling in a tangled mess of want and need. Her hands trembled.

He stood. "Want anything else?"

Her imagination rioted. What was he offering? "I can't eat another bite."

His lips curved. "Sure? There are fortune cookies."

He was clearing the dishes as if that look, that kiss, had never happened, as if she'd never mentioned waxing or her underwear, as if sex were off the table. She wanted him so much she was shaking.

"Perfect," she said. "Maybe I'll get lucky."

He turned from the sink, his blue eyes laser bright, and pulled her out of her seat. "Maybe we both will."

He slipped his fingers into her hair and kissed her, brushing her lips with his, making her blood pound and the words die in her throat. He felt so good, warm and hard, muscled and lean against her. She spared a thought for her underwear—what *had* she put on this morning? She hoped it was the good stuff—before his mouth moved on hers, firmly, deliberately. He parted her lips with his, and her mind stuttered and blanked as the heat in her rose everywhere. She clutched her fingers in his shirt, pulling him closer. He fisted his hand in her hair, licking deep into her mouth, feeding the hunger that flared inside her.

She kissed him back, using her tongue, and his hands slid down her back to her butt. He pulled her tight against him, rough and aroused, tasting her, taking her with his mouth, and she trembled because he was so hot, hot and insistent, his touch searing. She was burning up, she couldn't breathe, couldn't think. She pulled away—*Let's not lose our heads*—and instead of letting her go or lunging for her mouth, he wrapped his arms around her and held her, simply anchored her against his body and held on.

He was hard all over, his back, his hands, his erection pressing against her stomach, and immobile as a rock. A warm, living, breathing rock. Her personal statue. His heartbeat thudded in her chest. His breath stirred her hair.

She clung to him and felt . . . cherished. Safe.

Gradually, his heat seeped inside her. She was conscious of him in a way she'd never been aware of a man before, every breath, every twitch, every shiver communicating between their bodies, passing from him to her, awakening longings under her skin. She wanted him.

She wanted him to *move*. She wiggled against him, hoping he would get the message, and when he didn't, she made a sound of frustration and yanked his shirt from his waistband in back, seeking skin. His back was hot and smooth and sleekly muscled. His chest expanded with his breath. He raised his head from her hair, exposing the strong, tanned column of his throat, and she pressed her lips to his rapidly beating pulse, tasting salt.

LUKE SHUDDERED UNDER Kate's lips, under Kate's hands. He felt amazing, all powerful and out of control at the same time, his blood pounding, his heart too big for his chest. She was soft and warm against him. Her hair, tickling his chin, smelled exotic and comforting, like Chinese spice and soap, and he wanted to grab her up and do her on the table or against the wall, but there was something different and painfully arousing about standing there as she worked his shirt up over his ribs, as she ran her fingers through the hair on his chest, exploring him with her touch.

He helped her, yanking his shirt up and over his head, his body hers to do . . . whatever she wanted. And she wanted him, he could feel it in the tremor of her body, see it in her darkened eyes. He swelled under her gaze, under her touch, his skin tight, his dick pulsing against the fly of his jeans.

She dipped her fingers just under his waistband, light and cool against his bare, hot skin, and stopped. "Do you want . . ."

"Yes."

Her smile broke across her beautiful face. "To go into the bedroom?"

"Anywhere." *Anything. Anytime.*

She moved out of his arms, toward the door. He followed, determined not to lose contact, one hand sliding from her shoulder to the small of her back. She reached back and gripped his hand, hard, and his body jolted as if she'd wrapped those small, strong fingers around his heart.

He wanted to see her naked. To be with her, skin to skin. As soon as they crossed the threshold to her dimly lit bedroom, he put his hands on her sweater, under her sweater, feeling her pretty tits. She sighed and melted against him while he learned her shape through her bra. Nice. Soft. He plucked her nipples to tight little points and then eased her sweater up, over her head.

"Oh, yeah." She wore a little gold necklace that dipped into the shallow indentation between her breasts, her slight cleavage rising above the smooth, shiny cups of her bra, with a spattering of freckles like cinnamon on ice cream. He wanted to eat her up. "You're so pretty."

A flush started halfway up her chest. "Let me just get the light."

He caught her hands as she turned away. "I want to see you. You're beautiful."

"Not as beautiful as you." Her gaze slid over him, and he flexed a little, wanting to see the admiration in her eyes. "You're, um, really in shape."

"You're really sexy."

She made a disbelieving noise and moved away, toward the lamp by the bed. Her turn revealed a mark high on her right shoulder blade, dark against her smooth, pale skin.

"You have a tattoo," he said on a note of discovery.

"So do you."

"Wings?"

"Scales of justice." She popped her shoulder so he could see. "To celebrate passing the bar." Another shoulder hitch, like a shrug. "Not very original."

"Classic," he corrected.

"Like yours." She switched off the lamp and returned to him, her smile bewitching in the dark. Her fingers traced the eagle, anchor, and globe on his shoulder, reading the ink like braille. "When did you get this?"

"Marine Corps graduation."

She flattened her palm against his chest. "And this?"

Semper Fi. "After my first tour." He twitched under her hands like a racehorse, his muscles jerking under his skin. "Kosovo."

She kissed him there, pressing her warm lips over his heart, and he put his hands on her waist, pulling her hips into his, feeling the satin cups of her bra, the silk of her skin against his naked chest.

"Oh, God, Kate." He filled his hands with her, undoing the hooks of her bra as she tugged at his belt, bending to unlace his boots as she wriggled her jeans down her thighs.

She wore some kind of boy shorts, dark and brief, bisecting the smooth curve of her hip. He had to touch. To take. He plunged his fingers under the elastic, and she looked down. "Crap."

He froze.

She shook her head, obviously disappointed. "I was hoping I was wearing my good underwear."

A laugh filled his chest, strangled his throat. "Kate."

She glanced up.

"I don't give a fuck about your underwear. Except maybe how long it takes to get it off you."

Her smile made him feel like he'd won the lottery. "All right, then," she said, and pushed him, tumbling with him onto the bed, making the world go away, becoming his world, surrounding him with heat and light in the dark, all sensation, sleek and fast and hot.

He wasn't expecting . . . this. Her. Maybe in his head he'd had some fantasy of the uptight lawyer and the big bad Marine, but this was her show now. He liked it. She was different, focused and real and alive, better than anything he'd imagined.

She straddled him with a bounce. Her breasts gleamed above him, pale moons in the dark, and he cupped them. They were already tight and swollen for him, and he raised up, kissing her nipples, taking as much of her as he could inside his mouth, making her gasp and quiver, making her squirm and moan. Until she pushed his shoulders down on her pillows and took matters—took him—into her own hands.

His stomach muscles jumped. His brain blurred. "Condom. In my pocket."

She held up the foil packet. "Got it covered."

"Well, you will in a minute," he said, and she laughed.

He loved her laugh, rusty and surprised, like she didn't use it very often.

She fumbled with the condom. He let her have her way with him, arching his hips into her touch, losing himself in the beat of his blood and the brush of her fingers on his cock, stroking her now and then wherever he could reach. Her knee. Her hair. Finally, finally, he was ready. She leaned over him and kissed him hard, making his brain spark and burn, and while he was still sizzling from her heat, she sat up in one quick motion and rammed him inside her, taking him deep.

His mind detonated. *Bang.*

Everything was heat and light. She was slippery hot, melting down around him, and so tight he was afraid to move. His fingers dug into her damp thighs. They lay plastered together, fused, as her body adjusted to his. He listened to her ragged breathing in the dark, holding onto control, hot pressure building at the base of his skull and in his balls.

"Kate?"

She leaned forward and kissed him in answer, her mouth soft and tender, and his heart squeezed in gratitude. *Kate.*

Cautiously, she began to move, up and down, up, then— *oh God*—down again. And again, faster. He opened his eyes and watched her rocking above him, slick, wet, riding him, taking him in, taking him over, taking everything she wanted. Being everything he needed. She felt so good, connected to him. *Right.* He slid his hands down her back, pulling her closer, holding her tight. She could do any damn thing she wanted as long as she didn't stop. She was breathing faster, deeper, almost sobbing, and then he realized her movements were losing rhythm, becoming frantic. She wasn't quite there, she couldn't get there without him, she *needed* him. He reached between them, his hands urgent, insistent, wringing her response from her. With a cry, Kate dropped her head to his shoulder, clutched and convulsed and came, again and again. Her shudders grabbed and shook him. With a groan he thrust deep and emptied himself, holding nothing back.

Twelve

A HEAVY BEAT crashed Kate's dreams, blasting her out of her afterglow.

"That's mine." Luke surged up beside her, big and warm and out of place, reaching for his jeans, digging for his phone.

She snuggled deeper into her pillow, trying to hold on to an unaccustomed feeling of happiness. "Really? Because I always use rap as a ringtone."

He shot her a smile over his shoulder before he glanced at the display. "It's Josh." He rolled away from her, sitting on the edge of the bed. "I told him I'd be back by . . . Shit. It's almost ten thirty."

He switched on the bedside lamp. Kate winced. Squinted.

"Hey, Josh." Luke's voice was deep and easy. "How's it going?"

Holding his phone to one ear, he leaned down to search for his boxer briefs. The yellow lamplight slid over his smooth, muscled back as he bent, picking out the tattoo on his shoulder and . . . That was a scar, cutting like a sickle along his ribs. And another, like a constellation of stars under his arm. He'd been hurt. Wounded. Her flesh puckered in sympathy.

"Yeah, sure." Luke stood, his weight and warmth leaving the mattress, and tugged his jeans up over his hips. "Half an hour. Forty minutes, tops. Appreciate it, buddy."

He disconnected the call.

"What happened to you?" she asked.

"Nothing." He looked up from buckling his belt. "I'm really sorry. I have to go. I need to get home. "

She'd meant his scars. But of course he wasn't thinking about that. Or her.

She sat up, grabbing the pillow like a shield to cover herself. "Don't worry about it. No problem." No expectations, she told herself. No objections. But what came out of her mouth was, "It takes more than thirty minutes to drive from here to Dare Island."

"Traffic will be light." He pocketed his phone and keys. Hesitated. "I'll call you."

She smiled brightly. "Drive safely."

"Will do." He leaned down and kissed her—a hard, hot, brief kiss. "Sorry. Thanks."

Thanks for the best sex of my life? she wondered as he walked out.

Thanks for not making a fuss?

Thanks for putting the food away?

Impossible to know or to ask. She felt as though she'd been dragged down, tumbled, pummeled and submerged by an overwhelming wave of sensation. Her body felt weighted. Her mind struggled to surface.

She listened to him put on his shoes—and his shirt, presumably—on his way out the door.

Well. She climbed out of bed to lock up, breaking back into the real world with painful clarity. *That* certainly eliminated any morning-after awkwardness. No need to make eye contact or plans or conversation in the morning. No worries over whether the man she'd brought home the night before wanted eggs or orange juice. No nasty little beard hairs in the sink. It was practically the perfect evening.

Her space was her own again. As if she'd been tossed alone onto a familiar shore, naked and exposed, listening to the rough sound of her breathing and the beating of her pitiful heart.

Belting her robe, she wandered into the living room. Snowball crouched in the center of the dining table, eating shrimp out of a takeout carton.

"*Snowball!* Down!"

The cat scrambled off the table, sending napkins and silverware flying.

Kate lunged forward, grabbing at glasses. Thank God Luke had at least started to clear the table before they . . . before he left. She dropped to her knees to retrieve a fork from under a chair.

He left the cat.

Kate sat back slowly on her heels, a flutter under her breastbone like hope.

"He forgot you," she told the cat. *Us.*

But he'd be back. *I'll call you*, he'd said.

Kate gripped the fork as if she could tighten her hold on reality. It was just sex, she told herself. She could not let herself be swept away into some romantic fantasy simply because she wanted so desperately to believe. But the possibility tugged at her like the tide.

He'd left the cat. She had an excuse to see him again.

Snowball slunk out from under the end table.

"Don't even bother sucking up," Kate said. "You belong to Taylor. This thing with you and me . . . it's just temporary."

She didn't even have to wait for Luke's call. Tomorrow, she would drive out to Dare Island to give Taylor her cat. She wanted to see the little girl again. Almost as much as she wanted to see Luke.

The cat pressed close to Kate's knee. She stroked it absently. Really, returning Snowball was the best, the smartest thing she could do. Eliminate the obligations and pretenses. If Luke still wanted to see her after that, then that would mean . . .

But here her imagination floundered. She had no idea what it would mean. She had nothing in her experience to compare it to.

A thin, rusty sound vibrated from the cat's throat as it began to lick shrimp sauce from the floor.

HE SHOULD HAVE called, Luke thought the next morning. As soon as he reached the bridge and realized he'd forgotten the cat, he should have called Kate and . . .

Woken her up, probably.

Not a smooth move.

He was uneasily aware he could have handled things better last night. Not the sex. The sex was amazing. The talking and the dinner before that had been great, too. But the gotta-go-I'll-call-you bit at the end needed some work. Like the invasion of Iraq, the evening had been strong on shock and awe, weak on exit strategy.

He spooned grounds into the coffee maker; glanced at the display on his phone. Seven thirty on a Saturday. Too early to call. Kate was probably sleeping in.

He thought about her, warm and soft and naked against her pillows, and his body stirred. *Good morning.* He wanted to sleep in. With her.

But he'd had to get home to Taylor. And this morning he'd been up early to take the dog outside.

Luke regarded JD, sacked out under the table.

Last night Kate had blown him away. He still wasn't thinking clearly. He just knew he wanted to see her again, and that the logistics of any kind of relationship were going to be a bitch.

Good thing the Marines prided themselves on multitasking.

His cell phone rang while he was pouring his first mug of coffee.

His day suddenly looked bright. "Kate."

"Good morning." Her voice was brisk and cheerful.

"I was going to call you."

"Well, now you don't have to. Is it okay if I drop by this afternoon? With the cat."

His blood leaped. He wanted to see her. But she'd already done too damn much. "Not necessary. I'll come to you."

"I wasn't thinking 'necessary.'" Her tone slipped from brisk to hesitant. "I thought it might be fun. But if you're busy . . ."

"Not busy." They were both feeling their way, he realized. Both unsure of their footing in unfamiliar terrain. But he wanted to see her again. "I wanted to repay you for last night."

"Repay," she repeated, like she was testing the word.

"To thank you," he said hastily. Jesus, he needed more coffee. "For taking care of the cat. The vet and the flea bath and everything."

"You brought me dinner." Her voice warmed a few degrees. "And flowers."

"Hardly a fair trade." *Especially since we had sex. No, no, dumbass, don't say that.*

"I wasn't aware we were keeping score." Did she sound . . . amused?

Or was he totally in the doghouse because he hadn't called?

Before he could think of how to ask or what to say to make things better—*Sorry I stuck you with the cat, I shouldn't have fallen asleep on you, Do you want to have sex?*—his daughter walked into the room.

"We're not. I'm not. Taylor's here," he added desperately.

"Great. So I'll see you both this afternoon?" He was pretty sure he heard her smile this time.

"That would be good." He swallowed coffee. "Looking forward to it."

He disconnected, watching as Taylor poured cereal into a bowl, trying to drag his head back into the fatherhood game. "You're up early. I figured after your big Need for Speed marathon with Josh last night, you'd want to sleep in."

Taylor yawned. "You said we were going out with Uncle Matt on the boat today."

Shit.

He'd totally forgotten. Sam Grady's little sister Chelsea was getting married in two weeks, and Sam had arranged to take her fiancé out on Matt's boat. Luke had planned to tag along with Taylor. Not to crew—Matt had Josh and Tom for that—but to enjoy a day on the water.

JD pranced forward, roused by the sound of Taylor's voice, and attacked her slippers.

"Hey, JD." She grinned and sat cross-legged on the floor.

Luke got out the milk for her cereal, watching his daughter with the squirming puppy, wondering how they both would deal with Kate's visit. And the cat. "Yeah, about that . . ."

Taylor looked up, alerted by the tone of his voice.

"I thought maybe we'd stay home this afternoon," he said, testing the idea. "Grandma's making Christmas cookies."

She considered, her head cocked to one side like Bibi regarding a treat. "Can JD come?"

"Sure," Luke said, relieved.

JD had been banned from the fishing expedition because none of the *Sea Lady*'s life vests was small enough to fit the puppy. If having the dog along made up for missing a boat ride, Luke could square things with his mom.

"Okay." Taylor accepted this change of plan, scrambling up on a stool to eat her breakfast. "How come?"

"Miss Kate's coming over this afternoon."

Those big eyes fixed on his face. "Why?"

Luke considered his reply. He could go with the truth—*she's bringing Snowball*—but he didn't want to spoil Kate's surprise. On the other hand, he didn't want Taylor to worry. Even at ten, she knew a visit from a lawyer was not good news. "She just wants to see us."

"You saw her last night."

"Yeah, but she wants to see you."

Taylor dug her spoon in her cereal. "Josh says Miss Kate is hot."

His nephew had good eyes. And a big mouth. "Josh talks too much."

Taylor looked at him from under the brim of her hat. "At least he tells me things."

Ouch. "I tell you things," Luke said.

Taylor ate cereal.

He exhaled, leaning against the counter. "What do you want to know?"

"Is she your girlfriend?"

How did he answer that in a way a ten-year-old would understand? Or that Kate would accept? She was . . . Kate. Special. Why did that need a name?

"I like her," he said. "I'd like to see more of her. Does that bother you?"

"No, I like her, too. She was nice when I had to go to court." Taylor's voice was matter-of-fact, but her eyes were anxious in her thin face.

He'd seen that guarded look before in dozens of towns, hundreds of kids' faces. The eyes of a child who had seen too much, who had been forced to grow up too fast. It shook him, that look on his child's face.

He had to do a better job of taking care of her.

"You don't have to go to court again," he said, trying to reassure her. "Everything's going to be okay now."

Taylor slid him another sidelong glance. "I know. But if you had to go away again, Miss Kate could help watch me."

He studied his daughter's down-bent head, trying to find his place in this conversation. "There are lots of people who love you and can help take care of you."

"Yeah, but Miss Kate's a lawyer. And," Taylor added with devastating simplicity, "she knew Mom."

Luke's heart clenched like a fist in the center of his chest. Taylor needed as many connections with her mother as she could get. Maybe he ought to reach out to the Simpsons after all.

Unless you're bringing Taylor back, I got nothing to say to you, Jolene had said.

So that was kind of a dead end, at least until the hearing on Tuesday.

He poured more coffee, wishing he had a cigarette to go with it.

When he'd first learned of Taylor's existence, he'd been disbelieving. Okay, not simply disbelieving, he admitted. More like shocked and resentful. He liked his life just fine. He loved being a Marine. He didn't need a life lesson in responsibility.

But there was no way he could turn his back on Dawn's dying request. He'd returned home determined to do the right thing. Even then, he'd seen Taylor as an obligation, not a person in her own right. He wasn't prepared for this feeling that had ambushed him, deeper than instinct, this determination to protect her, this need to take care of her.

She's wonderful, Luke. The best thing that ever happened to me. I feel bad because you haven't had a chance to see her, how special she is.

Well, now he'd met her. His daughter. Now he knew.

Now he just had to make sure he was the dad she deserved.

"KATE DOLAN. HERE?" His mother turned from the stand mixer, spatula in hand, to face Luke. "*That's* the reason you didn't go with your father and the boys? You should have told me. This place is a mess."

By his mother's standards, maybe. To Luke's eyes, the Pirates' Rest could pass a field day inspection.

He shrugged sheepishly. "I'm telling you now. It's not that big a deal."

"Not a big deal when one of my sons invites a girl home?"

"Ma, it's not like that."

Tess narrowed her eyes. Heat flushed the tips of his ears.

His mother could usually see through them all. But she could hardly grill him now with Taylor standing at the counter, taking in every word.

"Fine. Go check the powder room. Guest soaps out, toilet seat down. And it wouldn't hurt for you to run the vacuum in the family room. I swear that Christmas tree drops needles every time I look at it."

He kissed the top of her head. "The house looks fine. The tree looks great."

"Powder room. Oh, Luke." Her eyes misted.

Luke knew where her mind was going. With Matt finally happy with Allison, and Meg reunited with Sam, he was next in line for the whole happily-ever-after deal. His parents had been married for so long that his mother thought everybody should march two-by-two, like animals onto the ark.

But all she said was, "She's a nice girl."

He cocked a smile at her. "She's a lawyer."

His mother glanced around the gleaming kitchen, obviously cataloguing every item that was in use or out of place, as though Kate were coming over to critique her housekeeping. "I'm in the middle of baking," she said somewhat helplessly.

Luke grinned. "So give her a cookie."

His mom melted. He knew she would. She always did.

Meg blew in the back door with her laptop under one arm and a grocery bag in the other. "Give who a cookie?"

Taylor looked up from sifting flour into the big blue bowl. "Miss Kate is coming."

Meg stopped dead. "What's wrong?" she asked, instantly protective.

Luke bit back another grin. He was almost thirty, a combat veteran, and his big sister still looked out for him as if they were on the playground. "Nothing."

"Then why is she coming?"

"Nothing to do with the hearing," he amended.

"She wants to see us," Taylor said.

Meg set the groceries on the counter. "I repeat, why?"

Because she fucked my brains out and I forgot the cat sprang to mind. But it wasn't like that.

It was . . . He didn't know what it was. Something different. Something special.

Something to think about.

"I'm going to clean the powder room," he said and escaped.

"HIS EARS ARE red. What's going on?" Aunt Meg asked, unloading lemons and walnuts from the bag. "Taylor?"

Taylor concentrated on her sifting. She liked Aunt Meg, but she liked Miss Kate, too. So did Dad. Taylor was pretty sure that Miss Kate was kind of like his girlfriend now, even though he hadn't said so. But she wasn't sure how much she was supposed to know or what she was supposed to say.

Everybody has secrets, she thought, and felt cold.

From the corner of her eye, she saw Grandma shake her head.

"What?" Aunt Meg batted her eyes innocently. "You think I would pump my ten-year-old niece for dirt on my brother?"

"Yes," Tess and Taylor said at the same time.

Meg laughed. "Yeah, okay. But only because I care."

"I'll take those lemons now," Grandma said.

"Fine." Aunt Meg zipped around the kitchen like a wasp, quick and buzzy, bumping into things. "You want me to zest them?"

"Do you have time? Don't you have work to do?" Grandma asked.

Aunt Meg had her own company. She worked really hard and she traveled a lot.

"It's two weeks before Christmas." Aunt Meg slipped out of her shoes and hugged Grandma. Carefully, because of Grandma's hip. "Nothing's happening in New York until after the holidays, and Sam's off doing manly-men bonding stuff. I want to bake cookies with my mommy." She winked at Taylor. "And my favorite niece."

Taylor ducked her head, a lump in her throat. She concentrated hard on the sifter, shaking it back and forth, back and forth, until the mountain of flour in the bowl cracked in the middle and ran down the sides like an avalanche.

She missed Mom.

She loved Aunt Meg and Grandma Tess and the puppy snoozing in Fezzik's usual spot under the table. But they weren't Mom. Nothing took the place of her mother.

Her chest ached and her wrist hurt a little as she shook the sifter, *back and forth*.

Last Christmas, Mom bought long tubes of sugar cookie dough already colored inside with pictures of trees and Frosty the Snowman. The snowmen had burned on the bottom, but her mother didn't care. She just laughed until Taylor giggled, too, and they'd covered everything with sprinkles and icing. Taylor's eyes stung. She could remember the icing—bright blue and white—but she couldn't see her mother's face anymore, not exactly. She couldn't remember her laugh.

The doorbell rang. Taylor heard her dad's footsteps in the hall as she tried to make the picture perfect in her head, the memory of her mom laughing, but everything was jerky and silent like a movie with the sound turned off. She had a photo of her mom now in a special frame by her bed, and that was better than nothing, but it wasn't the same, it wasn't *alive* . . .

A fat tear rolled down Taylor's nose and went plop into the flour.

"Kate is here," Grandma said.

And then her dad's voice said, "She brought you something," and Taylor looked up, and there was Miss Kate, standing in the doorway of the kitchen with Snowball in her arms.

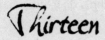

Thirteen

TAYLOR'S THIN FACE turned white, then red. Her mouth opened, but no sound escaped.

Kate's heart stuttered. Maybe she'd made a terrible mistake. Maybe this wasn't Snowball. Maybe . . .

"Snowball," Taylor whispered, and burst into tears.

"Snowball?" Meg said.

Kate jerked forward, jolted into action. "She's here. She's yours."

Taylor extended graceless arms. Kate shifted her hold, hunching over to support Snowball's weight as Taylor took the cat, sinking down with both of them on to the kitchen floor.

The cat squirmed once and then subsided into Taylor's arms, pushing its flat heat in a feline caress against her chin.

Taylor cried, cradling the cat to her chest.

"Hey. Hey, baby." Luke dropped beside them, scooping Taylor onto his lap. Her straight blond hair, her elbows and knees stuck out at all angles. Tears streaked her face.

Happy tears? Or cleansing ones. Kate eased back onto her heels, prepared to give them a moment together.

And Taylor's hand shot out and grabbed her hand, holding tight.

Kate's throat filled. Carefully, she squeezed back.

"It's okay." Luke met Kate's gaze over Taylor's head. If he was panicked by his daughter's crying jag, he didn't let on. His face was as impassive as a Marine's on the parade ground, but his hand, as he stroked his daughter's hair, trembled slightly.

Kate melted helplessly.

The puppy danced closer, drawn by Taylor's tears, desperately trying to join the cat in her lap.

Luke blocked the dog with one arm, keeping the other around his daughter. "She'll be fine in a minute. She's tough."

Taylor caught her breath on a sob, choking back tears.

Tess made a movement, rapidly checked.

Men.

"She will not be fine," Kate said with a fierceness that surprised everybody. Herself most of all. "She doesn't need to be tough. She can cry all she wants."

Tess gave a tiny nod of approval.

"It was just a surprise," Luke said.

"You don't need to apolo— Wait," Kate said. She rocked back, her gaze sweeping the kitchen. "You mean you didn't tell her?"

"I told her you were coming. Not about the cat," Luke said.

"Don't look at me," Meg said. "Nobody told me anything."

None of that mattered now, Kate thought. Nothing mattered but Taylor.

The little girl sniffed mightily and released Kate's hand. Her thin face was blotchy with tears, her skinny arms still wrapped around the cat.

Kate's heart constricted and then swelled. She was used to single parents and crying children. She saw them in her office every week. She sat behind her desk and dispensed tissues and candy and legal advice.

Only this time, her usual remedies weren't enough. Even Snowball wasn't enough.

She didn't know what else she had to offer.

Taylor sat up, pushing her hair from her face.

"Taylor," Luke prompted quietly. "Was there something you wanted to say?"

Taylor smiled wanly at Kate. "Thank you."

Kate swallowed. "You're welcome."

Taylor looked from Luke to Tess. "Can we keep her?"

Tess smiled. "That's up to your dad."

"Damn straight," Luke said.

"What about JD?"

"JD is used to cats. Plenty of kittens on base and in the shelter. You just have to give them both lots of attention. Once JD figures out that Snowball is part of the pack, they'll be fine."

"The vet said to let the cat control their interaction," Kate offered. "As long as she has freedom to retreat and hide, she won't feel so threatened."

Luke smiled at her slowly. "You sure the vet was talking about the cat?"

Kate narrowed her eyes. "She also suggested a leash."

Meg snorted with laughter.

Luke pulled out a bandanna to mop his daughter's tears. The tenderness of his gesture stole Kate's breath.

"Why don't you all sit down in the family room? Put on a movie," Tess said. "That way JD and Snowball can get used to each other while you can keep an eye on things."

"Works for me. You want to pick out the movie?" Luke asked Taylor.

She nodded and scrambled to her feet, still cradling Snowball. The puppy jumped up, too.

"Quit," Luke ordered, and JD plopped down.

"I'll be back," Taylor promised—her father? the puppy?—and crossed the bright, warm kitchen to the family room that extended off one end.

A big flat-screen TV was flanked by shelves of books. Bold, cozy cushions padded a worn leather sofa. Sparkling white lights and handmade ornaments crowded the Christmas tree. It looked like heaven. It looked like a home.

"Well." Kate swallowed and got to her feet, hugging her arms. It wasn't the cat she had exposed to danger by coming here. *Look, don't touch.* "I should go."

Taylor turned. "But you just got here."

"At least wait until the cookies come out of the oven," Tess said.

"We need you," Luke said.

For a moment, she let herself yearn and believe. "For what?"

"Buffer zone."

Kate looked at the puppy, who had given up its role as cowed orphan to stalk Meg's feet across the floor, and then at the cat, wary but content in Taylor's arms. *At least I got that right,* she thought with satisfaction. She could hold on to that when she was alone in her apartment.

"I think you've got the situation under control."

He looked into her eyes. "Stay. Please."

Heat pulsed inside her. Warmth suffused her skin. He wanted her. And she wanted . . . Too much. She could feel herself being drawn in, deeper and deeper, until she lost her balance. Until her desire to belong rose up and choked her. She didn't belong here.

But there was no place else she wanted to be.

Which is how she found herself sitting with Luke on the fat brown leather sofa, Taylor between them, watching *Miracle on 34th Street.*

The jaunty opening music played as that nice old man, Kris Kringle, strolled down the streets of New York and into Macy's. Taylor sighed and settled against Kate's side, nearly displacing Snowball. The puppy yawned and rested his head on Luke's thigh. Kate let herself ease into the cushions, relaxing by degrees, breathing in the lemony smell of the baking cookies and the scent of the Christmas tree.

Luke stretched his muscled arm along the back of the couch, his fingers brushing the ends of her hair, and a pleasant shiver chased down her spine.

"That's the movie Taylor picked?" Meg muttered behind her. "Jeez."

"Meg." Tess hushed her.

Kate frowned. What was wrong with Taylor's choice? Okay, the movie was kind of hokey. And in black-and-white. But *Miracle on 34th Street* was a classic, one of her favorites, a charming fantasy about a little girl who needs to believe and wishes for a house and a family . . .

Oh. She looked down at Taylor, leaning confidingly against her arm, and up at Luke. The reflection from the television made his eyes seem to glow with their own warm blue light.

Her breath went. *Yes*, she thought. And then, *Oh, no*.

She turned her head and stared fixedly at the screen, but her mind wasn't focused on the movie anymore.

The more you relied on someone, the more they could hurt you. Disappoint you. Kate could not encourage Taylor to become attached to her. To depend on her. Her relationship with Luke hovered somewhere between temporary and nonexistent. Who knew where it would go? Or when Luke would go. He was an active-duty Marine. He was leaving.

Life wasn't like Hollywood or fairy tales. There were no guaranteed happy endings.

Kate squirmed on the leather sofa as Maureen O'Hara argued with her handsome neighbor.

It was one thing to risk her own heart and peace of mind on an untested attraction. Quite another to risk Taylor's. The child had loved and lost too much already. She was happy with the Fletchers. She had a home and family. It would be irresponsible of Kate to encourage her to form a superficial attachment to her dad's temporary girlfriend.

A real house, said movie Susie, and Kate died a little inside.

As soon as this movie was over, she was out of here.

LUKE DIDN'T GET it. One minute everything was fine. Damn near perfect, in fact, everybody happy and comfortable on the couch watching the movie—okay, Kate and Taylor were watching the movie. He'd been more interested in watching Kate. She'd looked so cute, absorbed in the story, her eyes as wide and shiny as Taylor's, the rings of silky hair on the back of her neck making him want to touch. Stretching his arm across the back of the couch like he was Josh's age again, plotting his moves on his parents' sofa. Even with his daughter and the dog and the cat between them, it felt good simply to be with her. It felt solid and real and right.

And now she couldn't wait to leave.

"It's still early," he said. "What's your rush?"

She stood by the door to the hall, clutching a Tupperware container of cookies from his mother. "I have to go."

He narrowed his eyes. "Payback?" he asked softly.

"No, I . . . I need to get back."

On a Saturday night? But she'd said she didn't date. "Fine. When can I see you again?"

"Luke . . ." She caught her lower lip in her teeth. *Let me*, he thought. "This isn't going to work."

He fought a surge of . . . Frustration? Panic? "What are you talking about? It's working great."

"It's not fair to Taylor."

He turned, using his body to block them from the rest of the room, from his mother, sister, and daughter rolling strands of red and white dough. He lowered his voice. "This isn't about Taylor."

She put up her chin, a pulse jumping in her throat. "Well, it should be."

She was close enough to kiss, but she was already going away from him, shielded away from him by layers of jeans and sweater and the coat that said she would not stay. He wanted her naked.

"You're making problems where they don't exist. Taylor likes you."

Her pretty mouth set. She was making him crazy. "That's the problem. What happens when I'm not around anymore?"

He shook his head, baffled. "So don't leave. Stay for dinner."

"You're missing the point. I—"

The back door opened and Allison came in, bringing a draft of cold air into the hot kitchen.

Luke liked his brother's fiancée. *She sticks*, Josh had said. But right now, he wanted to snarl at the interruption.

Tess looked up from twisting red and white dough into the shape of candy canes. "Hey, sweetie. How'd the dress shopping go?"

"Not so well. No luck in Morehead City. Or in Jacksonville." Allison brushed a kiss on his mother's cheek, a hand over Taylor's shoulder. "I was hoping I could get some ideas, maybe some pictures to send to my mother so she'd let go of this idea that I have to come home to buy a wedding dress."

"It's natural for her to want to share this experience with you," Tess said. "You are her only daughter."

"I know, but . . . Philadelphia? It's not just the shopping. It's the fittings."

"Sam's sister bought her dress in Raleigh," Meg said. "Maybe if your mom were willing to fly in for the day . . ."

"There's an idea." Allison blinked as she spotted Kate. She came forward, smiling with her usual, unshakeable good manners. "Oh, I'm sorry. You must think I'm very rude. I didn't see you when I came in. It's Kate, isn't it? Allison Carter."

Reluctantly, Luke shifted out of her way.

"Hi, Allison," Kate said, releasing the cookie container to shake Allison's hand. "It's nice to see you again."

"Are you here to see . . ." Allison's gaze shifted to Luke. He didn't know what expression was on his face, but her brown eyes widened. "Oh."

"She brought Snowball," Taylor announced.

"Seriously?" Allison's face broke into a smile. "That's wonderful!"

"Look." Taylor grabbed Allison's hand and dragged her into the family room, where Snowball perched on the back of the couch, staring disdainfully down at the puppy.

"I have to go," Kate said again, taking advantage of the distraction. "Thank you so much for the cookies. Bye, Taylor!" she called and slipped out of the kitchen and into the hall.

Meg and Tess exchanged looks.

"It wasn't me," Meg said. "I was nice."

Luke followed Kate. The welcome banner was down. The white lights wrapped around the bannister twinkled against the early dusk. "You're really leaving."

Her slim shoulders straightened beneath her coat. "I think it's best."

He pressed his palm flat against the front door, preventing her escape. "What did I do?"

"Nothing." He watched the movement of her tongue as she moistened her lips. "I had a wonderful time. But you're not supposed to introduce your child to someone you're casually dating."

"I didn't introduce you."

"And you *wouldn't* have."

Women. "What are you talking about?"

"I'm just saying, when this . . ." She flapped her hand. "Thing—"

"Relationship."

"Is over—"

"You're jumping to the end when we're just getting started. Give me a chance. Give us a chance."

"And then what?"

He didn't know. How could he make guarantees? War was unpredictable and life was uncertain. But the thought of letting her go, of not seeing her again, twisted him up inside. "We'll find out together."

"It's not that easy. You must see that it's not. If it were just . . . I'd take that risk for myself. But I can't do that to Taylor. She can't afford to lose someone else she cares about."

"*Taylor* can't," he repeated, watching her face.

Kate nodded. "I'm worried she'll get emotionally attached."

"Oh, babe. Are you sure it's Taylor you're worried about?"

She stiffened. "What do you mean?"

If he pushed, she would run. Like the cat, she needed room to retreat to feel safe.

"You're complicating things again." He wasn't so good at talking things out, but he was afraid if he stopped, she'd leave. And he didn't want her to go. "Look, I appreciate everything you've done for Taylor. We both do. She likes you."

"And I like her. But—"

"No 'buts.' It's good that you like her. She *deserves* for you to like her. Plus, you knew her mom. You have a relationship with Taylor that doesn't have anything to do with me. The thing is . . ." He frowned, searching for the right words. "Taylor and me . . . We're a package deal now. That doesn't mean I always want an audience. Or a chaperone. I like you. I want to spend time with you. Not because of my kid or her cat or my ex-girlfriend. I want to see you. Only you." He leaned in, pressing her back against the door, one hand above her head. "Only me."

Her eyes were wide and dark, sparkling with points of light from the Christmas garland. He kissed her. She tasted like sugar and lemons, sweet and tart. She lifted her hand to touch his face as the kiss softened, deepened, as her body melted and turned pliant in his arms. His blood surged. His body hardened.

"See?" he whispered against her mouth. "Simple."

Her lips curved under his. "You're very convincing. As long as we can see each other without raising expectations—"

"Too late." He took her by the hips and tugged her closer. "My, uh, expectations are already pretty high."

That low, rusty gurgle escaped. "I did notice."

He grinned in triumph, drawing back to see her face. "So I'll see you."

"Yes."

"When?"

"You're coming to court on Tuesday."

He shook his head. "A permanent custody hearing in family court is not a date."

"I thought . . . I have a property settlement. Since we'll both be there anyway . . ."

"And a property settlement is not romantic." He kissed her again, taking his time. "What about Thursday?"

"I have meetings all day. Friday?"

"Taylor's out of school. Christmas break. You could come for—" He met her gaze. Stopped before she could refuse. She needed time to get used to the idea, he thought. In the Marines, you learned to be aggressive enough, quickly enough, for success. But you also learned to have a backup plan, because your first plan often didn't work. "I'll see you Tuesday. We'll figure it out then."

She exhaled, relaxing against him. And even though he wasn't getting what he wanted, her quick nod, her shy smile, felt like victory.

Fourteen

THE NICOTINE BURNED Luke's lungs as he dragged deep on his cigarette. He closed his eyes, holding on to the smoke to smother his nerves; opened them at the sound of his brother's footsteps crossing the courthouse parking lot.

Matt glanced at the cigarette and then at Luke's face and didn't say anything.

The lawyer had told Luke to wear his service uniform to court. To sway the judge, he knew. Luke didn't much like leveraging the uniform, but he accepted the lawyer's reasoning. *Always win. The only unfair fight is one you lose.*

Matt was in a jacket and tie. Luke couldn't recall the last time he'd seen his brother the waterman all dressed up. *Somebody's wedding? Somebody's funeral?* And then he remembered. *Josh's first communion.*

Tess Saltoni Fletcher might slip off by herself most Sundays to attend mass at the tiny Franciscan retreat house on the island. But she'd insisted that every one of her kids receive the Catholic sacraments.

Dawn hadn't been religious, not that Luke could

remember. He wasn't himself, beyond the muttered peti-
tions of every man on the battlefield—*God, don't let this
fucking M4 jam*—or prayers for the dead and dying.

He wondered abruptly if Taylor had been baptized.

His responsibility now.

He exhaled a long stream of smoke. "I'll be glad to get
this over with."

Matt smiled briefly. "It's never over. You're just getting
started."

"Ten years late."

"Yeah, but you have plenty of good stuff still ahead of you.
Wait until Taylor starts dating. Or gets her driver's license."

Luke raised his brows. "That's the good stuff?"

Matt's smile broadened. "It's all good."

"Yeah, maybe." He thought of Josh making out under
the blanket with the little red-haired girl. "Although Taylor's not dating until she's at least eighteen."

"Thirty-five," Matt said promptly.

Luke grinned. "Maybe twenty-one. I'll be out by then,
cleaning my weapon on the front porch when the boys
come by."

"Let me know how that works for you."

Their banter steadied him. Luke took one last drag on
his cigarette, the paper tip glowing, crumbling, the smoke
expanding his lungs.

"You ever think about what you're going to do between
now and then?" Matt asked. "Say, in two years? Or five?"

The thought had been circling, lurking in his mind like
an intruder. "I re-up in six months," Luke said. "I was
thinking I might put in for a lateral transfer. Something
that could keep me closer to home. But I can take care of
her best by doing my job. I'm halfway to retirement."

"If that's what you want," Matt said. "You've got the character, the commitment, the training to do whatever you want.
And now you've got the best motivation there is—Taylor."

Luke dropped his cigarette, crushing it underfoot. "It's
what Dad did. Twenty years. It didn't hurt us any."

"I was fifteen when Dad got out," Matt said. "You were

eight. And all those years he was away, we had Mom. We had each other."

"We still do," Luke said.

"Yes."

Their eyes met. "Thanks for having my six," Luke said quietly.

Matt shrugged. "That's what I'm here for."

Growing up in a military family, moving from base to base, the three Fletcher siblings had always stood by each other.

But Matt had been the responsible one, the one who came through. When Mom was in the hospital and Dad and Meg couldn't leave her side, Matt was the one who somehow kept things going, who ran his charter business and the inn and took care of Josh and Taylor. Everybody counted on Matt. Even his ex-wife, when she'd walked out on him and their three-month-old son, had counted on twenty-year-old Matt to do the right thing.

"That must get old after a while," Luke said. "You ever regret . . ." He shut his mouth. The last thing he wanted to do was question his brother's choices. Or lack of choice.

But Matt didn't appear offended. "You ever regret being there for your men?"

"Only when the bullets are flying," Luke joked. *Not even then. Especially not then.*

"Same thing."

Luke nodded to show his understanding. "Duty."

"Love," Matt said simply. "When Kimberly got pregnant . . . Whatever I gave up, whatever else I could have done, I got Josh out of the deal. To be able to raise him here on the island, to do work I love in the place I call home, to find Allison on top of everything . . ." Matt's rare smile broke. "I'm a lucky guy."

"Yeah. You are. Congratulations, bro."

"Thanks."

They shifted their weight, in the way of men under the burden of emotion.

"How long are you home this time?" Matt asked.

Luke tried not to read a challenge into his brother's question. "I've got a month's leave. Training after that, preparing for the next deployment. Maybe six months."

For the first time, he didn't feel the familiar adrenaline buzz at the thought of another mission, like a junkie anticipating his next fix. But he was just back from a ten-month tour. The anticipation would come, he told himself.

"Then you'll still be here at Easter."

"As far as I know. Why?"

"I've asked Josh to be my best man. But I want you to stand with me at my wedding."

It was so far from what Luke had been thinking that he gaped. Matt's first, rushed wedding, at the age of nineteen, had been small. The bride had been pregnant, the bride's parents had not approved. Luke had been . . . Shit, he'd been younger than Josh was now. Only Tom had stood with Matt that time.

This time around would be different.

"Ooh-rah," Luke said, his voice rough with emotion. "Back to back . . ."

"To back," Matt finished with him.

They grabbed each other in a hard, one-armed hug. Luke thumped Matt's shoulder. Matt patted Luke's back. They drew apart, clearing their throats.

They went into the courthouse together.

IN COMBAT, WAITING was the worst. But eventually a firefight broke out or a bomb exploded, and training and adrenaline kicked in and took over.

In court, it was all waiting.

Luke trusted this lawyer, chosen by Kate. He trusted Kate when she told him everything would be okay. But even when he had faith in his CO, when he believed in his mission, success had always ultimately depended on how Luke did his job.

Here, the outcome was out of his hands.

He hated that.

Even after the clerk called his name and he answered *Present*, there was nothing he could do but stand there with his back exposed to the crowded room while the lawyers talked.

Vernon Long gave him a quick wink and a squeeze on the shoulder before approaching the judge. The social worker, Alisha Douglas, smiled at him.

Nothing to worry about, Long had said.

Luke glanced across at the Simpsons, sitting with their lawyer. Tiny details imprinted on his brain, the comb tracks in Ernie's hair, Jolene's ankles swelling above her shoes.

He resisted the urge to turn around and look for Matt and Kate. She had cases of her own today, she'd told him. She might not even be in the courtroom now.

The Simpsons were questioned by their lawyer and by the judge. Luke listened to their replies, crafted to establish his own total lack of relationship with Taylor. *Dawn never talked about him. He never came, never called, Taylor never knew* . . .

And there were photos presented as evidence, Taylor with her grandparents and Dawn, not that many, but still . . . His gut clenched. Was it enough?

The clerk called Luke's name. Vernon smiled and nodded encouragingly.

Time slowed the way it did in combat. His vision narrowed, all his attention tunneling toward the judge as the extraneous sounds of the court faded away.

HE LOOKED GOOD, Kate thought from the middle of the rows of seats, as close as she could get slipping in as the proceedings started. Strong, safe, and dependable, like you could trust him with a kid. Like you could trust him with your *heart*.

Her heart fluttered anxiously.

Okay, maybe that was going too far. But the whole clean-cut Captain America vibe? Mm, yeah, definitely working for him. His cropped blond hair gleamed in the overhead lights. Pressed, polished, prepared, Luke looked like what he was, a man determined to do his duty. And even though Kate knew how deceptive appearances could be, she was impressed. So was the judge.

Luke answered Vernon's questions in a firm, quiet voice. There was a copy of Dawn's letter and of Taylor's military dependent ID, a record of her doctor's appointment on base, receipts for new clothes.

Judge Dixon leaned forward. "Staff Sergeant Fletcher, why do you think you're the appropriate person to have the care of a ten-year-old girl? Why should Taylor live with you?"

Luke's impassive expression flickered.

Because that's what Dawn wanted, Kate thought.

"Because that's what Taylor wants," Luke said. "And I want what's best for her."

Oh, good answer. After that, Alisha's testimony about the fabulous Fletchers—their warmth, their support, their growing bond with Taylor—was just icing on the cake.

Judge Dixon launched into his expected summation. "Natural parent . . . intact family . . . Absent a finding of unfitness . . . No reason to interfere with the right of Staff Sergeant Fletcher to have sole custody of his minor child."

Luke had won. Relief flooded Kate. She'd believed, of course . . . but she hadn't been sure. You could never be sure until you heard the words. That's what she loved and hated about her job.

Ernie Simpson listened to the judge's ruling with a blank face, as if he didn't yet understand. But Jolene did. Taylor's grandmother collapsed like punched dough, her face falling in toward the dark hole of her mouth, her protruding eyes swimming with tears.

Kate felt a twinge of reluctant sympathy. Jolene had already lost her daughter. Now it appeared likely she would lose her granddaughter as well.

Of course, Kate would have felt even sorrier for her if the Simpsons hadn't reported Luke to social services. But their complaint had totally backfired.

Judge Dixon, in fact, appeared to be scolding their lawyer for risking his clients' future relationship with their granddaughter by making unfounded allegations against Luke.

". . . would certainly be within his rights to deny them further contact with Taylor," Judge Dixon intoned. "For this reason, I am not including visitation as part of the custody order. However . . ."

Kate sat up, alerted by his change in tone.

"It *is* Christmas. In deference to the season, I would strongly urge both parties to arrive at some kind of agreement that would allow this little girl to enjoy the comfort and support of her family over the holidays. *All* her family," the judge said, with a stern look over the top of his glasses. "That means I expect you all to set up a visit before you leave here today."

Kate leaned forward, straining to hear, frustrated by her inability to listen in on the conference at the front of the courtroom. To participate. She could see the tension in the line of Luke's back as Vernon spoke in his ear. Matt half stood and then sat down again.

She clenched her hands together in her lap, trying to hold on to her emotional objectivity and failing miserably. She wished Luke would turn around, but he was nodding his head, listening to Vernon. She wanted to be up there with them. With him. Which wasn't possible, she wasn't Luke's lawyer, she wasn't his anything, really.

You have a relationship with Taylor that doesn't have anything to do with me, Luke had said.

But her relationship, such as it was, did not win her entrance into that magic circle.

She was on the outside, looking in. Precisely where she'd told Luke she wanted to be. Where she was safe and alone.

The next case was called. With a quick shake of her head, Kate went into the lobby to wait.

I want to see you, he'd said.

But he didn't need her anymore. She would offer Vernon

her congratulations on a job well done. She and Luke would go out some time to celebrate. And then he would go home to his family where he belonged.

Circumstances had catapulted them together in a kind of false intimacy. She knew details of his personal life that his fellow Marines did not. She understood pieces of Taylor's past in a way that his family could not.

But their relationship had progressed far too quickly to be real. It was a fantasy, fueled by the emotional circumstances of his return and her own loneliness. Now that Taylor's custody was settled, what did Kate have to offer him? What did they even have to talk about?

Luke left the courtroom, flanked by Vernon and his brother. They made an impressive exhibit: the old silver fox in his bow tie and pinstriped suit; the tall fishing boat captain in a navy blazer, his hair streaked brown and gold like oiled oak; and Luke, stone-faced and ramrod straight in his ironed uniform, every muscle and sinew rigid with coiled energy like a garage door spring.

She crossed the lobby, intercepting them. "Great work, Vernon." She looked at Luke. "Congratulations."

"Thanks."

Vernon was talking, saying something, but she couldn't look away from Luke. Despite the positive outcome, he was clearly holding tightly to control.

"Luke?" His gaze, fierce and burning blue, met hers. Her heart stuttered at the warrior intensity blazing in his eyes. "At ease, Marine," she said softly.

His impassive mask cracked. Ignoring their surroundings, he wrapped his arms around her and lifted her off her feet, burying his face in her hair.

She clung to his broad shoulders, trying to absorb his tension into her own body. She could give him this, she thought. The safety of her embrace, the reassurance of her body. For now, it was enough.

At last, he set her on her feet. His straight blond lashes veiled his burning eyes, giving him a sleepy, dangerous look. "Let's get out of here."

Vernon's eyebrows lifted.

Kate flushed, abruptly recalled to their surroundings. "I, um . . ." His brother was watching them, eyes narrowed in speculation, a smile tugging the corner of his mouth. "Don't you have to get home to Taylor?"

"She's still in school. I've got hours."

Hours. *Only you*, his eyes promised. *Only me*. Her flush turned into all-body heat. "But your brother . . ." she protested weakly.

"Drove separately," Matt said, looking amused.

"Let's go," Luke said.

"Right." She swallowed, flustered. "I have to get my car out of the county lot."

"You didn't walk?"

"No, I had files. For, um, court. But I'm done for the day," she added. "I'll meet you."

"Where?"

She glanced at Vernon, back at Luke. "My office?" *My place. My bedroom.*

He nodded. "Good."

"We still have a little paperwork to get through," Vernon said.

"You do that," Kate said a little breathlessly. "I'll, uh, I'll see you."

"Soon," Luke said.

"I didn't realize you two were dating," Vernon said.

"Oh, I wouldn't . . . We're not exactly . . ."

"We're together," Luke said.

Her face flamed. She said good-bye to Matt. She said something, she wasn't sure what, to Vernon, complimenting him on his handling of the case.

They were all looking at her, Vernon, with his shrewd eyes and bland face, and Matt with a little smile, and Luke.

She realized abruptly she had no idea what they were talking about. Or what she'd just said.

"Certainly helped with your friend Alisha," Vernon said. *For the second time?*

She smiled brightly. "I'm so glad."

Somehow she excused herself and escaped the courthouse without stumbling.

"You have a nice day, Miz Dolan," said the sheriff's deputy at the door. Deputy Bobby Ward, round as a well and nearing retirement.

Courthouse security usually fell to the old and out of shape and the newly hired. The deputy next to him looked barely out of high school.

"Thanks, Deputy Ward," Kate said. "You, too."

The cool December air kissed her hot face. The sky was bright and blue, with happy clouds splotched around like a child's painting.

She walked to the lot. All her life, she had been disappointed. By her father, her mother, herself. She *expected* to be disappointed. She *counted* on it.

We're together, Luke had said.

What did that mean?

She slid her bag from her shoulder to dig for her keys.

A man stepped out from the line of parked cars. A big man wearing a hoodie and a baseball cap. She recoiled even before she recognized his face, registered the threat before she recalled his name.

Will Brown. "I been waiting for you."

Kate's heart kicked into overtime. "Mr. Brown," she said, keeping her voice calm and pleasant. Professional.

"I come to say I was sorry," he said unexpectedly.

Kate swallowed the knot in her throat. "Did you?"

He ducked his head in apparent assent. "You know, Libby and me, we've had our problems."

Problems, yes. Black eyes and a broken nose, cracked ribs, a split lip. Kate had documented them over the eight months since Libby had found the courage to call her. And even so, Libby might have stayed with her husband because she had no money, because she had no job skills, because she had no confidence. Because he begged her. Threatened her. Because she'd loved him, once upon a time.

But then Will hit their oldest child, Cole, when the boy

got between them, trying to protect her, and that had been the last straw for Libby.

"Yes, I know." Kate glanced at the courthouse entrance, thirty yards away. No need to panic. Yet.

"But we always worked them out before," Will said. "She would've stayed if you hadn't been putting all those ideas in her head."

Deputy Ward was chatting with his trainee partner, oblivious to the drama in the parking lot.

"I'm sorry," Kate said. *Not sorry. Not sorry at all.* "I have to go."

"I'm not done talking," Will said. "I need to talk to her. I need to see her. She's my wife."

Kate's hands trembled. She tightened her grip on her keys. "I can't help you. You're not supposed to have any contact with Libby."

"But you could fix that." He looked at her, his dark eyes shining with tears. "I just want to go home."

"I'm sorry," Kate said, more sincerely this time. "I can't interfere with a restraining order."

"But you could talk to her. You could tell her how sorry I am."

"I really can't. You need to talk to your lawyer."

He slammed his fist onto the roof of her car. Kate cringed, nerves jumping in her stomach. "Don't you tell me what to do," he said, mean and low.

"Mr. Brown . . . Will—" *Keep him talking. Keep him calm.* The moment the confrontation turned physical, she lost.

"You quit talking. It's my turn to talk. Now *I'm* telling *you* what to do."

Kate backed against her car. She hated being vulnerable. Hated feeling afraid. Hated loud voices and the threat of violence. When she was little, she'd thought she could control it. That if she were good enough, smart enough, quiet enough, she could forestall it, stop it somehow.

She'd never figured out what would set her father off.

But she got very good at recognizing the signs, the bright, narrow eyes, the alcoholic flush, the rage that took over his body like an alien thing.

She recognized the signs now, in Will.

Her knees shook. She hated being powerless most of all.

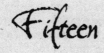

Fifteen

"Before Christmas, yeah, whatever. After Christmas, I don't care." Luke dragged his mind from Kate and the things he'd like to be doing with her, to her, right now, and tried to focus instead on Vernon Long's talk of visitation. "But not Christmas," he added, surprising himself.

It wasn't like he and Taylor had years of family holiday rituals that had to be honored. No special stockings to hang up, no Christmas Eve bedtime story, none of the stuff he remembered from his own childhood.

Maybe that was the point.

"It's my first Christmas home in two years," he tried to explain to Long. "Taylor's first Christmas with us ever." *Her first Christmas without Dawn.* "Things will be tough enough without . . ."

Jolene crying. Ernie drinking. Creepy Kevin and his Nazi tattoos.

Yeah, not on Luke's watch.

"Distractions," Vernon Long said.

"Yeah." Luke thrust a hand through his hair. Trust a

lawyer to come up with a three-syllable word that covered everything and said nothing.

He thought of Kate, talking on the phone in her office, using hundred-dollar words and her don't-mess-with-me voice, laying down the law with confidence and skill.

This was her world. He needed her. He wished she'd been beside him in the courtroom today. Even the judge's comments at the end—*Congratulations, Staff Sergeant. If you're half as good a father as you are a Marine, Taylor's a lucky girl*—had left him feeling unprepared for his job. For fatherhood.

He'd left the courtroom, hopped on adrenaline, trying not to sweat. Instinctively, he'd looked for Kate, seeking . . . What? He wasn't sure.

He only knew that when he saw her, solid as a lighthouse in her two-inch heels, her bright hair lighting the lobby, he'd felt like a sailor catching sight of his home harbor.

At ease, Marine, she'd said, teasing, reassuring, and everything inside him relaxed.

He wanted her. But more, he wanted simply to be with her, to be. *Only you. Only me.*

Long was still talking. Out in the parking lot across the street, somebody's car alarm went off.

Luke twitched. Home two weeks, and sudden noises still had the power to make him jump. He glanced through the glass-and-steel doors at the lights flashing on a red Mini Cooper.

Kate's Mini Cooper. His blood ran cold.

Kate was stumbling back, scrambling around the side of her car while some goon in a hoodie grabbed at her over the hood. She screamed, tripped, and went down behind the bushes that edged the lot.

The uniforms at the entrance froze like raw recruits under fire. The younger one fumbled for his weapon. Wrong move. Never draw unless you plan to shoot. And not when innocent civilians are in the line of fire. Luke shoved past him, bolting out the door and down the courthouse steps. Kate screamed again as he sprinted across the street.

"Stop!" yelled the uniform.

At him? At the other guy? Luke didn't look back, all his attention focused on the threat to Kate. At the shout, the guy's head jerked up. His mouth opened, his eyes widened before he braced, crouching for attack.

End it, Luke thought, and launched over the bushes, landing on his feet.

"Fuck off, soldier boy," the guy said. He was around Luke's height, maybe sixty pounds heavier, with a weight lifter's muscles and a beer drinker's belly. "This is none of your business."

Luke took a controlled step forward, not taking his eyes off the enemy, not daring to look at Kate. "Step away," he ordered.

"Fuck you."

The guy lunged, counting on his bulk to carry the day. Luke grabbed his wrist and used his weight against him, turning in, his back to the guy's chest, flipping him over his shoulder. The guy hit hard, with a grunt of pain, and lay stunned. Luke kicked him over and dropped down, securing his arms behind him.

The courthouse guards pounded across the street.

"Oh, God," Kate said from under the bushes. "Are you all right?"

Was *he* all right? She was the one who had been attacked.

He looked up, prepared to yell like his mom when one of them ran into the street. Saw Kate's white face, her glassy eyes. He took a breath to steady himself. What if he hadn't been here?

"Fine," he bit out. "You?"

She was already scrambling to her feet, like she could take on the world. She nodded.

"Good," Luke said and dug his knee deeper in the guy's back until the uniforms showed up with handcuffs.

THEY FINALLY ARRIVED at Kate's house nearly two hours later, after giving their separate statements to the sheriff's deputies. Kate felt numb, vulnerable, all the defenses she'd carefully constructed over the years suddenly knocked down. Stripped away. On autopilot, she made tea, her mother's coping mechanism in the aftermath of her father's rages.

Your daddy's just tired, stressed, under a lot of pressure, her mother would say. *If you'd only be quiet, come home on time, not argue with him, he wouldn't have to get so angry, raise his voice, lose his temper. Don't overreact. Don't make a fuss.*

Have some tea.

Kate wrapped her hands around her mug, craving its warmth.

Luke paced the confines of her apartment, his mug untouched. Violence pumped off him like heat.

She shivered, and he stopped in front of her chair. "Can I do anything? Get you anything?"

She shook her head.

"Do you want me to drive you to the hospital?"

She sighed. "No."

The sheriff's deputies had already catalogued her injuries, a sore hip, abraded palms, bruises on her arm where Brown had grabbed her. But it could have been so much worse.

Her mother used to say that. *It could be worse, Katie. At least you have food to eat and a place to sleep. Why do you always make everything into a big deal?*

Kate pushed the memory away. Will Brown was in a holding cell now on the top floor of the county courthouse, charged with Class 1A misdemeanor assault and battery. A conviction would likely only put him away for a month or two. But the jail time would buy a measure of peace for Libby and her children and increase his punishment if he ever threatened them again.

Kate cradled her mug, trying to keep the contents from sloshing. She couldn't seem to stop shaking. She wanted to curl into herself, the way she'd curled in bed as a little girl, burying her head in her pillow to block out the sounds of her father shouting and her mother's sobs. She roused herself to say, "You need to go. Taylor will be home from school soon."

He should go home and celebrate with his daughter. Taylor, who was safe now and protected and loved.

"I'm not leaving you."

"I'm fine. I don't need you to fuss over me." *I don't need you. I can't need you.*

Luke stiffened. "Too bad. You're stuck with me."

If she didn't know better, she'd say he looked almost hurt. As if she had the power to hurt him. Which was ridiculous.

On the other hand, she had been rude. He'd been nothing but kind to her. He deserved better.

Her hands fluttered on her mug. "I'm sorry." She forced the words out, each one sticking in her throat like a secret or a bone. "And I'm grateful. You were a real hero today. Thank you."

"No problem."

"You saved me."

Luke looked uncomfortable. "He wasn't armed."

"He still would have hurt me. It bothers me," she confessed, "that I was so . . . so helpless."

"You weren't helpless. You hit the panic button."

"And then you had to rescue me."

"Nothing wrong with that."

"Because you're a man." The unfairness of it broke through the cold shell encasing her.

"Because I'm a Marine. Hell, babe, we practice hand-to-hand to pass the time. You're not trained to fight."

"I shouldn't have to be." The spurt of anger was warm and welcome. "I'm a smart, strong, capable woman. I've spent my entire adult life using the law to protect women and children from violence. And then some abusive thug in the parking lot decides I'm responsible for breaking up his family, and I'm dependent on some man to save me."

Luke shrugged. "Pretty much."

"It's not *right*," she burst out, frustrated.

"No, it's not," he agreed unexpectedly. "But it's not on you that this guy is an asshole. Any man who hits a woman is no kind of man."

"I should have been able to handle it."

"You did. You kept your head, you called for backup." He dropped to a crouch in front of her chair. She felt the heat of his body through his uniform shirt, his breath warm against her face, his muscled thighs caging her knees. A little flame licked through her. "Nothing wrong with somebody having your six."

He raised his hand—to touch her hair? To cup her cheek?—and she flinched from the contact like a startled rabbit.

His eyes fired like gas burners, blue and hot. "You said Brown didn't hit you."

Mute, she shook her head.

Gently, his fingers feathered through her hair. Softly, his thumb brushed her scar. She could see him assembling the evidence, weighing, judging. "Then . . . who did?"

Shame clogged her throat.

Whatever horrors he'd witnessed as a Marine, Luke was his parents' son. His family's patterns of behavior were part of his psyche, imprinted in his DNA. He was a product of his upbringing, decent, normal, upright.

And she, God help her, was a product of hers.

She swallowed without saying anything.

Those brilliant eyes narrowed. "Your father?"

Don't exaggerate, Katie. It was one of her mother's favorite sayings. Along with, *He doesn't really mean it.* And, *It's only when he's been drinking. It's just his way.*

She lifted her chin. "He hardly ever . . . He only hit me a handful of times. Well, six. Less than two handfuls," she said, forcing a smile. Luke didn't smile back. "But that once—the first time—he was wearing his Naval Academy ring."

Fourteen stitches and a trip to the ER.

After that, he could reduce her to terror simply by taking off his ring and laying it on the table.

Sometimes she thought she'd imagined it. Mistaken

things somehow. Walked into a door, the way her mother always claimed she was doing, or bumped into a cabinet or tripped on a rug or the stairs.

She was his *daughter*.

She could still taste the surprise blooming in her mouth, sharp and metallic as blood.

Luke still hadn't said anything. Kate closed her eyes, unwilling to accept the vision of herself she would see reflected in his eyes. Weak. Diminished.

This was the cost of breaking the silence, the danger of letting someone in. If he rejected her now, he would be rejecting her true self, the real Kate.

"You said he died," Luke said.

She nodded.

"Two years ago."

"Yes."

"So I can't dig him up and beat the crap out of him for you."

Her eyes snapped open. "The solution to violence is not more violence."

"Sometimes it is. Not in this case, though."

"Because he's *dead*?" Outrage wrestled with humor.

"Yeah. Plus, he was your father. I'm not saying that would stop me, but—"

"*I* would stop you," she said. "I grew up and got away a long time ago. Sure, my childhood sucked, but it's over. I won't let myself be defined as a victim."

"I don't see you as a victim."

"No?"

He shook his head. "You're a warrior. A survivor." He held her gaze. "Like me."

He took her breath away. Nothing he could have said could be better calculated to restore her to herself.

A muscle tightened in his jaw. "It just eats me that you were hurt and I can't do jack shit about it."

She understood his frustration. Isn't that what she hated, too? To be helpless. Powerless. But he was wrong. "There is one thing you could do," she said.

"Sure."

His response was direct and generous. Like the man himself. Her lips curved. "Something that would make me feel a lot better."

"Name it."

Confidence unfurled inside her, like a line of pink along the bud of a rose. He knew, and he had not rejected her. He knew, and he still wanted her.

"Well . . ." She rested her arms on his shoulders, laced her fingers together behind his neck. "You could kiss me."

An answering smile started deep in his eyes. "I can manage that."

Their faces were almost on a level. He leaned forward slightly, still smiling, and touched her lips with his gently, softly, the way he'd touched her hair. She sighed and kissed him back, the bloom opening in her chest, her kiss warm and openmouthed. Luke surged to his feet, bringing her with him, pulling her flush against him, and she raised on tiptoe, finding their fit. He was tall and strong and hard against her, already aroused, the feel of him unexpectedly familiar, shockingly right. Sensation spilled inside her.

"Do you have time?" she whispered between kisses.

"Got five minutes?"

She jolted. "Um . . ."

He grinned. "It was a joke."

"Oh. Ha-ha."

He drew back his head, regarding her with half-closed eyes, all that beautiful blue smoldering behind straight, thick lashes. "Do you trust me?"

"Yes." Well, sort of. She didn't let herself rely on anyone. But she liked and admired him very much.

He kissed the tip of her nose and then her cheek and then her lips. "You can trust me." Another slow, melting grin. "I've never left a woman behind."

She flushed. Did he mean sexually? Or was he trying to tell her he didn't have a woman in every port? They'd already disclosed their sexual histories. She wasn't expecting him to make a commitment after one night.

His mouth came down on hers, harder, more insistent, and her thoughts were smothered, blanketed by heat. He picked her up, holding her butt in his big hands, and she wrapped her legs around his waist because, really, where else could they go? He carried her into the bedroom—he knew the way this time—while she held on to his shoulders, appreciating his strength and the lovely play of muscles in his arms and back and neck. Their bodies rubbed together lower down, and that was lovely, too. He set her down by the bed and unbuttoned her skirt. She helped, pulling her blouse over her head, shivering a little in her lacy bra and panties.

He hooked one warm, callused finger into the string over her hip and smiled into her eyes. "Very pretty."

Her heart beat faster. "I wore the good stuff." *For you.*

His smile deepened. "I wasn't talking about your under-wear, babe," he said and tugged it down.

He laid her down across her bed. Her knees fell apart, her feet barely touching the floor. She felt exposed. Naked. Well, of course she was naked. He was undressing, too. She watched him take off his clothes, savoring the sight of him, his solid chest, his washboard abs, the trail of coarse hair that led from just below his navel to his dusky, rigid sex. She had seen his tattoos before. Now, in the light, she studied his scars: the pale puckered slash like a sickle along his ribs; the constellation of small, dark, pitted scars under his arm; a half-dozen lines, nicks, and dents she'd only felt with her fingertips before.

You're a warrior. A survivor. Like me.

The thought of what he had endured, had survived, pressed like a weight on her heart.

He stood over her, damaged and beautiful, and her insides squeezed together with longing, as if she could pull him inside her. She held out her arms.

But he only pushed her legs wide, kneeling on the floor beside her bed. A quiver tensed her stomach. She didn't want . . . She didn't need . . . They didn't have time for . . .

That.

"Um, Luke?" She raised her head from the mattress.

His big hands slid down her thighs, lifting her legs over his broad, smooth shoulders. Her heels touched his back.

He smiled at her, his eyes gleaming. "Do you trust me, babe?"

The question took on a whole other meaning with his head between her thighs. She squirmed a little. "It's not a question of trust," she said with as much dignity as she could manage flat on her back with her knees apart, all of her on display. What was she supposed to *do* with herself while he was . . . down there?

"It's just not necessary," she assured him. "What we did before was fine."

His warm laugh gusted over her flesh, danced along her nerve endings.

"Let's see if we can do better than fine," he suggested and lowered his head.

Oh, goodness. He lavished her with sensation, making her body jolt and yearn, hitching closer, jerking away. He hunted her response, wringing it from her flesh, his hands and mouth relentless. Thorough. She raised her arm, shielding her eyes from the unbearable intimacy, but that only intensified the press of sensations, the sounds, animal, embarrassing, the rasp of her breathing and her moans, the wet, rich, intimate smells of sex. All her senses sharpened, focused, spiraling down, and she closed her eyes behind her arm and went into the heat and the dark, consenting and consumed. She gave herself up to the edge of his teeth, the play of his tongue, the searching, searing pressure of his mouth, and the tension inside her coiled tighter and tighter until it broke like spring, like a fever, drenching her in heat. So much, she couldn't bear it.

She lay in a kind of fever dream as he crawled over her, sheathing himself in a condom before he settled between her legs. His erection prodded her thigh, rubbed and slid against her sex. She was all soft, soft and wet and open under him. And empty. She felt so empty. She tilted her hips to meet his, wrapping her arms and legs around him, taking him for herself, all that muscle, all that strength and heat and determination, taking him inside her, hot and thick inside her. He filled her, stretched her, thrusting in a heavy rhythm that made her pant, and incredibly the tension was back, making her strain and twist against him as he pounded inside her.

"Oh, God, Kate," he said, and she opened her eyes and saw his face, taut and sweaty above her, his eyes dark and hot. Seeing her. Wanting her. She broke again in silky spasms, and this time he drove deep and shuddered with her into the dark.

KATE WENT OUT like a light after sex.

She didn't cuddle, Luke thought, regarding the curve of her spine, the inky black scales of justice rising like wings above her shoulder blade. She didn't want to talk about her feelings or go on about their relationship. She basically rolled over and conked out like a guy. *Thanks for the sex*, down and done.

He wasn't sure if he should take her reaction as a tribute to his awesome sex god skills or not.

She'd said she wanted to feel better. From the noises she'd made, he figured he'd done that for her, at least. Anyway, *he* sure felt good.

He raised himself on one elbow, tracing a finger along her shoulder. Not trying to wake her, just wanting to touch her. She was so pretty, her coppery hair bright against the pillow, her face relaxed in sleep. Freckles dusted her creamy skin like the body glitter girls used to wear back in high school, but soft. He rubbed his thumb over her arm, sniffed her neck. Everything about her was soft and smooth and warm. He could lay like this beside her forever.

Whoa. Where had *that* come from?

But he knew. The thing was, he'd always assumed that one day he would find what his parents had. That unspoken communication, that unquestioning trust, that rock-solid foundation.

He was twenty-nine years old, older than his dad when Matt was born, older than most of the guys in his unit who were married. Now that Matt and Allison had set a date, and Meg had dumped that loser in New York and looked to be settling down with Sam Grady, Luke figured he was next in line. Not that he felt any pressure to measure up to their example, to follow their lead, the way he had all through childhood.

He loved the island, but he wasn't at home there anymore the way that Matt was. Couldn't reconnect with his high school peers the way that Meg had. Islanders shared the same experiences, growing up with the easy rhythms of the coastal seasons, going to school or to sea, pairing up, having kids.

His ten years of service had set him apart.

The raucous cries of the seabirds made him flinch now. A whiff of diesel from the boats in the harbor could plunge him back into the streets of Afghanistan.

This last tour had changed something inside him. Or maybe he only felt that way now that he was back.

He wanted to be . . . normal. To have an ordinary life, a house and kids.

Well, he had the kid part down already. He had Taylor now.

And a house, if you could call his parents' rental cottage that. And a dog. And a cat.

All of them waiting for him.

He sighed and kissed Kate's shoulder. He wasn't making the mistake of rushing out on her again.

She made a little snuffling sound, too cute to be called a snore.

He grinned. "Babe."

"Mm."

"I've got to go."

"'kay."

She did not wake up like a Marine, alert and ready to fight. He tried again. "I'll see you."

She nodded, her head still firmly planted on her pillow.

If he left now, she could claim with perfect truth that she didn't remember him saying good-bye.

"I thought Christmas," he said.

Her eyes opened.

Yeah, he thought, amused. *That got your attention.*

"I can't come for Christmas." She sounded almost panicked. She rolled on her back to face him, so that her breasts moved in interesting ways under the sheet. "That's family time."

He lifted his gaze from her breasts. The best defense, he decided, was a good offense. "You don't like my family?"

"Of course I . . ." She glared at him. "That's not the point."

He knew that. Kate had spent so many years running away from family. He would have to work hard to make her accept being part of a family again.

"Just think about it," he said.

Once she got used to the idea . . . Everybody liked his family. If she'd just give them a chance, give him a chance, she'd see.

Sixteen

"I DON'T SEE why I have to clean up the yard."

Taylor's voice carried from the kitchen in the Pirates' Rest to the laundry room, where Luke was attempting to sort their clothes. Did he wash his daughter's red sweater with his khakis or with jeans? And what about her leggings?

"It's not like anybody's coming to stay," Taylor continued, sounding snotty.

"We don't just clean for guests," Tess said in an admirably patient voice. "And you promised your dad that you would take care of the puppy."

"I *am* taking care of him. I took him out twice today. He hasn't gone in the house hardly at all."

Luke had heard enough. He dumped detergent into the washing machine and stalked into the kitchen, delighted to have an excuse to take a break from laundry. "You're responsible for your own messes. And your dog's."

Taylor and his mother turned to him with nearly identical expressions of surprise. Tess didn't say anything.

Taylor's face turned tragic. "But I'm going to Madison's

this afternoon. Her mom got the new Wii dance game. She's *expecting* me."

He was glad his daughter was making friends. But that didn't excuse her from her responsibilities. "So you'll dance after you pick up the dog poop."

"Fine. I'll pick up JD's. But I don't see why I should pick up after Fezzik. Let Josh do it."

Josh would do it. Probably without treating them all to some big drama.

"Taylor," Luke said warningly.

She heaved a sigh. "All right. I'll do it when I get back."

Luke gave his daughter his best deadeye stare, the one that sent his men scrambling.

Her chin stuck out mulishly. "What? I said I'd do it."

"Now."

"Fine." She grabbed a plastic grocery bag from under the sink, slamming the cabinet with a crack like a gunshot.

Luke flinched. He tried to think of what Matt would say. Or Kate. But what came out of his mouth was, "And apologize to your grandmother."

"Sorry," Taylor muttered.

She banged out the back door.

Luke exhaled through his teeth. "Sorry," he said to his mother in almost the same tone Taylor had used.

Tess smiled. "For what?"

"I could've handled that better." Should have handled that better. What would Matt have done?

"You handled that fine." Tess patted his cheek. "I think it's wonderful that Taylor feels secure enough with you to act like a normal ten-year-old."

"Mouthing off like that is normal?"

"At her age? Yes. She's a preteen girl. Her hormones are just starting to kick in."

Luke felt the blood drain from his head. He was just getting used to the idea that he was a father. He didn't want to think about his baby girl with . . . hormones.

Tess laughed, taking pity on him. "You'll be fine. I expect she's still adjusting to having you home. Testing, the way you all used to whenever your father returned from a deployment." She smiled, a little ruefully. "It takes a while to establish the appropriate chain of command."

Luke thought of Corporal Danny Hill and his wife. *Stephanie's been handling everything on her own for eleven months . . . Have you told her how proud you are of her?*

He looked at his mom, her strong hands and frail frame, her face lined with humor and pain, her brave new hair color blazing like a battle standard.

Her cane, resting against the kitchen counter.

He'd accepted that his coming home would be an adjustment for Taylor. But until this moment, he had still regarded his own mother with the eyes and habits of a child. Matt had tried to tell him. But Luke hadn't fully appreciated what his going . . . and coming . . . and going again would mean for Mom. For both his parents. They would soldier on, without question or complaint. *Back to back*, the way they had taught their children. But after so many tours of duty, they must be getting tired.

He felt as if the ground had shifted under his feet, changing forever his internal landscape.

"Mom . . ."

She smiled at him, brows a little arched, the same questioning, patient look he remembered from his childhood. *Who left out the lunch meat? Did you study for your chemistry test? How did tryouts go?*

What could he say? *Sorry for taking you for granted*? *Sorry for taking so long to grow up*? "Thanks."

Her cheeks turned pink with pleasure. "Oh, honey. You're welcome. What else?"

"What?"

"I know that look. Something's on your mind."

He barely resisted the urge to shuffle his feet. "I, uh, invited Kate Dolan for dinner."

Tess tilted her head. "Really?" An interested trill like a bird's.

Manfully, he continued. "On Christmas Day."

Her eyes widened. "Tom! Tom, come here."

Oh, shit.

His father appeared from the living room at the front of the house, where he was setting up the train set around the big tree.

Tess took his arm. "Tom, Luke's invited Kate for Christmas."

His father's bushy gray eyebrows climbed. "You dating the lawyer now?"

Dating. Having sex with. "Yes."

Tom nodded, hearing what Luke did not say. "You could do worse. Bit soon to have her around for Christmas dinner, though."

He could tell them she didn't have anywhere else to go, play on their sympathies. Or he could tell them the truth. "I want her here. She hasn't said yes yet."

Tess's eyes narrowed at this perceived slight to her younger son. "Why not?"

"She doesn't want to horn in on family time."

"Hm," was his mother's only comment.

"You haven't known her long," Tom said.

Luke held his father's gaze. "Longer than two weeks."

It was one of their family's stories. Tom Fletcher met Teresa Saltoni when he was at Great Lakes Naval Base and she was waiting tables at her parents' restaurant in Chicago's Little Italy. Two weeks later, they were married.

Tom grunted. "I hope you know what you're doing."

So did Luke.

Kate was itchy enough over this whole family business without taking flak from his folks. He loved them a lot, but as a group, they could be pretty overwhelming. There was no telling what Meg would say. Or Josh. Or Taylor.

He glanced out the window at his daughter, scooping poop in the yard.

His life right now.

He went out on the deck to supervise.

Taylor glowered and bent to her work. He was still not forgiven, then. But the puppy wandered over the grass to greet him, tail flopping cheerfully. Luke rubbed its tummy. The dog, at least, was delighted with the poop-hunting game. As soon as Taylor stooped with her trowel, JD bounded over to investigate before licking her face. Taylor jerked her head away and then grinned, pure kid.

Luke relaxed, feeling less like a prison guard. He reached for his cigarettes, glanced at Taylor and shoved his hands deep in his pockets instead.

A blue-and-white patrol car crunched over the oyster shell drive and parked behind the inn.

Dare had its own police department now, Luke remembered. The town had taken the unusual step of incorporating to give the residents more control over the forces of tourism and development on their island, to protect them against outsiders.

But the cop who got out of the patrol car was a stranger.

Luke shouldn't have been surprised. He'd been gone a long time. And the population on Dare shifted over time like the barrier islands themselves, constantly eroded and renewed by the tides.

He watched as the cop came up the walk, not swaggering, but moving deliberately, aware of his surroundings. Midthirties, Luke judged, boxer's build, a little over average height. Dark and closely shaved in navy blue uniform pants and shirt. Unassuming. Confident. Like he knew what he was doing.

What was a guy like that doing writing traffic tickets for drunk tourists on Dare Island? And why the hell was he here?

He stopped a few yards away from the bottom of the steps. *Out of the kill zone.* Ex-military, maybe. "Staff Sergeant Fletcher?"

Luke hid his surprise. "Luke."

"Jack Rossi."

They shook hands. Rossi's grip was solid and strong, nothing to prove. His gaze was dark and direct. Nothing to hide.

"Hi, Chief," Taylor said.

Rossi glanced down, his hard face softening. "Hi, Taylor. How's it going?"

"You know each other?" Luke asked.

"I swing by the school most days," Rossi said easily. "Part of the job."

"Hearts and minds," Luke said.

They exchanged looks. "Exactly."

"The chief came to talk to our class about drugs," Taylor said.

"In fourth grade?" Hormones and drugs. Jesus. Couldn't she stay ten forever? At least until he got the hang of this fatherhood thing.

"Early intervention," Rossi said.

Taylor gave Luke a pointed look. "We learned about smoking, too."

Ten, going on thirty.

"Nice dog." Rossi squatted and offered a hand to JD, who promptly peed in excitement. "Yours?"

Taylor nodded. "My dad brought him home. From Afghanistan." From the pride in her voice, Luke deduced he was now forgiven for making her clean the yard. She looked at him directly. "Can I go to Madison's now?"

"Wash your hands first."

She nodded and ran to the cottage. JD trotted after her.

"Nice kid," Rossi said in the same tone he'd used for the dog.

"Yeah." *Enough with the pleasantries.* "What can I do for you, Chief?"

"Jack." He stood. "Heard you had a little excitement at the courthouse the other day."

"That's out of your jurisdiction, isn't it, Jack?"

The chief shrugged. "I've got friends in the sheriff's department. I was wondering—now that you're on this side of the bridge—if there's anything else going on I haven't heard about yet. Some guys get back, they don't handle things too well. They hit their wives, they drive too fast, they drink too much. I just want you to know I'm here."

Reassurance? Or threat?

"Everything's fine," Luke said.

Those dark eyes met his. "I was in the Tagab Valley myself—2004, before I got out."

The Tagab Valley in the Surobi District of Afghanistan. In 2004, Luke had been on embassy security in Kabul. "MP?" Luke asked.

"Sniper."

O-kay. All Marines were riflemen. But even among Marines, the brutal intimacy of the snipers' job set them apart.

Jack smiled briefly. "I'm not much for war stories. But if you need an ear, I'll listen."

Every day a vet committed suicide. More Marines were falling to the enemy within than to the Taliban. It was easy to understand the chief's concern.

And hard not to resent it.

Sniper. If anybody should have problems adjusting, it should be a guy who made a personal ID of each kill.

"Appreciate the offer," Luke said. "But it's not necessary."

The back door opened.

"Chief Rossi!" Tess said. "I thought I saw your patrol car. Is everything all right?"

"Yes, ma'am. Was just welcoming your son here home."

"Well, that was nice of you. You'll be going home yourself soon, won't you?"

"Ma'am?"

"For Christmas. Don't you have family up north? New Jersey or someplace."

Luke narrowed his eyes. Was his mother *flirting* with the new police chief?

"Pennsylvania," Rossi said. "But I won't get up there this year."

"Too far?" she asked sympathetically.

"Too busy." Another brief smile. "I've got one part-time officer for backup. Until I can hire more staff, I'm working a lot of holidays."

"Then you'll have to come here for dinner. You do get time to eat, don't you? On Christmas Day?"

"I'll eat, yes." He glanced at Luke. "But I don't want to intrude."

Well, hell. Luke didn't want Jack Rossi here for Christmas. He wanted Kate.

But Rossi was a fellow Marine, alone for the holidays.

Luke smiled. "Looks like we'll have a chance to swap war stories after all."

A THIN RAIN fell over Beaufort harbor. Many of the boats had been dry docked for the season, and those that remained were shrouded, floating on the gray water like gulls with folded wings. But the drab scene outside only made the inside of the bar seem snug and warm. The beer signs and Christmas lights glowed and twinkled.

Kate swirled her pink Moscato d'Asti cocktail. She'd never had one before. She was doing all kinds of things she'd never done before, including grabbing a holiday drink with Alisha.

Alisha took a sip of gingerbread martini. "I'm just saying, I'd be happy if Luke Fletcher was coming down my chimney."

Kate smirked. "Ho ho ho."

"'Ho,' yourself," Alisha retorted. "So, how often is Staff Sergeant Sexy stuffing your stocking?"

Kate laughed and almost choked on her drink. She swallowed hastily. "'Stuffing my stocking'? Where do you come up with this stuff?"

"All those long, lonely nights with nothing to do but paint my toenails. You know how it is in this job. Half the guys I meet are deadbeat baby daddies and the other half are junkies. So tell me everything. And give details. I want to live vicariously."

Kate felt her face heat. "There's not much to tell. I've only seen him a couple of times since the hearing."

"So, where did you go?"

"We don't go anywhere. He comes over."

"Well, that can be good," Alisha said. "Long, romantic evenings in front of the fire . . ."

"No fire. I don't have a fireplace."

"But you're having hot sex."

"Amazing sex," Kate confirmed.

"And now you're just being smug," Alisha complained. "So, are you like a booty call? Or friends with bennies? Or what?"

Kate toyed with her orange twist. "We're definitely friends." *Friends* was good. She needed more friends in her life. "I don't want to . . . We're not rushing into anything."

"Does he spend the night?"

Kate shook her head. She had been the one to set limits on their relationship. She couldn't complain if they occasionally felt . . . limiting. "He has to get home to Taylor."

Alisha picked thoughtfully at the cookie crumbs on the rim of her glass. "Maybe you should go to his place. Then you could fool around after his little girl goes to bed."

"He says he doesn't want me to have to drive home alone late at night."

"Then sleep over."

"Alisha, you're a social worker. Are you honestly suggesting we have sex while there's a young, impressionable child in the next room?"

Alisha grinned. "Honey, how do you think most parents have sex?"

"I'm not Taylor's mother."

"But you like her."

"She's a wonderful little girl. That's why I'm trying to protect her. I don't want her to be hurt. Or disappointed. In case things don't work out."

"How can they work out if you don't give them a chance?"

"Now you sound like Luke."

"Do I? Good. I was afraid maybe he was the one dragging his feet."

Kate thought of Luke, laughing, urgent, doing her against

the wall of her apartment last night, and a blush worked its way from her toes to her hairline. "No, he's more the 'full speed ahead and damn the torpedoes' type."

Alisha arched an eyebrow. "Torpedo, huh? And you had problems with 'Christmas stocking.'"

Kate laughed. Drew her finger through the water ring on the table. "He wants me to come for Christmas," she confessed. "To his parents' house."

"That's great."

"I haven't said yes."

"Why not?"

"It's too soon."

"Too soon for what?"

"Too soon for me to know how I feel. Certainly too soon to trust how he feels."

"Honey, it's obvious how you feel. It's all over your face."

Kate felt a jump in her belly that could have been pleasure or panic or acknowledgment. Or all three. "What if I go and it's a bust?" she blurted.

"What if you don't go and regret it?"

Kate exhaled shakily. "Is that a social worker thing? Answering a question with another question?"

"Is that a lawyer thing? Not answering at all?"

They smiled at one another.

Kate took a solid gulp from her glass. "We should have done this before."

"Never too late." Alisha raised her martini in a toast. "Or too soon."

"Sneaky," Kate decided.

"All I'm saying is, you think about it. But if you decide you're not ready for his family, you come with me to my mother's." Alisha reached across the table and patted Kate's hand. "Nobody should be alone on Christmas."

NOBODY SHOULD BE *alone on Christmas.*

Alisha's words followed Kate home to her empty apartment. Luke's flowers gleamed white against the gloom, breathing the fragrance of roses and pine into the still, chill air. Kate stood listening to the rain against her windows, but the sound did not fill the silence.

Kate sighed. Maybe she should get a cat.

But it wasn't Snowball she was missing.

Before she could talk herself out of it, she pulled her phone from her bag and hit CONTACTS.

Three rings. "Hello?"

"Hi, Mom. It's Kate," she added, even though her name and number must have shown up on her mother's phone display.

Silence.

Kate swallowed. "How are you?"

"I'm fine, dear." Brenda Dolan sounded faintly puzzled, as if she couldn't imagine why her only child would be calling two days before Christmas.

Kate tried again. "How was your drive?"

"Traffic was terrible. Well, you know how it is around the holidays."

"I'm sorry." Kate tried to find another, more pleasant subject. "And Aunt Sharon? How is she?"

"Very busy with her family. Everyone is here," Brenda said. "Julie and Christopher and the children."

"That's great," Kate said, squashing her feelings of guilt. Her aunt had not invited her for Christmas. And Brenda had turned down Kate's offer to come home, claiming there was no point in cooking a big meal and putting up a tree for just the two of them. She preferred to go to her sister's, where she could enjoy all the trappings of the holiday without any painful reminders of Christmases past.

"I guess you all have a lot to catch up on," Kate said.

It was the only verbal cue her mother needed. Brenda launched into the news of her sister's family, her monologue like one of those Christmas newsletters. Lots of accomplishments, no awkward confessions or messy emotional details. No unpleasantness.

See? The list said. *I made the right choices in life. I don't need your pity.*

"Mom," Kate said abruptly.

"Yes?"

"Don't you want to ask about my day?" *My life.*

"I assume you went to work."

"Well, yes. I mean, I met with clients today."

"Breaking up families? Taking children away from their parents? Why would I want to hear about that?"

"Protecting children in abusive situations? Yeah, I can see that wouldn't be an interesting topic for you."

An offended silence rolled from the phone.

"Mom. Mom, I'm sorry."

"I think this conversation is over," Brenda said with chilly dignity.

"Mom." The words stuck in Kate's throat like a hair ball. "I love you."

"Oh. Well, I . . . Well, thank you, Kate." Brenda's voice shook slightly. "I have to go. It's almost dinnertime. Tenderloin tonight."

Kate closed her eyes. "Merry Christmas, Mom."

"Merry Christmas to you, too, dear."

Kate sat a long time, gripping the phone. Whatever it was she wanted, she would not get it from her mother. Ever.

You could find substitutes, surrogates, for a mother's love. But the hope, the expectation, never went away.

And the wound never healed. If your own mother could not love you, who would?

Eventually, Kate ordered herself to move, to put on the kettle for tea, to sort the day's mail.

There was a Christmas card from the Blakemores, the wronged wife, the cheating dentist, and their three beautiful children, picture perfect in matching holiday sweaters.

Kate sighed. She'd had another tearful phone consultation with Tammy Blakemore this week. *I can't leave him,* Tammy had sobbed. *Not at Christmas. How would it look? Where would I go?*

And so Tammy stayed, letting her fear keep her with a man who did not love her the way she deserved to be loved.

Kate wanted to scorn the dentist's wife for her decision. But was Kate any better, was she any braver, letting her fears keep her away from seeking love at all? Keep her away from Luke.

Her phone lit up and buzzed on the counter. Kate tensed until she recognized the number.

Her heart lifted. It was Luke. Maybe he was calling to tell her he could get away tonight after all. *Booty call?* Maybe.

Whatever he wanted, whispered her heart.

Whatever she had it in her to give.

"Hi," Kate said breathlessly. "Are you coming over?"

"I wish. You coming for Christmas?"

The word escaped before she could catch it. "Yes."

"Yes?"

She bit her lip. "If it's not too much trouble."

"No trouble. That's . . . God, that's great. I'll tell Mom." His response warmed her. "She won't mind a last-minute guest?"

"Are you kidding? She'll be thrilled. They all want to get to know you."

"Oh, God." A trickle of panic leaked through the warmth. "What should I do? What should I wear?"

"Besides the good underwear?"

"They're not going to see . . . Luke, I'm serious." But a smile tugged her mouth.

"It's casual. We do the whole church thing Christmas Eve, so the day is pretty relaxed. When we were kids, we didn't even get dressed until lunchtime. We just stayed in our pajamas and played with our toys."

"Really?" She was fascinated by this glimpse of a family so different from her own.

"Yeah. Unless we got bikes or rollerblades or a new basketball hoop. And even then we put our jackets on over our pajamas."

A new thought struck her. "Presents. I have to buy presents."

"Kate, I don't want you to get clutched up about this. It's not that big a deal."

"Right." She attempted a joke. "It's not like you're bringing me home to meet the family."

"Well, no. That would be dumb."

Right. She winced.

"Seeing as you've already met them," he continued. "They already like you. They appreciate everything you've done for me and for Taylor. Mom would have invited you even if we weren't seeing each other."

A little flush of nerves and pleasure washed through her. "Are we? Seeing each other?"

"Hell, yeah. We're sleeping together."

"I meant . . . Exclusively."

"We're together," he repeated. "I thought that was a given."

Oh, boy. She took a deep breath to steady herself. "Then I'm definitely bringing flowers."

She might not know the rules of normal family life. But flowers for the mother of the man you were seeing—*exclusively*—seemed like a no-brainer.

"That'd be great." She could hear his smile.

"Or wine. Do your parents drink wine?"

"Mom's Italian. Of course they drink wine."

"And I should bring a gift for Taylor."

"If you want to, and you have the time to shop, fine."

"What does she like?"

"I wish I knew."

"What did you get her?" Kate asked.

"A Wii. And some dance game."

There was a terse note in his voice that hadn't been there a minute ago. "That's a wonderful gift. She'll love that."

"Hope so. She played it at some friend's house." A pause. "I had to call the friend's mom to find out the name. I don't know my own daughter well enough to pick out a damn present."

This wasn't, she realized, about the game.

"You'll figure it out," she said gently. "The way you did with Dawn's picture and the cat."

"You gave her the cat."

"Because you came looking for it." *With your big muscled arms and your big generous heart and your tight-lipped determination to be what Taylor needs. How could I resist you?*

He sighed. "I'm glad you're coming for Christmas."

Her heart jerked. "Are you?"

"It'll be fun."

She was no good at fun. She had no idea how a regular family behaved at Christmas.

But he already knew that. He wanted her anyway. Maybe it would be all right.

"So." She heard the intake of his breath. "How was your day?"

Breaking up families? Taking children away from their parents? Why would I want to hear about that?

"Can I take the Fifth?"

"That bad, huh?" His tone was sympathetic. And then it sharpened. "Nobody's bothering you, are they? That Brown guy—"

"No. No, nothing like that."

No man wanted to hear a woman whine. Whining was not sexy. Or productive. Luke had enough troubles of his own without listening to Kate maunder on about her relationship with her mother. That's what she paid her therapist for.

"Crickets," Luke said into the silence.

"What?"

"Tell me about your day, Kate."

"Well . . ." Tentatively, she told him about some of the clients she'd seen that day, consciously choosing the good stories, the happy endings. A couple she had talked into trying mediation, a brother and sister who would be able to spend Christmas with their loving foster parents. As the call went on, as he asked questions and made comments, she found herself editing less, sharing more.

He didn't weigh everything the way she did. She operated from her head, by logic and rules, while he reacted from instinct and training. But he had a quick understanding of people and a deeply held code of personal behavior that she admired. It was nice to have someone to talk to as she brewed her tea, as she sat down alone at her table. It was helpful to hear his perspective.

"And then I had drinks with Alisha," she concluded.

"Christmas celebration?"

"Yes." Ridiculous to feel proud of that, like a kindergartner boasting of a new friend at school.

A silence opened.

Her hand grew sweaty on the phone. "I talked to my mother today."

Another pause. Waiting.

"How'd that go?" Luke asked at last.

"The way it always does. We don't . . . connect. I think I remind her of a part of her life she'd rather not think about."

"I'm sorry." His voice was deep and gentle.

Her eyes stung. "It is what it is. I'm thirty-two years old. I'm never going to please her. I need to stop wanting her to change. I need to stop expecting her to give me what I need."

"You don't call her because you expect something."

She blinked. "I don't?"

"No. You call because she's your mother and it's the right thing to do. You do it for you. Because doing the right thing is important to you. That's your payoff."

She gave a choked half laugh. "Then how come I still feel lousy?"

"Because you deserve better."

His quiet response brought a lump to her throat. No one had ever told her that before, besides her therapist. Hearing the words from Luke was both far sweeter and more dangerous. To be valued, to be validated like that . . .

She could not speak. She must not let herself hope. Hope led to disappointment, always.

"Kate . . . Drive out tonight. Or tomorrow. There are rooms at the inn. You could spend the day, go to church with us tomorrow."

Temptation seized her. She wanted badly to say yes. And maybe that was reason enough to say no. She'd already made the emotional decision to come for Christmas Day. She must not depend on him for more.

And she would not take this time away from his family.

"This is your time," she said. "Yours and Taylor's. You should do the traditional Christmas Eve thing together."

"She's ten. I'm pretty sure that's too old for Santa. And we don't have any traditions."

She heard the stubborn tone that masked his insecurities.

"Remember the other day when we were watching the movie?" she asked. "You said you wanted me to stay as a buffer zone."

"Between the dog and the cat. Yeah. So?"

"You don't need a buffer zone between you and Taylor. You need to be getting as close to her as you can get. And that's what she needs, too."

"Yeah." He exhaled. "Thanks."

"My pleasure," she said with absolute sincerity.

The silence this time was deeper, richer. No longer empty, but brimming with possibilities. Even the rain against the windows sounded cozy.

"What are you wearing?" he asked and made her laugh again.

"This is not turning into one of those phone calls."

"Why not?"

Her skin bloomed. Her mind stuttered. She pressed her thighs together. "I am not that kind of girl."

"You could be. All I have to do is hear your voice and I get hard."

Her face flamed. "Oh."

"I've embarrassed you."

"Yes." Honesty compelled her to add, "But I like it."

His chuckle raised all the little hairs on the back of her neck and along her arms. "So. Want to have phone sex?"

"Um." Her throat closed.

She had spent years guarding her words, keeping secrets, divorcing her emotions from her speech. The more she felt, the less she could say. And with Luke, she felt . . . so much.

"Too soon?" he asked.

Maybe. "Yes."

"Okay. Later for that, then. I'm not the world's most articulate guy, anyway."

"You do all right," she said breathlessly.

They talked a while longer. She couldn't remember afterward exactly what they said. Her mind kept circling, returning to his words. *All I have to do is hear your voice and I get hard.*

When they ended the call, she was flushed and dizzy and short of breath. Almost as if they'd had phone sex after all.

What was she doing?

He got to her, she admitted. He reached her on some basic level she could not defend against.

It wasn't his looks. Okay, maybe his looks had something to do with it. What woman wouldn't lose her head over that hard, disciplined body, those burning blue eyes, those amazing arms?

He had impressed her from the first by his willingness to shoulder his responsibilities, his determination to do the right thing. She liked his directness. His sense of humor tickled hers into being. His passion—in and out of bed—challenged hers. With very little effort, he could probably even talk her into phone sex. She smiled. *Later for that.*

But she could have liked and admired him for all those things, his looks and his character, without loving him.

What got to her was his loyalty to his family. His tenderness with Taylor. His generous, teasing affection.

His heart.

Kate had always imagined that if she ever let her guard

down with a man, she would do so with clear eyes and a cool head after a considerable period of time and testing.

She wasn't prepared for a man like Luke.

She hadn't counted on love that wasn't a careful, deliberate step, but a hard, fast fall.

Seventeen

"THERE ARE EIGHT bathrooms in this house," Tess said, hands on her hips. The dinner dishes were done, the leftovers put away, and she was engaged in the eternal struggle of getting her family to church on time. "Would someone please explain to me why it takes twenty minutes to get out the door?"

Matt gave her his slow, rare grin. "Because there are nine of us, Mom."

Tess bit her lip to contain her answering smile. "*I'm* not using a bathroom. I'm standing here waiting for the rest of you."

"Maybe you should try to go," Luke suggested straight-faced, the way she'd said to him a thousand times growing up. "Just in case."

Taylor, so serious all afternoon, smiled.

"That's it," Tom said. He rolled his shoulders under his navy blazer, a plough horse adjusting to the yoke. To please her, he was actually wearing a tie tonight. He looked so handsome. Handsome and dear and uncomfortable. "Everybody out."

And with a last-minute rush of *where are my keys* and *I need my shoes* and *did someone take the puppy out*, they spilled out the door and into the quiet night.

The sun had set. The icy sparkle of a million stars soared above the glow of the Christmas lights. A little breeze carried the scent of the sea.

"Shotgun!" Josh called.

"In your dreams, cutie," Meg said. "No way am I riding in back."

Sam put his arm around her. "I always wanted to make out with you in the backseat of your parents' car."

"Ew," Taylor said.

"Josh, get in the truck," Matt said. "You can ride with me and Allison."

"What about Luke and Taylor?" Allison asked.

"We'll take the Jeep," Luke said.

"Let's go. We're late," Tom barked from beside Tess.

Despite their hurry, she stood a moment longer on the deck, watching her family on the walk, stumbling and laughing in the dark. Matt, broad and solid, and Allison in lace like a bride. Josh, almost as tall as Matt now, beside them. Meg in her little black dress, smiling over her shoulder at Sam. Luke in his dress blues with Taylor, a little stiff, a little apart.

Her heart yearned and ached for them. The stars sparkled and blurred.

"Oh, Tom," she said. "They're all home."

He looked at her warily. "Nothing to cry about."

"Look at them, all paired up."

"Except for Luke."

"Tomorrow," she said. That girl, that lawyer, would come, and they would see. "What do you think of her? She seems a little . . ." Tess hesitated. *Cool. Abrasive.* "Prickly to me."

"Our Meg's prickly. This girl's tough. And careful."

Tough was good. A Marine wife had to be strong. And careful was a better word. "But is she right for Luke?"

"That's up to him. You can't choose for them, babe."

Tess sighed. "No."

But Luke was her baby. The youngest of their three, he needed to be needed. Needed a cause to give him purpose, a direction that could mean as much to him as the Marines. He'd never understood his own importance or his strengths.

Meg turned on the walk. "Mom?"

The word summoned so many memories. All those years when Tom had been the one in uniform or overseas, when the children were small. All the old, beloved stories hovered close tonight, pressing on Tess like the rush of angels' wings. The stories of Christmas, the bewilderment and wonder of the unexpected birth, the courage to give and accept love.

Stories about families, messy and imperfect, mismanaged and real and wonderful.

Somehow it all came right in the end.

"Babe." Tom put his hand at the small of her back. "You ready?"

Tess looked into the face of the man she had loved for forty years. Four decades of love. She gripped Tom's hand and followed their children in the starlight.

THEY GOT THROUGH that okay, Luke thought with relief as he drove home along the dark road. A mist hung over the water and wreathed the half-moon.

At Easter and in the summer months, when the tourist tide swelled Dare's Catholic population, the Franciscans conducted Sunday services on the beach in a structure that resembled a campground's picnic shelter. But in the still of winter, the friars offered mass in their own chapel. The small wooden church had been filled with the glow of candles, the scent of flowers and incense. *Smells and bells*, Tom called it. The handful of island Catholics had been there, along with a smattering of visitors.

Even in such a small congregation, it had been hard to get away. Luke's uniform attracted attention. People he'd known most of his life wanted to hug him and wish him well. Even the newcomers and Yankees wanted to shake his hand and thank him for his service.

It had been pretty great, actually.

Jack Rossi had been there, alone at the back of the church, in a charcoal gray suit and a crisp white shirt like a federal agent or a funeral director. With a name like Rossi, it figured the guy was Catholic. He caught Luke's eye over the crowd and smiled briefly.

Taylor had fumbled through the unfamiliar rituals of the mass, stayed quiet through the unfamiliar prayers. But she kneeled when the family kneeled, sat when the family sat. And sang the old, traditional carols in a clear, high voice that about ripped out Luke's heart.

He'd heard Meg sniff a couple times, and Mom and Allison both got misty. Well, Mom always cried whenever she managed to get them all to mass. It was practically a tradition.

But Taylor didn't cry. Not when he'd taken her to the front of the church to visit the crèche with its carved wooden statues of Mother and Child. Not even this afternoon when he'd told her the Simpsons were blowing off their scheduled visit to deliver her Christmas presents. *Car trouble*, they said.

Whatever.

All he cared about was Taylor, who was missing her mom.

He glanced at her slumped against the passenger door, staring out the window at the colored lights flickering through the trees, looking like the weight of the world was pressing on her thin shoulders.

She'd left off her camouflage cap tonight. Her pale, straight hair was shiny in the glow from the dashboard.

On impulse, he reached into the backseat for his peaked white uniform cap and plopped it on her head. She looked up, startled, her hand flying to the shiny brim. And then her eyes met his and she smiled a tiny smile.

The ache in his chest intensified.

You don't need a buffer zone between you and Taylor,

Kate had said. *You need to be getting as close to her as you can get. And that's what she needs, too.*

He turned down the beach road.

Taylor sat up. "This isn't the way home."

"We're taking a detour."

He switched the headlights to bright, driving slowly in case one of the shy island deer bolted across the road. No hitting Rudolph on Christmas Eve.

A wavering line of erosion fence was pitched along the side of the road. He pulled onto the shoulder and cut the engine. The silence rushed in, sounding like the sea.

They got out of the Jeep. The breeze was edged with salt and damp and chimney smoke, but compared to Afghanistan's mountain nights, the air felt almost warm.

Taylor shivered with cold or excitement, her little face pale in the dark.

Luke shrugged out of his uniform jacket and slung it around her shoulders.

She hopped from foot to foot. "Where are we going?"

"Not far."

They climbed the stairs to the beach access, a long boardwalk stretching over the silver and gray dunes. Above the beach, the walkway widened to a deck with built-in benches on two sides.

Luke stopped.

"This is so cool." Taylor ran to look over the rail. The half-moon threw a spotlight on the sea that shimmered to the horizon. The waves whispered and withdrew. "We're, like, the only ones here."

He sat on the bench. "Look up."

She sat beside him, obediently tilting her head. The stars whirled and pulsed above them, points of light against the velvet sky. No streetlights. No pollution. No choking desert sand.

"Dad."

He lost his breath.

Taylor twisted to look at him. "We're not searching for Santa's sleigh or anything, right? Because I'm ten."

Luke grinned. "No sleigh. I brought you to look at the stars."

"Cool." She settled against his side. "Like the wise men."

"Yeah." He put his arm around her. So she wouldn't get cold. "You know, before we moved here, Grandpa was in the Marines. Uncle Matt and Aunt Meg remember that better than I do. But there was this one Christmas, right before he got out . . . He couldn't come home. He was in Iraq. The first go-round. I was pretty disappointed. Well, I was only eight. Younger than you are now."

Luke cleared his throat. "Anyway, after Grandma went downstairs, I climbed out on the garage roof and looked at the stars. I thought, wherever he was, he could see them, too. I picked out one star to be, like, my Dad star. Because the stars are always there. Always with you. Even in the daytime, when you can't see them, they're there."

Taylor looked at him blankly. Oh, God, he was screwing this up. Did she get what he was trying to say?

"Your mom . . . I figure she's like one of those stars. Watching over you."

Taylor nodded slowly, her eyes shining in the moonlight. When the shining threatened to overflow, she squeezed her eyes shut, burying her face against his side.

Luke tightened his arm around her. "She'll always be with you," he said hoarsely.

And so will I.

"Is THERE ANYTHING I can do?" Kate offered.

She wanted to help. To belong. Allison, Josh, and Taylor were shouting and shaking to the Wii in the family room. Meg was arranging veggies and prosciutto on a tray, talking about some wedding—his sister's?—with Sam, while Fezzik haunted the floor at their feet, hoping for food to drop. Luke had just rescued a spitting Snowball from JD. The whole scene was noisy, cheerful, and slightly overwhelming.

Very different from TV.

Tess smiled and pulled the plastic wrap off a bowl of

dip. "Table's set, the roast is resting, and we have another twenty minutes before we have to do anything with the potatoes. Why don't you give Taylor her present? Sam, do you want to open a bottle of this nice wine Kate brought?"

"Got it." He winked and reached for a glass.

Josh wandered in, put his arm around Tess and stuck his finger in the dip. "Mm. Good."

She smacked his hand and then shoved the bowl at him. "Take this into the family room. Taylor's going to open her present from Kate now."

Kate's stomach hollowed. Because the pressure of picking out the perfect gift wasn't enough without an audience to critique her choice.

Luke returned from putting the puppy in timeout behind a baby gate. "Time for presents?"

Tess nodded. "Get your father."

"He's playing trains with Matt."

Tess whipped off her apron. "Tom!"

Allison came in, flushed and lovely from the dance game, and poured herself a big glass of water. "Nice flowers," she said to Kate.

"Thanks," Kate said. The poinsettia she'd chosen with such care overwhelmed the kitchen table. Too big. Too much.

She always told her clients in a custody battle to save the expensive gifts. You couldn't buy love and acceptance.

But she hadn't followed her own advice. She desperately wanted the Fletchers to *like* her.

She let herself be steered into the family room. Nudged onto the couch. Luke sat beside her.

"Here." Sam handed her a glass. "You look like you could use this."

Support? Or recognition of her outsider status?

She took the wine gratefully. "Thank you."

Taylor tore at the paper, ignoring Kate's carefully tied ribbon.

"It's a book." More tearing. "Three books." Her voice was bright. Polite.

Kate set down her glass, clasping her hands tightly together in her lap. "There are some DVDs, too."

"*Anne of Green Gables*," Allison said.

Meg leaned forward to see. "Oh, I loved those when I was a kid. Or maybe I just had the hots for Gilbert."

"Who's Gilbert?" Sam asked.

Taylor turned the books over in her hand, glancing at the photos and the back cover blurb. "Cool."

Luke's hand rested on the back of Kate's neck, warm and reassuring. His thumb stroked idly under her hair.

"I thought . . ." Kate shrugged awkwardly, not sure if or how much she should explain. "It's about a girl who goes to live with a family on an island, and how she changes their lives. She's ten, like you, and smart and brave. Kind of a 'kindred spirit,'" she said, borrowing a phrase from the books.

"Thanks." Taylor's smile flashed. "What did you get Dad?"

"Oh. Um. Another book." Kate reached down by her feet and handed Luke's present to him.

He ripped it open with the same careless disregard for paper and ribbon that Taylor had shown.

Kate smiled ruefully. Next time she wouldn't worry so much about her wrapping job.

Her breath snagged. *Next time?*

Luke stared down at the handsome coffee table book. "It's Dare Island."

"To remind you of home," Kate said. *When you deploy again*, she thought, her throat constricting. "The photos are by Adam Scott. He—"

"Hey, we have that book," Josh said. Tess shot him a look. "Well, we do. Upstairs. That guy, the photographer, he stayed here, didn't he?"

"Oh." Kate bit her lip. "Well, you can exchange—"

"*I* don't have this book," Luke said. "Thank you."

He leaned forward and kissed her, hard and sweet.

"We got you something, too." Taylor scrambled to her feet and returned with a small box from under the Christmas tree.

A jewelry box. Small, square, unmistakable.

Kate's heart slammed into her ribs.

Luke was watching her, his eyes intensely blue. "Open it."

She couldn't breathe. She picked at the paper, aware of his family, watching. Her hands trembled. *We're not rushing into anything*, she'd said to Alisha. *It's too soon.*

"It's a cat," Taylor said when Kate opened the box. "You gave us Snowball, so we gave you a cat."

"To go on your chain," Luke said.

Kate let out her breath in relief and pleasure and . . . No, that wasn't disappointment. The gold charm was beautiful. And thoughtful. The perfect gift.

She beamed at them. "It's beautiful."

"He skipped a step," Meg murmured.

"What do you mean?" asked Allison.

"A man works his way down your arm. First earrings, then necklace, then bracelet, then ring." Meg shrugged. "Luke went straight to necklace."

Kate couldn't help it. She looked at Meg's hands.

Meg caught the direction of her gaze and grinned. "Ta-da." She held up her left hand. Waggled her fingers, flashing a huge emerald-cut stone in a diamond setting. "Merry Christmas to me."

Sam caught her hand and kissed it. "And to me."

"They're so cute," Matt drawled.

"Congratulations," Kate said sincerely. "I hope you'll both be very happy."

"Gee, Uncle Luke, does this mean you're going steady now?" Josh asked.

"What did you get your little redhead for Christmas?" Luke asked.

Matt hid a grin with his hand. Josh's ears turned red.

The doorbell chimed.

"I'll get that," Josh said and escaped.

"Do you like it?" Taylor asked Kate.

Kate looked into those big blue eyes, Luke's eyes, and closed her hand on the box. "I love it."

She loved everything. The presents, the noise, the teasing, the love. Luke's family was so nice. So *normal*.

She couldn't stand it. She didn't see where she fit in. How she could possibly fit in.

"I think I'll go upstairs and put it on," she said.

"There's a bathroom with a mirror right here," Meg said.

"Thanks. I just . . ." She had to get away. She needed a minute to compose herself. "My purse?"

"With the coats. William Kidd Room," Tess said. "Left at the top of the stairs."

Kate nodded blindly and bolted.

Alone in the handsome guest bedroom, decorated in deep shades of green, she pressed her hands to her hot cheeks. What was the matter with her?

She took a deep breath and threaded the charm through her chain with shaking hands.

Yeah, okay, her childhood sucked. But she was a competent, confident, professional adult. She didn't fall to pieces in the courtroom. Why should a simple family celebration shake her assurance and turn her into a whimpering idiot?

She met her eyes in the mirror. Because it was Christmas.

Because the contrast between Luke's family and her own broke her heart.

"Everything okay up here?" Luke asked.

She blotted her lower lashes with her fingertips before she turned and saw him leaning in the doorway. "Fine."

"Uh-oh."

"What?"

He smiled at her. "In my family, 'fine' means they haven't amputated yet."

She smiled back. "I'm really okay. We should go downstairs."

"No rush. The police chief just got here." He shut the door and strolled forward. "Let him take the heat for a while."

"The police chief? Is everything all right?"

"Yeah. He came for dinner. My parents always invite at least one stray for the holidays."

She bit her lip. "I see."

And she did. *At least one stray.* She must be the other one.

Luke studied her. "I don't think you do." He nodded toward the chain in her hands. "Want help with that?"

Nothing to do but put a good face on things. "Yes, thank you." She turned her back, gathered her hair out of the way.

His fingers were light and warm on the back of her neck. Helplessly, she closed her eyes as longing spilled inside her. His lips brushed the side of her throat, and she shivered and moved away.

Luke frowned. "You sure you're okay?"

"I'm . . ." *Not fine, don't say fine.* "I'm not used to being around so many people at the holidays. I don't know how to react. How to behave."

"You could try to relax and enjoy yourself."

"I am. Enjoying myself." *Not relaxed. Not relaxed at all.* "It was lovely of your parents to invite me. I'm just a little tense."

The corners of his eyes crinkled. "Let's see if I can relax you."

He kissed her again, a soft and undemanding kiss, intended to comfort.

And everything inside her turned to flame. She opened her mouth, angled her head, and inhaled him. There was no other word for it. She wanted to absorb him, ingest him, take him inside her. His arms came around her, hard as rope. The ridge of his erection dug into her stomach. He felt so good that her eyes brimmed in gratitude. They kissed again, deep and wet, and she sucked his tongue into her mouth.

"Shh, shh," he whispered, and she realized she was moaning, grappling with him to bring him closer, to take him in, frustrated by her tight skirt. The fine wool abraded her skin. She was liquid, melting, dying inside.

He spun her around and yanked on her skirt, bunching it over her hips, exposing her thighs and the thin triangle of her panties. The cool air kissed her hot, flushed skin. He was hard behind her, hard and close. His strong hands shaped her butt, his calluses raising goose bumps, before he reached around, rubbing her from the front, long fingers sliding over wet satin. His arms shook. Or maybe that was her legs.

"Kate."

She could not speak. She had gone to some dark place beyond words, into the extremity of need. She bent forward from the waist, dropping over the bed, resting her arms on her discarded coat with her butt up in the air.

"Oh, God, Kate."

His zipper rasped. She could feel him, blunt and smooth at her entrance. They both shuddered.

"Condom," he said hoarsely.

"In my purse."

"You're amazing."

She turned her head sideways on her bent arms, closing her eyes, listening, waiting, hotter and more turned on than she'd ever been in her life. Her blood beat, hard and fast, in her ears and between her legs. His fingers curled under lace and elastic, stretching her panties out of the way.

"This okay?" he whispered.

"*Do it.*"

He positioned himself behind her, sliding up and down, making her twist and pant. She angled her hips, pushing back, desperate to take him in, and he grabbed her hips, entering her in one thrust, gliding deep. She bit on her coat to keep from crying out. He took her in short, sharp digs, grinding, pushing, until his strokes hit something good, high inside her, and she saw stars and flew apart, all her tension unraveling in long, silky skeins of pleasure.

Maybe she passed out. Probably not. She could feel him shaking above her, riding her spasms, until his own release broke over them both, and he followed her over the edge.

His weight relaxed on top of her. His heart thudded against her back. He turned his head and kissed her shoulder blade. Her heart quivered and surrendered.

She never wanted to move again. She lay quiet, in a kind of sexual torpor, surrounded by the scent of clean linens and hot sex.

Merry Christmas to me.

Soon—*too soon*—Luke sighed and pulled away, separating from her by degrees. He bent and pressed his lips to the base of her spine, making her hips hitch reflexively.

His hands tightened on her flesh. And then he tugged her panties into place and smoothed her skirt back down over her hips.

"Best. Christmas. Present. Ever," he said.

Her laughter hiccupped, surprising them both. "Better than a bicycle?"

"More fun to ride."

She snorted and then pressed her fingers to her mouth.

"Shh," he said again, teasing. "You don't want anyone to guess we're having fun up here."

"Oh, God." She dashed into the bathroom to make appropriate repairs.

"It's no good," Luke said when she came out.

"My hair?" She reached up self-consciously. "Lipstick?"

He shook his head. "It's me."

She looked at him blankly.

He met her gaze. "All they have to do is look at me and they'll see I'm falling for you."

She flushed all over. Her heart fell at his feet.

After that, Christmas dinner was pretty much— *ha-ha*—an anticlimax.

Kate sat, smiling fuzzily, as the Fletchers carved the roast and passed the potatoes and talked about . . . Well, she kept losing the thread of the conversation. Whatever nerve Luke had struck inside her had obviously shorted her brain.

She managed a polite conversation with the new police chief, Jack Rossi, dark and sober in his uniform. *Her fellow stray.*

But the word had lost its power to sting. *All they have to do is look at me . . .*

"Where are you from, Chief Rossi?"

"Jack. Delaware County." Her face must have looked blank, because he added, "Outside Philly."

"Oh, are you from Philadelphia?" Allison leaned across the table, not flirting, but . . .

Aware, Kate decided. The chief had something that made women aware. Testosterone or something. Even a woman deeply in love or newly engaged or still giddy from breath-robbing, heart-stealing, drums-beating sex could notice.

"Allison's family is from Philadelphia, too," Meg said.

"So I'm not the only dingbatter," Kate said.

Jack's eyes narrowed slightly. "Dingbatter?"

"Someone who is unfamiliar with island life," Allison said diplomatically. "Generally used to refer to Yankees, uplanders, and anyone from Away."

"How long have you lived here?" Jack asked.

"This is my first winter."

"I warned her it was quiet," Matt said.

Allison smiled, curling her hand around his on the table. "It has its attractions."

"Impressionable children present," Josh said. "Do not corrupt our pure young minds."

"Pure?" Luke said.

"I'm trying to protect Taylor," Josh said with dignity.

"What about you, Jack?" Tom asked from the head of the table.

"I like quiet," the chief said.

"Well, you won't find it in this house," Tom said.

"Don't you miss your family?" Tess asked.

"I miss Philadelphia," Jack said in a neutral voice. "What about you, Miss Carter?"

"Allison, please. Actually, I'll see my mother very soon. She's flying into Raleigh tomorrow to take me shopping for a wedding dress."

"That's three hours away, isn't it? You drive carefully," he said.

"Mom and I are going with her," Meg said. "We're making an overnight out of it. It'll be fun."

Allison pulled a face. "Even if it is at the most inconvenient time. I told Mother you had a full house this weekend, with all the guests coming for Sam's sister's wedding. If she'd only wait a couple weeks . . ."

"You'd have even less selection," Meg said. "I've been

browsing wedding sites. Most of them recommend ordering your gown a year before your date. Six months, minimum. You only have four months left."

Sam grinned. "You've been browsing wedding sites?"

Meg tossed her head. "I like being prepared."

"Anyway, the timing's not a problem," Tess said. "The rooms are all ready. And we'll be back Thursday afternoon. It's natural for your mother to want to see you over the holidays."

"Speaking of holidays, what happened with Ernie and Jolene?" Tom asked. "I thought they were coming yesterday to see Taylor."

Kate glanced sharply at Taylor.

Luke had his Marine face on. "They couldn't make it. Car trouble."

Taylor stared down at her plate. *Oh, baby*, Kate thought.

"Anyone ready for dessert?" Tess asked.

Tess had just served the rum cake, when Jack's cell phone buzzed.

"Excuse me," he said and went into the hall to take the call.

"Want to play Just Dance after dinner?" Taylor asked.

Meg groaned. "Not if it involves moving. I ate too much."

"Not unless it involves blowing stuff up," Josh said.

"Maybe after I digest dinner," Allison said.

"I'll play," Kate offered. She glanced at Tess. "Or I can help with the dishes."

"I've got 'em," Tom said. "You girls go play."

Exactly, Kate thought, amused, as if she were Taylor's age.

"I'll play if Matt plays," Luke said.

"You're on."

Josh snickered. "Old white guys dancing? Let me stick a fork in my eye."

"Wiseass," his father returned without heat.

"Let me take on your old man in dance," Luke said, "and then I'll beat your ass in Call of Duty."

Josh grinned. "Bring it."

Jack returned to the dining room. "I have to go. Tess, Tom, thank you for a wonderful dinner."

"Anytime."

"Nothing serious, I hope," Tess said.

He shook his head. "Noise incident with possible pyrotechnics."

Sam raised his brows. "Which means . . . ?"

Jack smiled. "Somebody setting off fireworks on the beach. Merry Christmas, everyone. Good night."

"Merry Christmas."

It really was, Kate thought as they trooped into the family room to dance or jeer.

Best. Christmas. Ever.

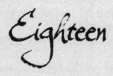

Eighteen

THE NEXT AFTERNOON, Taylor sat on the cottage steps, throwing a ball for JD while Josh practiced free throws in the driveway. The steady *thunk, thunk, swish* kept her company.

It was warm in the sunshine. JD was so goofy, galloping over the grass after the ball, his puppy ears flopping. Out of habit, Taylor checked for the knot in her stomach that had been there since Mom died.

It was still there, but it was looser. A lot looser.

Later today, when Dad finished cleaning the gutters for Grandma, Miss Kate was coming over and they were going out to dinner. Like a family. The thought made Taylor feel kind of funny, because they weren't a family, she and Mom were a family.

All we need is each other, Mom used to say. *We don't need anybody else.*

Taylor swallowed. Except Mom was wrong.

The thought felt weird, disloyal almost, but Taylor was only ten. She needed people to take care of her.

And that was okay.

Last night, she'd started reading that book from Miss Kate, about Anne of Green Gables. Anne was an orphan until she went to live with Marilla and Matthew. Like Taylor coming to live with Grandma and Grandpa, only not really, because Taylor wasn't really an orphan, she had her dad and Uncle Matt and Aunt Meg and Josh. All her family. And Snowball and Fezzik and JD, running toward her in the sun with the ball in his mouth.

Taylor clapped her hands. "Good boy, JD. Now come. Come here, JD."

She reached for the ball and the puppy danced away, his whole body wagging in delight.

"No, no." She giggled. "You have to give me the ball or I can't throw it again."

She heard the noise of a car out front.

Josh grabbed a rebound and watched them. "Dopey dog."

"He's good at catch." Taylor defended her puppy. "It's just his fetch needs a little work."

Josh set down the basketball and dropped to a crouch. JD jumped him, and Josh snatched at the ball in the puppy's mouth. A car door slammed. Taylor thought she heard the rattle of Dad's ladder and voices coming from the front, but her attention was on Josh, wrestling with the puppy.

"Drop it. Drop it," Josh said.

JD play-growled, delighted with this new game.

Josh grinned at Taylor. "He's not so good at letting go, either."

Something moved in the corner of her vision. A man, walking along the side of the house. He stopped when he reached the back yard, and Taylor turned her head to look at him, a tall man in a black jacket with a scraggly blond beard and a tattoo on his neck.

Terror blinded Taylor. She felt a flood of shame and then . . . She could smell her own pee, feel her jeans damp and warm between her thighs. She'd wet herself like a baby. *Helpless baby.* She wanted to throw up. Or cry.

Josh stood slowly. "Who are you?"

"I'm Taylor's uncle. Why don't you leave us alone to say 'hi,' boy?" He smiled, revealing ragged brown teeth. His breath, Taylor knew, would smell like a dirty drain. "Don't you have a hug for your Uncle Kevin, sweetheart?"

LUKE WAS ANNOYED.

Bad enough that Ernie and Jolene had blown off their scheduled visit with Taylor before Christmas. They couldn't be bothered to drop off her presents on time? Fine.

But to show up, unannounced, the day after Christmas, when his mother was out of town, and his brother and Dad were out on the boat, and Luke himself was up to his elbows in gutters . . . Yeah, that pissed him off. Plus, Kate was supposed to be here in less than an hour, and he'd had his mind on a lot better things than the Simpsons.

He shot a quick glance at the car. When they first pulled up, he thought he'd seen three people. But by the time he climbed down the ladder, there was only Ernie and Jolene puffing up the porch steps.

He sighed and wiped his hands on his jeans.

The judge had said Taylor deserved to enjoy the comfort and support of her family over the holidays. So Luke would make nice. The Simpsons were her grandparents. For Taylor, he could do the right thing.

"Come on back to the kitchen, and I'll put up a pot of coffee," he said. "I'll let Taylor know you're here."

Jolene clasped her hands together over the brightly wrapped package in her arms. "Where is she? Where is our grandbaby?"

"Out back, playing with the dog. This way."

He led them through the front hall and into the kitchen. Sure enough, through the window he could see Taylor sitting on the cottage steps. The back of his neck crawled. Something wasn't right. There was the puppy, pressed close to Taylor's legs. There was Josh, with a basketball at his feet. And . . .

Luke frowned. "What's he doing here?"

"Kevin?" Jolene lowered her bulk into a chair. "Oh, he drove us in his car. I told you we had car trouble."

Outside, Kevin said something Luke couldn't hear. Josh's hands half curled into fists at his sides, as if the boy wasn't quite sure what to do with them. JD, who had the aggressive instincts of a ball of wax, chose this moment to show his puppy teeth, his hackles rising.

Taylor grabbed for the puppy's collar, her face white.

Go time.

Luke went straight to Taylor, one eye on the target, and crouched down, putting an arm protectively around her shoulders.

JD growled deep in his throat, squirming to get away. Kevin's foot twitched.

"Kick the dog, and I'll break your leg," Luke said quietly. He looked at Josh. "What's going on?"

Josh opened his mouth. Shut it. Gave a quick hitch of his shoulders. *I don't know.*

Under Luke's arm, Taylor was shaking. He smelled urine. *Jesus.* She'd wet herself.

His brain started to put it all together. The nightmares. The baggy clothes. The way she woke up screaming and swinging.

She misses her mother, they'd all said, convinced it couldn't be anything else, confident that they were doing their best.

But she'd wet herself.

"Taylor?" he asked gently, his mind dark with possibilities, his body pumping with unused adrenaline.

She shook her head, her mouth tight, her eyes glassy with unshed tears.

"Take Taylor inside," Luke told Josh, keeping his voice calm. "She doesn't feel good. JD, too."

Josh swallowed and nodded. He collected Taylor and the puppy and got them in the cottage.

Luke stood and took a step toward Kevin. Not close enough to lose the advantage of distance, but enough to communicate a threat. He lowered his voice. "I haven't liked you since I saw you. I don't want to see you again. Get the fuck out."

Kevin apparently didn't know enough to be afraid. He sneered, exposing his jack-o'-lantern teeth. "I'm little Taylor's uncle. I have a right to see her."

"Bullshit."

"Judge said—"

"Your parents can stay." Maybe they could tell him what the hell was going on. "I'll bring them home. You get the fuck out of here."

"They won't let me leave without them."

"Then you all go."

For the first time, something flickered in Kevin's face. "Whatcha going to tell them?"

"I'll tell them you upset Taylor so much she wet her pants. Now get out. I don't want to see you here again."

It took five minutes, maybe ten, to get the Simpsons out of his parents' house.

Jolene kept crying. "But we just got here. I want to see Taylor. This is all your fault," she accused Luke.

Ernie's face wrinkled like an old apple. "Where's Taylor? What happened?"

Luke couldn't tell him. Because he didn't fucking *know*. He was acting out of instinct, from the sick fear in Taylor's eyes and the ball of ice in his gut.

He wanted to smash things. A wall. Kevin's face.

But he had to get to Taylor. Talk to her. Reassure her. Anything else, everything else, had to wait on that.

Finally he got rid of them and could return to the cottage.

Josh was on the floor with JD, giving and receiving comfort. When Luke came in, he stood, his face somber. "What can I do?"

Luke regarded him, nearly a man with his broad shoulders and outsized hands and the boyish worry in his eyes. "You've already done it. You did good. Where's Taylor?"

"In her room. I, uh, I put her jeans in the laundry basket."

Luke nodded. "When your dad gets home, tell him we have a problem. I might need him to watch Taylor for me tomorrow." *While I go to the cops. Or hunt down Kevin Simpson and kill him.*

"Is she okay?" Josh asked, with a child's need for reassurance.

Luke didn't know. His ignorance terrified him. But he was the adult here. It was his job to make things right. "She will be."

Josh nodded, young enough to be satisfied with the promise.

"Josh?"

He turned at the door.

"Thanks," Luke said quietly.

His cheeks turned pink. "No problem."

Luke was still cranked up. He remembered driving at night in Afghanistan over bumpy mountain roads. You couldn't see anything, not the road lurching beneath you or the insurgents out there in the dark. No headlights, just eerie images through night vision goggles, the ghosts of the vehicles before you or behind. But you knew you were fucked, that bad things were coming.

Only this time, he suspected, the worst had already happened. To Taylor.

He took a deep breath, willing himself to calm, focusing the way he did before a mission, and went down the hall to his daughter's room.

Taylor sat with her back to the headboard and her knees drawn up, Snowball cradled against her chest. He spared a moment's silent thanks to Kate, for bringing her the cat.

"Taylor?"

She closed her eyes and turned her head away.

A wave of helpless love and fury shook him. He thought of all those kids, in Haiti, in Iraq, in Afghanistan, the ones with the dead eyes and the wounds that would never heal. He thought of Eric Cordero, struggling with the memories of war, and Aaron Short, who'd shot himself rather than live with his pain.

He thought of Kate.

He hadn't saved them. What made him think he could save his daughter?

"It's okay, baby." He tiptoed into her pretty, girly room with the picture of Dawn staring at him reproachfully from beside her bed. "Daddy's here."

Too late.

KATE WAS SMILING as she climbed the steps to the cozy yellow cottage and knocked on the soft blue door. A late-blooming rose scaled the side of the house, its pink faces turned to the afternoon sun.

She felt like those flowers. Happy. Hopeful.

Yesterday had been perfect, the best Christmas ever. She'd been welcomed and accepted by a normal family at last. Her heart beat high with anticipation as she listened to Luke's footsteps crossing to the door.

"I'm sorry." His face was set in full Marine mode. His expression almost drove her back a step. "I should have called."

Trouble. Her childhood had taught her the signs. Her body reacted with old, remembered tension. "What is it? Is everything all right?" Her stomach dropped. "Taylor?"

A crack appeared in his warrior façade. He ran a hand over his cropped hair. "She won't talk to me."

She tried to wall off her emotions, to retreat into her professional role, where she would be safe. Where she could be effective. But the misery in his eyes sliced her in two. "What happened?"

His breath shuddered out. "I don't know."

She took his arm. His muscles were rigid under her fingers. "Let's go inside," she said gently, "and you can tell me."

They sat together at the kitchen counter while he told her, tersely, about the Simpsons' visit and Taylor's reaction.

Kate had to draw on every ounce of her training and experience simply to listen, to ask the right questions, not to react with shock or anger or fear or disgust.

Emotion would not help Luke or Taylor.

But her heart broke and bled for them both.

"The son of a bitch did something," Luke said, his eyes dark with guilt. His voice rasped with frustration. "Hurt her. Scared her. And I didn't know. She won't talk to me."

"You don't," Kate said.

He looked at her dumbly.

She moistened her lips. "Dawn never talked about her childhood. I never talked about mine. She grew up in that house. She left Taylor in your care. She must have had reasons. But she never shared them with me. We had this bond we never knew about, never spoke of. Because you don't. Because you think you're different. Because you believe you're alone. Because you wonder if what happens is somehow your fault."

His eyes flamed. "I'll fucking kill him."

Kate wrapped her fingers around his hand, clenched on the counter. "You have to stay calm. If you get angry, if you get upset, it will be that much harder for Taylor to talk to you."

He bowed his head, gazing down at their clasped hands. His jaw worked. He looked up, his gaze locking with hers. "Will you talk to her?"

Her heart jolted.

It was the ultimate trust. The most intimate of invitations. She was agonizingly aware of what he was asking and her own limitations. The more she involved herself in Taylor's life, the greater the risk of letting the child down, of not being there, of not being what she needed.

Kate was terrified of failure.

"Her mother's not here," Luke continued quietly. "My mother's not here. I don't know what to say. You'll know what to say. Will you talk to her?"

Once she committed to this, she was committed forever. There was no going back.

"Let's talk to her together."

Taylor was curled in a defensive posture on her bed, her face buried in Snowball's fur. Kate looked at the tension in those thin shoulders and was filled with murderous rage at anyone who dared hurt this child. She couldn't approach this case with professional detachment. She wanted to growl and rage like a mother bear defending her cub.

But Taylor didn't need her anger. She needed love and acceptance and support.

Kate tapped lightly on the open door. "Hey. Can I come in?"

Taylor hitched a shoulder. *Whatever.*

Kate sat gingerly on the side of the bed. She judged it was too soon to touch Taylor, so she stroked the cat instead. Snowball stretched out her chin, purring. Kate scratched it. "I hear you had a tough day."

Taylor raised her head, doing a good imitation of her father's stone face.

Kate cleared her throat. "It's okay if you want to talk about it. Remember when we talked about feelings before? Feelings are never wrong, they're just feelings. As long as you're honest . . ." *Everything else will work out.*

But Kate couldn't bring herself to say the words this time. Taylor had been through so much in the past four months. Some of it Kate knew about. Some things she could only guess at. How could Kate promise that everything would be all right ever again?

Taylor gave her a too-adult look out of her child's face. "Is this because I wet my pants?"

Kate kept her expression neutral. It was vitally important not to make accusations, not to interrogate. The only purpose of this discussion was to gather enough information to help Taylor.

And to make an informed report to the police.

"It's because you were upset," Kate said. She waited a beat. Taylor didn't respond. Kate touched the back of her hand, gently. "What upset you, sweetie?"

Taylor hid her face again in Snowball's fur. "Uncle Kevin," she muttered.

By the door, Luke made a movement, abruptly stilled.

Kate swallowed. "What did he do to upset you?"

No response.

Kate tried again. "Are you upset about something he did today?"

Taylor shook her head, her face still hidden. "I thought it would stop," she whispered. "It did stop when I came here."

Oh, God.

Kate glanced at the doorway. Luke was in agony. You could see it in his face. But he didn't say a word.

"What would stop, honey?" Silence. "Taylor. Did somebody touch you in a way you didn't like? Or make you do anything you didn't want to do?"

"He didn't touch me."

Kate sucked in her breath, torn between relief and dread. "Okay." *Don't push. Don't pressure her.* She withdrew her touch from Snowball, folding her hands together very tightly in her lap to hide their trembling.

"He used to come into my room," Taylor said. "At Grandma Jolene's. And . . . and touch himself. His thing. The first time, I was asleep, so I didn't really know what he was doing. I'd wake up and he'd be . . . there. Doing it. And then he said he would tell everybody that I let him do it. That I let him . . ." Her voice broke. "But I *didn't.*"

Luke swore quietly, viciously. *"Son of a bitch."*

Kate shot him a look.

Taylor turned to her father. "Do you believe me?"

"Of course I believe you." He pushed away from the doorway and sat on the bed, taking her carefully in his arms, holding her safe.

Kate blinked back tears.

"I'm sorry," he said. "Jesus, baby, I'm so sorry."

Taylor sighed and laid her head against his chest. "It stopped. After you came. After you took me away."

"I should have protected you."

Taylor raised her head. "I didn't stop him."

"You're not to blame. You're ten. What were you going to do? That's not on you. It's him."

"If I slept on the couch, then he wouldn't come. Because Grandma or Grandpa might see."

"That was really smart," Kate said.

Taylor threw her a grateful look.

"Why didn't you tell somebody?" Luke asked. "Why didn't you tell them?"

Taylor's lips trembled. "He said they wouldn't believe me. And he said if they did, it would kill Grandma Jo. Because she's old and her heart is sick. And Grandpa Ernie is too old to take care of me by himself. So then it would just be him and me."

Kate felt sick.

Luke looked ready to commit murder, his body braced, tension rolling off him in waves. But his voice was gentle. "You could have told us. Grandma or Uncle Matt."

"I didn't know them," Taylor said. "I didn't want everybody to know. Or to think I was a liar. And anyway, it stopped."

"You could have told me."

Taylor looked at him. "You weren't here," she said, so simply it broke Kate's heart.

Luke went white.

Kate wanted to put her arms around them both, to hold them, hug them, protect them. But this wasn't about her. She patted Taylor's knee. "You were really brave to tell us now."

"I wasn't brave," Taylor said truculently, using anger to mask her shame. Kate knew how that went. "I peed my pants."

"Marines do it all the time," Luke said.

Taylor frowned. "What?"

"Pee their pants."

Kate's throat filled. If she hadn't loved him before, she would have fallen in love with him now for his kindness, for his restraint. His matter-of-fact tone was exactly what Taylor needed.

"When you're in danger, you pee your pants," Luke explained. "Hell, I've been in tanks under fire that smelled like latrines."

"Gross," Taylor said. But she sounded more amused than revolted.

Luke shrugged. "It's normal. You saw the enemy, you had a stress reaction. What matters is that you didn't let it stop you from doing what you had to do." Somehow he managed to smile down at her, giving her exactly the right reassurance. "You looked out for yourself when there wasn't anybody else to do it. You protected JD. And you told us, which was really brave. You did the right thing. I'm proud of you, Taylor. And I love you."

She laid her head against his chest. Her voice was muffled. "I love you, too, Daddy."

Kate swallowed tears. Maybe things would work out after all.

"I'LL KILL HIM," Luke said after Taylor had finally fallen asleep.

His rage was like a fireball inside him, incandescent, all consuming, sucking all the oxygen from his lungs.

Kate turned from wiping the counters. Five hours and a lifetime ago, he'd expected to take her to dinner at The Fish House. Instead, she'd fixed scrambled eggs and toast. No one had had much of an appetite. "You can't."

Luke set Taylor's milk glass carefully in the top rack of the dishwasher. Because if he didn't do it gently, he was going to hurl it across the room. Crush it in his hand. *Can't?* He inhaled carefully, feeding the fire. He knew lots of ways to kill people. Never with more justification. Or a greater desire.

"Taylor needs you here," Kate continued. "She's lost one parent already. You're no good to her in jail."

He knew that, damn it. His frustration wrung his gut in knots. "I'm supposed to protect her. What the hell do you think I should do?"

"Go to the police," Kate answered promptly. "Defendants in criminal cases are usually under court order to have no contact with the victim while the case is pending. And Taylor needs counseling."

He nodded heavily. Counseling, fine. And her pervert uncle put away in prison as some other guy's bitch.

Kate bit her lip. "You asked me before if I had any recommendations. For counselors. I . . . Well, I made a list of names. Back in my office."

She looked anxious, like he could possibly get mad at her for remembering and caring. Like he might resent her interference. He wasn't resentful. He was grateful. He didn't know how they would have gotten through this without her. But he couldn't find words through the fog of anger to tell her so.

"Thanks."

"And she might need a medical exam," Kate said in her precise, painstaking way.

Luke twitched like she'd applied electrodes to his privates. "She said he didn't touch her."

"Taylor may not have told us everything." Kate's gaze was steady on his. "It would be a reasonable precaution to check her for STDs."

Shit. His gut cramped. A couple days ago, he'd been worried about his ten-year-old being exposed to drugs. But this . . .

"I told her I believed her," Luke said. "Let's get her to the shrink. If the shrink says she needs to see a doctor, then okay."

He watched her weigh, nod, consider. She would never compromise her judgment to please someone, he realized. Not even now. Not even him. God, she was great.

"All right," she said.

"Kate." He struggled to say something. She deserved more from him than scrambled eggs and lukewarm appreciation and filtered rage. "Thank you. This isn't how I pictured us spending our first night together."

She smiled wanly. "I probably should go."

"Stay." He gave her own words back to her. "Taylor needs you here." *I need you here.*

Her gaze met his, her beautiful hazel eyes soft with compassion. Her tender mouth curved. "Then I'll stay."

"Kate." He stopped, at a loss.

"It's all right," she whispered, putting her arms around him.

He bowed his head to her shoulder, clinging to her like a sailor lost in a dark, turbulent sea.

Nineteen

"SORRY, FOLKS, BUT you don't have any kind of case here."
Police Lieutenant Wade Franklin hitched his paunch comfortably, regarding Kate and Luke over the almost-clean surface of his walnut veneer desk.

The Twisted Creek Police Department was an annex of the town hall, a one-story brick building with a red tin roof, grimy blue industrial carpet, and stained acoustic tile. If it weren't for the wanted posters and the bulletproof glass, Kate thought, they could have been visiting the street maintenance department down the hall or the building inspector's office.

She didn't mind the run-down décor. But Franklin's weary pragmatism made her want to torch the building.

"The alleged abuse happened over three months ago," he continued. "You've got one child witness, the alleged victim, who doesn't say boo about shit until yesterday. By her own account, her uncle never actually laid a finger on her. Miz Dolan, you've seen these cases. You know how hard they are to prove. Sometimes kids living in a house with grown-ups see things they're not supposed to see."

"He jacked off in her bedroom," Luke said, his voice tight with anger.

Franklin sighed. "Were you a witness? No. You weren't there. Will her grandparents corroborate her story? No. They won't. But here's what I'll do. You get your little girl a medical exam or a psychological assessment, something that can establish that abuse has occurred, and I'll take that to the DA. Then we'll see if we can go forward with a case."

"What about her safety?" Kate demanded.

"That's not a concern. According to what you told me, she doesn't live in the same house with the alleged abuser anymore. They don't even live in the same town anymore."

"That won't stop a child predator."

"Then neither will a court order. You're a lawyer, Miz Dolan. You've seen enough broken restraining orders to know that."

He was right. And that only made her angrier. And more afraid. "Which is why Kevin Simpson needs to be prosecuted."

Franklin heaved another sigh. "Even if you're right, even if this Simpson guy is scum, I can't lock up people on your say-so. My best advice is take your kiddie to the doctor, get me something the DA can work with, and I'll see what I can do."

Kate stalked out of the police department, vibrating with frustration.

She knew the system didn't always work. She couldn't save everybody. But she wanted desperately for her efforts to make a difference this time. To do her job for Luke. For Taylor.

"I'm so sorry," she said to Luke as they got back in the Jeep.

He slid her a look. "Why?"

"Because I told you we should come here." She shook her head. "I know the DA. Let me give him a call."

"That would be good. Thanks."

"Aren't you angry?"

He shrugged. "I'm disappointed. But I'm not surprised.

I'm a Marine staff sergeant. I'm used to the brass screwing up."

"And?"

"I'm a Marine staff sergeant," he repeated. "I fix screwups. I don't need some pissant, parking-meter cop to help me put the fear of God in some asshole."

She regarded him uncertainly. He looked capable of anything, including murder. A quiver tensed her stomach, worked up her spine, an atavistic reaction to the threat of violence. She had to trust him. She *did* trust him. Only . . .

"Don't do anything that could get you arrested."

"I won't." His smile didn't reach his eyes. "I'll hide the body real well."

Kate smiled back uneasily, unsure if he was joking or not.

"APPRECIATE YOU KEEPING Taylor this morning," Luke said to Matt when he and Kate got back to the Pirates' Rest. They stood outside his brother's work shed, where he kept his classic Harley.

"Nice to have her around." Matt smiled down at Taylor, wiping grease off her hands with a rag. She looked better this morning, Luke thought with relief. More relaxed. "We changed the plugs on the bike."

Matt had always tinkered when he had a problem to work out, Luke remembered. Obviously, he'd taught that technique to Taylor. Thank God for his brother.

He owed Matt—and Tom and Josh, who had finished off the gutters this morning and were putting the ladder away in the shed—a debt he could never repay. Because of them, Taylor would not regard every man who came into her life with distrust and suspicion. He owed her healing to them. He could never take her away from them.

But he didn't want to live without her. What would they do when his leave was up and he had to head back to Lejeune?

"What's for lunch?" Josh asked, coming out of the shed.

"You eat up all that roast beef from Christmas already?" Tom asked.

Josh grinned. "Not all."

"Then go make sandwiches."

Luke and Kate exchanged glances. He wanted to talk with his father and brother without the kids listening in.

And Kate, bless her, didn't miss a trick. "Taylor and I can help. If that's okay with you," she added to Taylor.

Taylor hitched one shoulder. "Sure."

The three men watched as they walked across the grass into the house.

"That's a good woman," Tom said.

"Yes."

"What are you going to do now?"

About Kate? Luke wondered. Or about this mess with Taylor? "Have you told Mom yet?" he asked, avoiding the question.

Tom rubbed his jaw. "She and the girls get back from their wedding dress trip this afternoon. I figured that's soon enough."

"Taylor doesn't want to talk about it," Luke said.

"She doesn't have to," said Tom.

"It wasn't her fault," Matt said.

"I know that." Luke turned his head from side to side, working out a kink in his neck. He'd picked a hell of a time to quit smoking. But he'd done it for Taylor. Everything he did now was for Taylor. "But if you could have heard this police guy, the things he said . . . I don't want everybody on the island looking at and speculating about my daughter."

Matt scowled. "So you're just going to let it go?"

"No. Kate's going to talk to the DA."

"And then what?" Tom asked. "You gonna put that little girl through a trial?"

"Kate says it won't come to that. They'll probably work out some kind of plea bargain."

"As long as they put the son of a bitch away," Matt said.

"He'll serve a couple of years, at least," Luke said. "But he hasn't even been charged yet. Which means there's no court order to protect Taylor."

Tom raised his eyebrows. "You satisfied with that?"

"No."

Their eyes met.

"Talk to Rossi," Tom said.

Luke shook his head. "No point. Simpson's not in his jurisdiction."

"Unless Simpson sets foot on the island," Matt said.

"Fine. I'll talk to the chief. But that won't stop me from paying Kevin a visit."

"Didn't expect it to," Tom said.

"You want backup?" Matt asked.

"No backup. I'm not going to hurt him." *Much.* "I just want to put the fear of God into him."

"You can leave Taylor here," Matt said. "I'll watch her."

"Thanks, bro. But Kate already offered."

And that was a first, Luke reflected, as they all trooped into the inn for lunch. To turn to someone outside his family. To know she had his six.

A good ally, Luke had thought the first time he'd seen her.

But she was more than that. Somehow she had become more. She was necessary to him now, to his happiness, to Taylor's.

Now all he had to do was convince Kate that they were necessary to hers.

TAYLOR WATCHED HER dad pocket his keys and his phone, and felt her throat get tight.

She thought that after she told about . . . that after she told, things would get better, and in some ways they were, a little, but in some ways they were worse. Because everybody knew now, they looked at her and felt sorry for her and knew. *Josh* knew.

Taylor's face got hot just thinking about it.

It wasn't so bad when she was working on the bike with Uncle Matt. And over lunch, Josh had taught her how to burp the alphabet, which made Taylor laugh, even though swallowing all that air kind of upset her stomach. She'd hoped maybe things were getting back to normal.

But now her dad was leaving—*again*—leaving her with Miss Kate, who was nice, but she wasn't Dad.

"I thought we were going to watch the movie," Taylor said, not even caring if she sounded whiny.

"I need to go out for a little while," Dad said.

"Why?"

He bent and kissed the top of her head. "I'll be back before dinner. I just want to talk to Chief Rossi."

Roast beef lurched in Taylor's stomach. She could only think of one reason for her dad to talk to the police chief. "Is he going to arrest Uncle Kevin?"

"He can't do that. But he can help keep you safe, and that's the most important thing."

"What about Grandma Jo?" Taylor asked.

"He won't arrest her, either," Dad said, kind of joking, but sort of mad, too.

You can't ever tell, Uncle Kevin whispered in Taylor's head. *Your grandma has a weak heart. You don't want to kill her, do you?*

Taylor swallowed. She hated Uncle Kevin.

"Nothing's going to happen to your grandparents, honey," Kate said soothingly. "They'll be fine."

Taylor wanted to believe her. But how did she know? "Then why do you have to go?" she appealed to Dad. "Can't everybody just forget it? I'm fine now."

"That's not the way it works," Dad said.

"Why not?" Her throat hurt. "You said I was safe. You said it was over."

"You are safe. But it's not over. People who do bad things have to face the consequences."

"I don't care," Taylor said. "I just want to forget about it."

"Taylor, you don't have to be ashamed of what happened," Kate said. "You're not responsible for the bad things your uncle did. It wasn't your fault."

Taylor's eyes burned. Her face burned. "I don't want to talk about it. I don't want to think about it. I want it to be like it never happened."

"Yeah, I get that," Dad said.

"No, you don't." Taylor could hear her voice getting louder and louder, but she couldn't seem to stop. "You don't understand. Nobody understands."

There was a kind of awful silence.

"I do," Miss Kate said.

"Kate." Her father sounded shaken. "You don't have to—"

"Yes," Miss Kate said firmly. "I do. Taylor needs to know that she's not alone. What happened to her does not define her."

Taylor wasn't sure what they were talking about.

Miss Kate's chin stuck out the way Aunt Meg's did sometimes, and she looked Taylor straight in the eyes. "When I was a little girl, my father used to hit me."

Taylor caught her breath. *Okay, that was bad.*

"I'm not talking about spanking," Miss Kate said. "He *hit* me. Hard. That's how I got this scar on my cheek. My mother used to say it wasn't my father's fault. It was because he was drinking or he was upset or . . . Well, the reasons don't matter now. Maybe they never did. The thing is . . ." Miss Kate swallowed, and Taylor realized this stuff was hard for her to talk about, too. "Because my mother said the hitting wasn't his fault, I grew up thinking it must be mine. That there was something I could do to stop it. That if only I were quieter or cleaner or nicer or prettier, he would stop hitting me.

"But he didn't. Because his hitting wasn't about me. It was never my fault. Just like what your Uncle Kevin did to you was never your fault. Okay?"

"He still *did* it," Taylor whispered. "And now I feel . . ." *Dirty. Helpless.*

"Look at me," Miss Kate commanded. "Do I look like a victim to you?"

Taylor shook her head. Miss Kate was strong. And she

was smart. Maybe as smart as Aunt Meg. Anyway, Mom always said Miss Kate was the smartest person *she* knew.

"Having bad things happen to you doesn't make you a bad person. It doesn't change who you are. *You* are a wonderful kid. *You* are a warrior. *You* are a survivor. Like your daddy." Kate looked at Taylor's dad. "And me."

Taylor sighed. That sounded pretty good. "Kindred spirits." Like in that book Kate had given her.

Kate's eyes were really bright, like she might cry, but she smiled instead. "And bosom friends."

Taylor smiled in satisfaction. That was in the book, too.

Dad looked confused. "Right."

He kissed her head again and then he kissed Kate. Right on the mouth. And it wasn't so embarrassing. It felt right. Like they were all in this together, like they were a team. His girls.

"I'll be home before dinner," he said.

Twenty

"NICE PLACE YOU'VE got here," Luke said to Jack Rossi.

"Thanks," the chief said dryly.

Luke stuck his hands in his pockets, surveying his surroundings. There were obvious differences between the Dare Island Police Department and the one in Twisted Creek. It was next to the fire department, for one thing, instead of the town hall. The walls had been painted sometime in the last decade, the acoustic tile was clean, and the chief's office didn't smell like somebody had taken a piss in the wastebasket. Obviously there was more tax revenue in tourism than textiles these days.

But certain features came standard. Same file cabinets, same wanted posters, same industrial carpet.

"Of course, I've been living in a hooch, so my requirements aren't that high," Luke said.

A gleam of humor lit Jack's dark eyes. "Let me know if you want a tour of the cells. You didn't come here to talk about the accommodations. What can I do for you?"

I don't want to talk about it, Taylor had cried. *I don't want to think about it. I want it to be like it never happened.*

Luke's jaw clenched. *Right there with you, kid.*

But Kevin Simpson had bargained on Taylor's silence. Had preyed on her in silence. The only way to defeat the son of a bitch was to speak up.

Jack Rossi listened, grim faced, sniper cold. Occasionally he nodded or made notes. "You should notify the school that you don't want Simpson to have contact with your daughter," he said when Luke was done. "If he does, if he calls the house, comes by, threatens her in any way, I want to hear about it. Unfortunately, without a protective order, there's not a whole lot I can do."

Luke wouldn't let himself feel disappointment. He'd pretty much expected that response. "Right. Thanks for your time."

Jack typed on his computer. "Of course, if I see a vehicle with his plates drive onto the island, there's no reason I can't . . . Oh, yeah. There he is. Kevin Simpson. Bunch of minor drug charges, all dismissed. That might affect sentencing, if you get that far. Possession, possession of paraphernalia, possession with intent to distribute . . ." Jack's eyes narrowed. "I thought you said he lived in Twisted Creek."

Luke nodded. "That's right. With his parents."

"Not according to this. His address is listed just outside of town."

"What difference does that make?"

"None, in terms of a case. That's county jurisdiction, but the alleged abuse still took place in the grandparents' home. It means we can pay him a visit without upsetting the grandparents, though."

Luke had told Matt he didn't need backup. The same went for a witness. "'We'?"

Jack stood from behind his desk. "I'm riding along. I can't do a lot for you officially. But maybe seeing the uniform will tell Simpson we mean business."

Luke's hands curled into fists at his sides. *He* meant business. He didn't know if the chief intended to back him up or get in his way.

Don't do anything that could get you arrested, Kate had said.

"I take it there's not a lot of heavy crime on the island this time of year."

Jack smiled thinly. "I think Hank can handle traffic stops without me for a while."

They got in Luke's Jeep.

"You must miss the adrenaline," Luke said as they pulled out of the lot.

"No." One word, flat, uncompromising.

Luke stole a glance at the chief's profile. He didn't look like a fish out of water. More like a hawk in a flock of gulls.

A sniper. What was he doing on Dare Island?

"How long were you in the Corps?" Luke asked.

"Two tours. I joined up after 9/11."

"How'd you know it was time to get out?"

"I come from a family of cops. My dad was a cop, my uncles are cops. One brother's a cop, one's State Bureau of Investigation." Jack shrugged. "And I was thinking of getting married."

Luke blew out his breath. "Yeah. Me too."

The admission came without conscious thought. But it sounded right. Felt right.

"Kate Dolan," Jack said.

"That obvious, huh?"

The chief smiled slightly. "When the two of you came downstairs? Yeah."

"I've got another six months left in my enlistment," Luke said abruptly. "After that . . . I don't know."

He'd always been a Marine. And now he was a daddy, and his daughter needed a father full-time.

You could have told me, he'd said to his daughter last night.

And she'd looked at him. *You weren't here.*

His grip tightened on the steering wheel. If you didn't reexamine your priorities after that, there was something wrong with you.

"Well, you've got a nice place to come home to," Jack said. "Your family's here. And the hometown hero angle works for you, too."

"I'm no hero." It was a point of pride in the Corps: other branches got medals; Marines got the job done.

"You are to the folks around here," Jack said. "I saw you Christmas Eve. Everybody wanted to shake your hand."

Luke remembered. It felt good to be welcomed home—not just as Tom and Tess's son, as Matt and Meg's brother, but for himself, in recognition of what he'd done. "At least nobody threw rocks."

"I guess you got a lot of that in Afghanistan."

"Some." The memory tightened his gut. "I spent the last couple months on patrol, providing training and support for the ANP."

The flat winter fields rolled by.

"You know, I could use somebody in the department who knows the island," Jack said.

Luke had never thought that far ahead. Never considered a future on the island that didn't involve working at his parents' inn, his brother's boat. The idea was unexpectedly appealing. "Too bad I don't have any training."

"You're a Marine. You can shoot, keep a cool head, and command respect. Everything else is paperwork."

Luke turned his head to look at the chief. He was serious. "You making a job offer?"

"I'm making a suggestion," Jack said. "Think about it."

Luke found it hard to do anything else. The possibility of doing meaningful work on Dare Island, available to his daughter, near to his family, close to Kate . . . How could he *not* think about it?

He'd always wanted to be like his dad. A career Marine. *Moving around with a wife and three kids, deployment after deployment . . .*

Okay, maybe that wasn't going to work. Taylor needed stability. Kate had a house and a law practice in Beaufort.

Luke stared out the windshield. "This girl—the one you left the Corps for—what happened with her?"

"We got married. And divorced. Turn here," Jack said. "Cotton Hill Lane."

Luke turned down a rutted gravel road off the highway.

Kevin Simpson lived in the middle of nowhere, surrounded by stubbled farm fields, migrant workers' trailers, ditches full of turtles and seeding cattails.

Nice enough if you liked scenery. Or you didn't like neighbors.

Kevin's single-wide was set back between a windbreak of trees and some fallen-down outbuildings. If Dawn had moved up in the world from her parents' place, Kevin had definitely slid down. The windows were boarded or bare, the yard littered with junk.

Luke parked the Jeep in the weeds by the road, twenty yards from the house.

"Those are his plates," Jack said. "That's his car in the driveway. Guess he's not visiting his parents today. And . . . Well, well. Look at that."

"What?"

"See those big yellow circles of dead grass? Your creepy Uncle Kevin is a meth cook. He's been dumping chemicals."

"The ammonia smell," Luke said.

"Oh, yeah. Oh, this is good." Jack reached for his phone.

Shit. "Last time I visited Jolene, I thought she'd been cleaning."

"Maybe she was. Or, if the son comes around, he could have cooked a batch right there without his parents knowing. The thing about meth is it's portable. With the right ingredients, you can mix it up in a two-liter soda bottle."

"Convenient."

Jack looked up from his phone. "Unless it explodes. Meth is highly toxic, highly volatile. Knew a trooper did a stop on a guy mixing up a batch in his car. Blew out the windshield, killed the guy, trooper wound up in the hospital." He turned his head, spoke into the phone. "Hi, Eddie. This is Jack Rossi, Dare Island police. Got a present for you guys out on Cotton Hill Lane."

Luke listened as Jack did a SITREP over the phone.

"Now what?" he asked when Jack ended the call.

"Now we wait for the sheriff's department to show up with a warrant."

Adrenaline demanded Luke storm over the burned-out grass, kick in the door, and eliminate the target. He inhaled slowly. Released it. "What about Kevin?"

"He's out of luck. See, indecent liberties with a child, even if he's convicted, he serves maybe ten months, tops. But manufacture of methamphetamine, plus possession, plus whatever other charges the DA can cook up—possession of meth precursor, drug paraphernalia, probably weapons—well, with his priors, he could be locked up for years."

Years for Taylor to grow up free from fear.

Luke released his breath. She wouldn't have to testify. It was a best-case scenario.

But the idea of doing nothing, sitting with his thumb up his ass, waiting for some overweight sheriff's deputy to ride in and save the day, made him itch.

Minutes ticked by. The December sun beat down on the Jeep. With the windows rolled to keep out the smell, the inside heated like a microwave.

Luke looked at Jack, so cool he apparently controlled his own sweat. "Waiting for a warrant, you said."

"That's right. We're out of our jurisdiction, we're not wearing vests or hazmat suits, and we don't know how many people are in there. Meth heads tend to be twitchy. And paranoid. And armed." A corner of Jack's mouth curled up in a smile. "Didn't you ever watch *Breaking Bad*?"

"I've been out of the country," Luke said tersely. His fingers drummed the steering wheel. "We should contain him. There's got to be another point of entry in the back."

Jack sighed. "I'm not leaving the vehicle. I won't risk

Kevin Simpson seeing the uniform and getting spooked. But you don't report to me. If you want to circle around back and make sure he doesn't go running across the fields after the sheriff's deputies show up, I won't stop you."

LUKE POSITIONED HIMSELF with a view of the door in the cover of the falling-down shed, next to a rusting boat trailer with a tarp and no boat. Snakes below and spiders above, he bet. There was some kind of gray chemical slag pile that looked like Mordor, and an aluminum pot with the bottom burned out.

The smell was much worse back here.

He fished the bandanna from his pocket. He was tying the cloth over his nose and mouth when he heard the first vehicles approach. No sirens, thank God, but he saw rotating blue lights and flashing orange ones and then a long red ladder truck, its chrome gleaming in the sun.

Jesus. Must have been a slow day for law enforcement. They might as well have announced their arrival with a brass band.

Car doors slammed.

The back door burst open and Kevin Simpson bolted down the trailer steps holding a green two-liter soda bottle.

Luke stepped out of concealment, sweat under his arms and in the small of his back. *Highly toxic*, Jack had warned. *Highly volatile.*

Kevin skidded to a stop. The bottle slid from his hands. Hit the hard-packed ground. And exploded like an IED.

Flash. Boom.

Fuck. A ball of heat, a burst of flame.

Luke dropped. Debris rained down. Scalding toxic fumes rolled over the yard. He could hear Kevin screaming.

Voices shouted. Luke staggered to his feet, eyes swollen and streaming, and ripped the tarp from the trailer. The familiar, sickening stench of roasting flesh and singeing hair joined the putrid chemical stew. He heard sirens now, or maybe that was the ringing in his ears. His mouth tasted like metal.

On the ground, Kevin was burning, jerking, shrieking.

Luke ran toward the son of a bitch and threw the tarp over him, smothering the flames.

Twenty-one

SHE WAS WAITING for her man to come home.

Another first, Kate figured. She looked out the cottage window, where the sun was going down in a great orange ball, and felt an answering warmth radiate in her chest.

She'd never been willing to wait before. Growing up, she'd never known whether to anticipate her father's home-comings with relief or dread. As an adult, she spent enough time at the mercy of the court. She didn't need to sacrifice her personal time to someone else's schedule or convenience.

It made a difference, she found, when you weren't waiting alone.

Her lips curved into a smile. And when the man you were waiting for was Luke.

"Go faster, go faster!" Taylor yelled from in front of the Wii, now hooked up to the cottage TV.

The screen beeped, bleeped, revved and sparkled.

Josh groaned. "What's with the banana?"

The two of them were playing Mario Kart. Kate had been playing Mario Kart, too, until she crashed off track for the billionth time. She was better at the dance game, where she understood the rules, where she wasn't racing blindly into the unknown. But none of that mattered. She was part of the action. Not detached. Not merely an observer. She would rather be here than answering email, checking voice mail, writing court briefs in her empty apartment.

"What? Wait! No, no, no!"

"Shells to you, buddy!"

Kate's smile broadened as she listened to the kids' trash talk. Evidence, she thought, that Taylor would be all right. A survivor. She would need counseling, of course. But supported by the Fletchers' unconditional acceptance, she was already moving beyond her trauma, eager to embrace happiness, to accept love.

Could Kate do any less?

"Kindred spirits," she murmured.

I'll be home before dinner, Luke had said.

Maybe tonight they'd go to the Fish House. Or better still, she could have dinner waiting. She would cook. At least, she thought ruefully, she cooked better than she played Mario Kart. Maybe steak and a salad?

She opened the refrigerator. *Eggs, milk, bread*. No meat. No lettuce. She closed the door. "How do you guys feel about pizza?"

"Pizza? Yay!"

"Cool."

Kate sighed in relief. *See? She could do this*.

Headlights arced across the glass.

Taylor scrambled from the floor. JD leaped up with a joyous bark. "Dad's home!"

Kate's heart beat faster. The door opened.

"Luke?" she whispered.

He looked . . . My God, he looked awful. Was he actually wearing *scrubs*? Baggy green pants and a too-tight top that exposed a V of dark blond hair. His beautiful blue eyes were red-rimmed and swollen.

Her pleased anticipation vanished in concern. "What happened to you?"

"Hey, babe." He strode forward swiftly to give her a hard, brief kiss. "Sorry I'm late. I had to drop off Jack."

She wanted to grab him and hold him, to reassure herself he was here, he was really all right. To inhale him, to breathe in the secret scent of his skin and hair. He smelled different, antiseptic and unfamiliar. "Are you all right?"

"I'm fine."

Her eyes narrowed. "'They haven't amputated yet'?"

His swift grin acknowledged her gibe.

"What happened to your clothes?" she asked.

"There was an accident. They gave me these at the hospital. But everything's fine. Everything's great." He opened his arms to Taylor. She ran to him, wrapping her arms around his neck, and he lifted her off the ground.

Hospital. Kate's stomach hollowed. She swallowed. "What kind of accident?"

Luke hesitated.

Josh had muted the sound on the TV and stood, his eyes tracking their interaction as if they were on screen.

Right, Kate thought. *Children present.* She smiled at the teenager brightly. "Do you want to go get that pizza now?"

"Hell, no," Josh said. "I want to hear this."

"Was anybody hurt?" Taylor asked.

"No. Well." Luke looked at Kate, a help-me-out-here look.

What did he want her to say? She had no clue what was going on.

Because he hadn't told her, damn it.

"You know I went to see Chief Rossi," Luke said to Taylor.

Taylor nodded, her blue eyes fixed gravely on his face.

"We went together to talk to your uncle Kevin."

Shock swam in her eyes as tears. "Oh, no."

"It's okay," Luke said.

Taylor buried her face in his neck.

"Honey, no, really, it's really okay," Luke repeated firmly. He raised Taylor's head from his shoulder. Their gazes locked, blue on blue. "Your uncle is never going to hurt you, he is never going to bother you again."

Kate sucked in her breath.

"Is he dead?" Taylor whispered.

"No, he's in the hospital. In the burn unit. He was cooking drugs in his trailer and there was an accident. An explosion. He was burned—real bad. He's not going to be a threat to anybody ever again."

Burned. "I don't think the children need to hear the details," Kate said. They had enough material for nightmares already.

"'To the pain,'" Josh murmured.

Taylor looked at him.

"What?" Kate asked.

"Like Humperdinck," Taylor said.

"It's from *The Princess Bride*," Josh explained. "The fate worse than death."

Taylor smiled a small smile against her father's shoulder.

My God, thought Kate, a little shaken by the children's bloodthirsty acceptance. But maybe there was healing there, too. In fairy tales, the ogre was always slain, the monster vanquished. *He is never going to hurt you again.*

To the pain.

Yes.

"I WISH YOU had called," Kate said to Luke much later, when the pizza had been eaten, and Josh had gone home, and Taylor was in bed.

They were seated together on the couch, one of his arms extended across the sofa back, her head against his shoulder. She let herself relax against his warmth as if she belonged there, settled against his side.

He played with her hair, pulling and releasing the tiny springs. "It happened kind of fast. I told you I'd be home for dinner."

"And the fact that you were blown up and hospitalized in the meantime wasn't something you felt you needed to share." She forced herself to speak lightly. "What really happened, Luke?"

"It went down pretty much like I told you. Kevin was mixing up a batch of meth when the sheriff's deputies arrived. He ran out the back door." Luke shrugged. "The bottle just slipped."

She was a lawyer. She could recognize an evasive witness. There was something he wasn't telling her. "How do you know the bottle slipped?"

"I was there. Jack was watching the front, I staked out the back. To make sure he didn't get away."

"Oh. Oh, *Luke*." The realization of his danger made her shiver. "What if he'd had a gun?"

"He didn't. Not on him."

"Meaning, there were guns in the house."

Luke didn't answer.

Fear and frustration raked her like claws. Did he really imagine that by keeping silent, he was protecting her? "Even if he wasn't armed, you exposed yourself to terrible contamination." Too often in her work, she saw the corrosive, destructive effects of meth. "You could have inhaled poison. You could have burned your lungs. You could have . . ."

Died. Her voice failed her. The thought of never seeing him again, never holding him again, opened a hole in her chest. She could not bear it.

"I wasn't really thinking about me. I was more worried about Taylor." His free hand covered both of hers. He held them, linked together on his thigh, his clasp warm and sure. "The whole time I was at the hospital getting checked out, I kept thinking, what if things had gone the other way? It meant a lot, Kate, knowing Taylor was safe with you. Knowing you were here for her. It meant everything."

She swallowed the lump in her throat. "I'm so glad." He had his whole wonderful, functional family to count on for support. She was beyond moved and humbled that he'd chosen *her*. That he trusted *her* with his daughter. "I'm happy to be here for you."

"We're a great team."

"Yes."

"The three of us." His face was set, his tone determined.

Kate had been thinking the same thing. So why did she feel a quiver of unease? "Ye-es," she said again, more slowly.

"Right." He nodded once, decisively, like a soldier accepting his duty. Or a prisoner, she thought, resigned to his fate. "So I've decided to leave the Corps."

She sat up. Pulled away. "What? When?"

"That's what you wanted, isn't it?"

Yes, but . . . "When did I ever say that?"

"From the beginning. You said Taylor should be my top priority. And I agree."

He sounded tense. Shouldn't he be happier, if this was his decision?

She studied his face, his deep blue eyes sunken with exhaustion, his cheeks stubbled and drawn. The trauma of the past two days had obviously taken its toll. Not to mention that he'd nearly gotten himself blown up in a meth lab explosion. Concern twisted her insides. No matter how much she selfishly wanted him to stay, Luke was in no condition to be making important life-changing decisions.

"We should talk about it later," Kate said. "When you're rested."

"There's nothing to talk about."

Now he was just being stubborn. "So you've made up your mind. Just like that."

"I talked to Jack Rossi."

The police chief? "What does he have to do with it?"

"He told me the community college is offering the Basic Law Enforcement Training program in January. Six weeks if you go full-time, six months if you attend night school. By the time I get out, I could be certified." He looked at her expectantly.

She didn't know what to say. Her brain felt like she was on a Mario kart, rushing along, crashing into barriers. After the chaos of her childhood, it was important to her to dot every i, to cross every t, to think through every decision. And Luke had already made up his mind.

After talking to Jack Rossi. Whom he barely knew.

He'd never mentioned anything to her.

"The Dare Island PD would sponsor me for the program," Jack added. "Tuition would be free."

"That's great," she said heartily. Even to her own ears, her enthusiasm sounded forced. "If that's what you really want. But why . . ." *Would you leave the Marines? And if you can leave something you love, just like that . . .*

But she couldn't complete the thought. He'd never said he loved her.

Luke's smile twisted. "Would Jack make me the offer?"

She knew why. He was wonderful. With his compassion and quick thinking, his sense of service and ability to connect with people, he would make a terrific cop.

"He thinks I'd make a good law officer," Luke said. "When that meth bottle exploded . . . Jack said he watched me run toward it, not away. Kevin was burning, right? Screaming. And I was next to this tarp. So I used it to smother the flames."

She stared at him, stunned. "You mean, you saved his life."

"The life of a pervert who molested and terrorized my daughter." He met her gaze, his eyes dark. Almost bewildered. "Yeah."

Her heart swelled like a balloon in her chest. *The solution to violence is not more violence*, she'd said to him, talking about her father's abuse. She'd never expected this Marine, this warrior, to agree with her.

He hadn't, not in words. He'd merely done everything in his power to protect Taylor, and then demonstrated his principles at the risk of his own life.

She curled her fingers around his broad hand. His knuckles were rough. Her hand looked small and pale against his. "What it makes you is a man who's determined to help others," she said firmly. "Whose training and whose honor run so deep, you will run into danger even for an enemy you despise. You got that training as a Marine. Is leaving the Corps what you really want?"

Say yes, she thought. *Make me believe.*

Luke was stone-faced. "It's what I've got to do. Taylor's already lost her mother. She can't lose her father, too."

Kate loved him for his determination to do the right thing. She wanted him to stay. But she wanted him to *choose.* "Do you really think being a cop is that much safer than being a Marine? Especially after today."

His jaw tightened. "At least I'd be home most nights. I can't marry you and then go off for six to ten months at a stretch, leaving you to take care of my kid."

Marry? The bottom dropped out of her stomach. Her heart soared.

"If . . . if we were ever in that situation, Taylor wouldn't be *your* kid," Kate pointed out carefully. "She would be *our* kid."

He nodded. "Agreed. But we're not going to be in that situation. Taylor needs a full-time mom *and* dad."

Kate's hands were cold. Her stomach felt as if she'd swallowed hot coals. She adored Taylor. *Kindred spirits.* But why couldn't Luke say that he loved her? That he wanted to be with her?

"Don't offer to marry me because Taylor needs a mother. Don't stay with us because we require some big sacrifice from you. We both deserve better than that."

Luke's jaw knotted. "What do I have to do to prove myself to you? After three weeks, I'm willing to change my life for you. What more do you want from me?"

Tell me you love me. Reassure me.

She gritted her teeth so she would not cry. So she would not give in. She was used to being disappointed. But she'd be damned if she begged. She wanted him so much. But not if he didn't love her. Not if he would grow to resent her for encouraging him to give up the career he loved in favor of the life they could have together.

"I want you to change your life for yourself," she said. "Because this is what you want. Because *I* am what you want."

His gaze clashed with hers. His body vibrated with masculine frustration. She half thought he was going to pick her up and cart her off somewhere, to bed or to Vegas. She half wished that he would.

Pathetic, that's what she was.

Something happened behind his eyes. A light. A click. The connection sparked along her veins.

He released his breath, shaking his head. His mouth twisted. "I've been doing this all wrong, haven't I?"

"Don't ask me." She was not sulking. She did not sulk. "I'm not exactly a relationship expert."

His smile broadened. Softened. "Kate." He took both her hands again, between both of his. Large, warm hands, strong and callused. "I want you. I need you. I love you. Being back home has made me realize that I miss this. I want to be home every Christmas. I want to live closer to my family. I want to raise my daughter on the island where I grew up, and show her where to catch fish and where to watch the stars. I want to serve and protect in a community where I don't get rocks thrown at me every day on patrol. I can make a life here, a good life. But it won't be a whole life without you. I want to marry you. What do you want, Kate?"

A swarm of butterflies rose inside her, all color and motion.

She opened her mouth and . . . stuck. She was terrified to count on him. On anybody, but on someone she loved most of all. All the lessons of her childhood chattered in her head, drowning out his beautiful words and the plea of her own heart.

If you never asked, you were never disappointed.

If you didn't rely on someone, they could never let you down.

If you never admitted how desperately you wanted something, it didn't hurt so much when it was taken away.

Yes, she loved him. *But . . . marriage?* whispered a voice like her mother's. Look at all the marriages that failed. Kate saw them in her office every day.

"I like what we have together very much," she said, picking her words like shards of glass. Her hands trembled in his. "I've let you into my life farther than I've let anyone. I want to be like you. I want to be able to commit to things. But I'm not. I can't. It's too soon. I need time."

"Do you love me?" His voice was hoarse. The vulnerability in his question cracked her chest wide open.

"Oh, God, yes."

He kissed her, his lips a little rough, a little chapped, infinitely tender. "Then trust me," he said against her mouth. "Trust what we could have together."

"I do trust you." Hot words, hot tears, pooling at the back of her throat. Her voice was thick with emotion. "I don't know if I trust myself. My judgment. I don't want to hurt you. I don't want to disappoint you. I think I'm more afraid of that than anything. I don't know if I can be what you want. What Taylor needs."

"So many *don'ts*. That only tells me what you're afraid of. What do you *want*, Kate?"

She met his gaze, his blue eyes dark and steady and sure.

She did not have his confidence. She didn't have that strong family foundation that made it easy to believe. Her doubts did not magically disappear, her scars did not vanish. They were part of her, she acknowledged. Maybe they always would be.

But now her love was part of her, too. Her love for Luke was bigger than her fears. And his love was worth the risk. Was worth everything.

"I want you," she said, speaking from her heart. A survivor after all, ready to fight for the love she deserved. That they all deserved. "I want Taylor. I want us to be a family."

"That's what I choose," Luke said. "I will always choose you. But I can wait until you're ready."

She placed her hand on his chest, sliding her fingers beneath the loose V-neck of the hospital scrubs to touch his warm flesh. Her fingertips traced the ink on his skin. *Semper Fi*. His breath caught. Her heart quickened. She leaned up and kissed him, a kiss that simmered with tenderness and promise.

"Don't wait too long," she said.

Luke laughed and pulled her close. "I get out in six months."

She smiled and settled against his chest, contentment settling into her bones. "I guess that's enough time."

She felt him swallow. His arms tightened around her. "Whatever you need. You're worth waiting for."

All her life, no one had said those words to her. No one had made her feel like this, safe, protected, and loved.

Kate raised her head and smiled. "It's not what I need," she explained. "That's how long your sister said it takes to shop for a wedding dress."

Luke's grin widened. His eyes blazed with heat and joy.

After that, no words were necessary for a long time.

Epilogue

LUKE STOOD NEXT to Matt between Josh and Sam, watching his brother's bride walk toward them.

The spring green lawn rolled to a tiny strip of beach. Beyond the live oaks, wax myrtle, and waving reeds, Pamlico Sound sparkled and gleamed in the April sun. Yesterday, Josh and Luke had spent a couple of hours helping the florist, Rowan Whitlock, haul tubs of flowering dogwood trees and pots of freesia, ferns, azalea, and hydrangea into place. A light breeze fluttered the sides of the big white rental tent and caught the edge of Allison's veil.

She was beautiful. Luke didn't know squat about dresses, but hers—a flowing, deep-cut column of lace—made her look like one of those tulips she carried, long-stemmed and fresh. Sweet without being fussy.

But it wasn't the dress or the flowers that made throats catch and Tess beam through her tears in the front row of chairs. It was the joy in Allison's eyes, the absolute confidence in her smile as she floated across the grass on her father's arm.

Matt, usually so serious, looked like the happiest guy in the world as he stepped forward to take her hand.

Luke wanted that. He was ready—*eager*—to take that next step with Kate. He didn't mind—*much*—that she needed time.

He looked for her in the row next to his parents.

She grinned at him, shy and happy, her shields down, and a shiver of hope, of impatience, jolted through him. He wanted her so much. He stood straight and still in his dress blues, his collar chafing, and made himself listen to Allison's aunt, the Episcopal priest, begin the words of the marriage ceremony.

"The union of husband and wife in heart, body, and mind is intended by God for their mutual joy . . ."

He met Kate's eyes and smiled back at her. He didn't doubt that she loved him. He just had to love her and trust her and wait for her to trust herself.

And hope to God it didn't take too long.

"That each may be to the other a strength in need, a counselor in perplexity, a comfort in sorrow, and a companion in joy," Allison's aunt said in her deep, educated Yankee voice.

Tom cleared his throat noisily.

"Amen," everybody said.

There were more words, more tears, more smiles, more kissing. A lot of kissing, which gave Luke an excuse to grab Kate in the front row. Her lips were warm and soft. Her fingers tightened on his arms.

Despite his parents' warm acceptance, he knew she sometimes still felt awkward among so much family.

"You doing okay?" he murmured as he drew back.

Her face was rosy. She nodded.

His mother poked him in the side with her finger. "Get up there. They're ready for the blessing."

And after that there was no time to speak, no chance to get her alone, until the pictures were taken and the toasts were made.

He could wait.

He was good at waiting, patient and stubborn as any islander. Kate was worth waiting for.

But watching Matt pull Allison close in their first dance, he wanted what they had. What his parents had. That love. That trust. Now and forever. His throat tightened.

"Damn it, boy, smile. It's a wedding, not a funeral," his father said.

"I know it's a wedding," Luke said. "Mom wouldn't get you in a tie otherwise."

Tom's weathered face cracked. "It's more comfortable than that uniform you're wearing."

Luke moved his shoulders uncomfortably. "I won't be wearing it much longer. Not like you."

Tom had served in the Corps for twenty-five years. All Luke had ever wanted was to be the man his father was.

"Because that was right for me," Tom said. "Like this is right for you. I'm proud of you, boy."

"I thought—" Luke clamped his jaw shut. *You'd be disappointed.*

"I was proud when you enlisted," his father said. "Proud when you deployed. Proud of you now, doing the right thing for your little girl. You got a lot of years to make up for there."

"I'm looking forward to it," Luke said honestly.

Tom's faded blue eyes narrowed. "And the job?"

Luke smiled. "Looking forward to that, too."

Tom grunted. "Good."

They stood, shoulder to shoulder, as the music changed and Allison danced with her father.

Matt led a glowing Tess onto the floor. They made some picture, Luke thought, his tanned, rugged brother with his big hands and feet, their tiny mother with the old spring in her step. Matt twirled Tess carefully under his arm and Luke's smile broadened. Matt must have taken dance lessons.

"I'm cutting in," Tom announced. "You should dance with your daughter."

Luke glanced at Taylor standing with the rest of the wedding party, wrinkling her nose at something Josh had said. She looked cute as a bug in her pale pink junior bridesmaid's dress. *My daughter.* A great wave of thankfulness swamped his chest. She'd changed his life, his parents' lives, everything.

In her first pair of heels, she almost reached his shoulder. They'd put some gunk on her hair and gloss on her lips. She smelled sweet and unfamiliar and alarmingly grown up.

"What were you and Josh talking about?" Luke asked as they shuffled across the floor. More couples joined the dancing. He scanned the crowd for Kate.

"Who's getting married next, you or Aunt Meg."

His attention snapped back to Taylor.

"Josh says it's gonna be Aunt Meg and Sam, because they're already engaged," Taylor said. She tilted her head back, fixing him with her big blue eyes. "But I want it to be you and Kate."

Luke's heart pounded. "Why is that?"

"Because then she could stay with me when you have to work and stuff. And we need a bigger house. With a yard. For JD."

JD was almost the size of Fezzik now and still growing.

"Taylor, you can stay with Grandma and Grandpa. Or Uncle Matt and Allison. Or—"

"I know." Her pointed little chin stuck out. "But I want Kate."

Luke exhaled. "Yeah." *So do I.*

Had he done enough to convince Kate of that? He'd been so damn busy the past few months. Had he taken the time to show her how much she meant to him, to reassure her in all the ways she needed to be reassured?

The music switched up, pounded out, as the DJ coaxed more people to the dance floor.

"Hey, shorty." Josh appeared at Luke's elbow. "Wanna dance?"

Taylor's face radiated joy. She sniffed. "If you think you can keep up."

Josh grinned. "Whatever. Let's see you break it down without your Wii to follow."

Luke watched them jump into the dance before he turned to search for Kate.

She was there, standing there, waiting for him, smiling and solid and so beautiful his chest hurt. It was all he could do not to grab her and kiss her. And then he thought, *What the hell*, and grabbed and kissed her hard.

She got into it, too, twining her arms around his neck, kissing him back.

He raised his head. "Sorry I've been tied up."

"It's your brother's wedding," Kate said a little breathlessly. "You have things to do."

"I don't mean today. The last three months. Driving to the base for training, taking law enforcement classes at night . . ."

"Do you regret it?" she interrupted.

He took a step back onto the dance floor, using the excuse of the music to hold her close and sway. Maybe they weren't moving to the beat, maybe he wasn't going to score any points on Wii. But she felt good against him, warm and soft. "That I've barely seen you for more than a couple hours at a time? Yeah."

"That you're taking the class. That you're taking the job."

He shook his head. "No. I thought it would be tough. It's been a long time since I was in school. But I like it. Community policing—most of it's problem solving. Making a difference, helping people make better choices. It's challenging."

She smiled up into his eyes. "And you like a challenge."

He grinned back. "Ooh-rah."

"When will you start?"

"July. Middle of the tourist season."

"That doesn't give you much of a break," she observed.

"Four days." Over by the three-tiered cake, Jack Rossi was chatting up Jane, the pretty blond baker from the Sweet Tea House. Luke shrugged. "Jack needs the help. It's what I want. Why wait?"

Kate regarded him thoughtfully.

Sam spun Meg and pulled her close. Meg laughed and

slipped off the dance floor, smiling at him over her shoulder. Sam caught her hand and followed her out of the tent.

"Where are they going?" Kate asked.

Luke grinned at her slowly.

She blinked. "Wedding sex? But Matt and Allison haven't cut the cake yet."

Luke chuckled and held her closer. "It's the wedding mojo, babe. Puts you in the mood."

"You're right." She swallowed. "Let's do it."

He drew in a deep breath. Let it out in a rush. "Okay."

She flushed. Dimpled. "I meant . . . Let's get married. In July. You have four days."

He stopped. His feet simply would not move. Now he couldn't breathe at all. "Kate. Are you sure?"

She met his gaze, her beautiful hazel eyes shining with confidence and trust. "'It's what I want,'" she quoted back at him softly. "'Why wait?' I think when you finally know that you want to spend the rest of your life with someone, you want the rest of your life to start as soon as possible."

"I love you."

She touched his cheek. "I know. I love you."

The words sank into his bones, wrapped around his heart. "I want to make you happy."

"You already do. And sometimes we'll fight and maybe we'll hurt each other. Bad things could happen, and that's okay. It's really okay. Being around your family, watching your parents together, taught me that. I'm not searching for guarantees anymore," she told him. "All I need is your promise that you'll stand by me. That you'll be with me. That you'll love me."

They stood together, surrounded by his family, the cool salt air, the warm spring sun, the sound of music and the scent of flowers.

"Forever," he promised and laid his lips on hers.

Turn the page for a preview of
Virginia Kantra's next Dare Island novel

Carolina Blues

Coming soon from Berkley Sensation!

LAUREN PATTERSON OCCUPIED the corner table of Jane's Sweet Tea House, barricaded behind her laptop, a latte, and a Glorious Morning muffin.

Facing a blank computer screen wasn't nearly as terrifying as confronting three masked men with guns, she told herself firmly. She hadn't frozen then. There was absolutely no excuse for her to be paralyzed now.

The July sun pooled like syrup on her little table. Beyond the window, the waters of Pamlico Sound gleamed. Vacationers packed the bright bakery, seeking an air-conditioned respite from the North Carolina heat. A young couple, broiled pink by the sun, held hands at the next table. A father lifted his little daughter onto his shoulders in line. All of them happy. Together.

Lauren's muffin stuck in her throat.

Behind the counter, a pretty teenager in geek-girl glasses struggled to meet the stream of orders for iced espresso drinks. Before Lauren's fifteen minutes of fame, she'd worked as a barista to make ends meet. Her graduate student stipend had barely covered her tuition. It definitely hadn't stretched for luxuries like cable. Or even food.

Lauren tore little strips from her napkin. She would be happy to show the teenager working the Cimbali machine how to pull a proper shot. Or jump up and bus tables. Anything, really, to avoid the cursor blinking on her screen.

The cheerful silver bells on the door chimed, announcing the arrival of another customer.

She looked up, seeking a more positive direction for her thoughts. Or maybe, she admitted, she was simply searching for a distraction.

A man stood silhouetted against the bright glass door, dark against the light. Thick, close-cut hair. Lean, muscled body. Dark mirrored sunglasses.

Her heart beat faster. A cop.

Save me, she thought.

She took a deep breath and looked away. The sudden sight of the law was never good news. A uniform at the door, blue lights flashing in the rearview mirror . . . Anybody could get sweaty palms and a dry mouth. There was nothing unusual about her response.

He entered the shop, moving with a quiet, contained authority more menacing than a swagger. Among the soft, pink, underdressed tourists, he stuck out like an assassin in a ballroom.

He promised safety. He promised danger. An irresistible combination.

She rolled the shreds of her napkin into tiny balls and dropped them on her plate.

He nodded to the young woman behind the register; she had a fat blond braid and the dreamy gray eyes of a princess in a fairy tale. The blonde nodded back, never losing her rhythm or her sweet, rather vague smile.

Lauren didn't understand why the girl wasn't melting into a puddle at his feet. Okay, so he wasn't Prince Charming. Not the kind of guy you wanted to meet at midnight, unless you intended to lose a lot more than your shoes.

But hot. Very hot. Smoldering, in fact.

Given the slightest encouragement, Lauren would have followed him home, like one of the island cats that seemed to hang around the bakery's back porch, lean and hungry and hoping for handouts. *Pet me. Rescue me.*

She shook the thought away. She was *not* a police groupie. Before that horrible day almost a year ago, she'd always gone for the bad boys, tortured, sensitive souls with lousy home lives and pierced tongues and nipples. She didn't *do* authority figures.

"This isn't peppermint schnapps," complained a thin woman at the head of the line.

"No, it's Irish cream syrup and whipped cream," the blonde said.

"But I ordered Irish coffee. There should be peppermint schnapps."

Not in Irish coffee, Lauren thought.

The blonde blinked. "I'm afraid we're not licensed to serve alcohol," she said with doll-like calm. "But I can add a touch of mint syrup if you'd like."

"I don't want any damn syrup," the customer said loudly. "I want my drink. I want to speak with your manager."

The people behind her in line shifted away. Lauren had seen that kind of body language before. They didn't want to get involved. They didn't want the drama.

Lauren, on the other hand, had already proved she was a total sucker for other people's problems. Not just where her family was concerned. She had a master's degree in psychology—practically a license to meddle. And even though she knew better now, her muscles tensed in instinctive sympathy.

"I'm Jane. The owner," the blonde was saying. "If you'd like me to make you another drink—"

"What I'd like is a real Irish coffee," the angry woman said. "It's false advertising, that's what it is."

The blonde flushed scarlet.

Lauren couldn't stand it. She stood to bus her empty mug, breaking the tension with action.

Hot Cop spoke. "This is a bakery, not a bar." His deep

voice raised all the little hairs along Lauren's arms. "You want a drink at ten in the morning, you'll have to take your business elsewhere."

Okay, so his by-the-book attitude wasn't going to win the bakery any patrons, Lauren acknowledged. But at least he was stepping in, defending the princess against attack.

The unhappy customer folded thin, tanned arms across her skinny bosom and turned to give the interloper a piece of her mind. But faced with Hot Cop's cool air of authority, she faltered. "But I'm on vacation," she said almost plaintively.

He regarded her impassively from behind mirrored sunglasses. "Yes, ma'am. Have a nice stay."

"Carolina sea salt caramel latte to go," the owner, Jane, said, setting a drink with a clear domed lid on the counter. "On the house."

The customer pursed her lips. "Skim?"

It was important in negotiations, Lauren had learned, to give the hostage taker an opportunity to save face.

Jane nodded. "And whipped cream."

The thin woman took the cup without thanks or payment. The door bells rattled in her wake.

Hot Cop looked at Jane. "You really want to start rewarding customers for bad behavior?"

Jane's flush deepened.

Lauren dumped her dirty mug into the bus tray. "I'm pretty sure she just wanted to get her out of here before she made more of a scene."

The sunglasses turned in her direction. "You don't stop bullies by appeasing them."

Memory tightened Lauren's chest, constricted her throat. *Lying flat on the bank floor, her face pressed to the cool tiles, the smell of fear rank in her nostrils . . .*

She smiled, because that had worked for her in the past, and because Hot Cop so obviously needed to lighten up. "Sometimes you do whatever it takes to survive."

His dark brows flicked up. "Her survival isn't in question."

Lauren shrugged. "It is if a customer decides to trash her bakery online."

"Thank you," Jane said.

Hot Cop didn't budge. "So, in your opinion, she should compromise her principles to avoid a customer lying in a bad review."

"I wouldn't say lying. Exactly. Everybody tells their story in a way that makes them the hero." *Or a victim.* "I think she should go with whatever makes people feel good."

"Here's your coffee," Jane said, setting it on the counter. "Black. No sugar."

Lauren glanced from the cup to the cop's hard face. A smile tugged at her mouth. "I guess you don't worry about stereotypes, huh?"

For a moment she thought that he wouldn't answer. That he didn't get it. And then his smile flashed, robbing her of breath. "I didn't order donuts," he pointed out.

She tilted her head, challenging, flirting. Enjoying the freedom of her anonymity. "You don't like sweet things?"

He surveyed her coolly from behind dark mirrored glasses. "I like them fine. I'm watching my weight."

Was he kidding? Her gaze dropped to his lean waist. He had the flat stomach and disciplined body that came from serious gym time.

Several months ago, Lauren had started working out as a way to deal with the stress, the constant meals on the road, the loneliness. But recently she'd realized that exercise wasn't fun anymore. The routines she'd adopted to make herself feel better had become another obligation. So she'd quit. She still ran sometimes or did a little yoga, but her compulsive fitness days were over.

"Yeah, I can see how that would be a problem," she said.

"Occupational hazard," he agreed, straight-faced.

"Jack is our chief of police," Jane put in from behind the counter.

Not just a cop. The top cop.

"I'm impressed," Lauren said.

"Don't be. We're a small department. Until last week, it was just me and one part-time officer." He removed the glasses. His eyes were sharp and dark in a hard-featured face. Stern jaw, strong cheekbones, bold, prominent nose. Her heart beat faster.

"Jack Rossi." He introduced himself.

Italian. It figured with that face.

"Lauren." *No last name.* To make up for her omission, she offered her hand.

His hand enveloped hers, sending a shock of warmth up her arm. Lauren swallowed, resisting the urge to tug back her hand. He did not recognize her. No one had. She didn't look anything like the pictures that had flashed on the news or the girl who had appeared, smiling and made up, on all the talk shows. She'd taken out the little ring in her left eyebrow. Her hair was shorter now and darker, almost black.

"What brings you to Dare Island, Lauren?" he asked.

"Oh, you know," she said vaguely. "Work."

His gaze narrowed slightly on her face. "What is it that you do?"

Even after all the media interviews, she hated that question. At thirty, she should be able to answer with certainty, *I'm a cop, I'm a baker, I'm a doctoral candidate in psychology.* Anything other than, *I'm famous for being in the wrong place at the wrong time.*

She couldn't be sorry that her presence in the bank that day had saved lives. But the whole hostage thing had changed her in ways her family couldn't see, her friends refused to accept. After her appearance on *Dr. Phil*, her book *Hostage Girl: My Story* had spent forty-eight consecutive weeks on *The New York Times* bestseller list. She was as isolated by her fame as she had been by her captors.

"I'm a writer."

Who couldn't write. Her stomach cramped. Her follow-up book, *Hostage Girl: My Life After Crisis*, was supposed to come out in six months. Before—her agent had explained with brutal honesty—no one was interested in her anymore.

That sexy little indent at the corner of his mouth deepened. Even his smiles were cool and controlled, she thought wistfully. Everything in her life felt so out of control. She was jealous.

"Guess you don't worry about stereotypes, either," he said.

What? She followed his gaze toward her table before understanding clicked. *The latte. The laptop.* Her lips eased into an answering smile. "The whole coffee shop scene is kind of cliché," she admitted.

Jane looked up. "We're a bakery. We're not a coffee shop."

Jack Rossi angled his body, shifting his attention to the woman behind the counter. His smile softened, making his strong features even more attractive. "I don't come for the coffee, Jane."

Oh. *Oh.* Lauren glanced from his hard, dark face to Jane. The baker blushed. If he didn't want donuts . . . and he didn't come for the coffee . . . He wasn't wearing a wedding band. Clearly he was after whatever else the pretty blond baker had to offer.

Lauren's lungs deflated. So did her ego.

Which was stupid. Even before the hostage incident, she didn't date blue-collar cops with Italian-sounding last names. No, she attracted musicians, losers, and weirdos.

Anyway, she was here to write. She had a deadline. She didn't have time for a fling or even a flirtation. It was just that her defenses were low, her confidence shaken, her energy depleted. Was it any wonder she wanted to borrow someone else's for a while?

Don't overthink it, her publicist, Meg, had urged. *Everything will be fine. You'll be fine. Just move on.*

It was good advice. Lauren sighed. If only she could figure out how.

IT WAS A beautiful day. Too bad his job was to ruin it for somebody.

Jack sat in his cruiser, running the AC and the driver's

license and registration of the seventeen year old who'd just blown through a stop sign on her way to the beach.

The ID checked out. The BMW belonged to her daddy. Jack could have let her off with a warning. He might have, too—he'd been young and dumb once—if so many other kids without cars didn't walk this road.

And if she hadn't tried so hard to flirt her way out of a ticket.

The law existed to protect everybody. The sooner Miss Teenage BMW learned the consequences of her actions, the better.

For some reason—for no reason at all—he thought of that writer, Lauren Somebody, in the bakery this morning. *I think she should go with whatever makes people feel good.*

A dangerous philosophy. It used to make him feel good to get drunk and hit things. No more. These days he restricted himself to one beer and the heavy bag in the back room of the station house.

Her face slid into his memory, the wide, soft mouth, the gleaming, intelligent eyes, the tiny scar that pierced her left eyebrow.

After almost eleven months, he knew most of the residents on the island. Lauren No Last Name was no more from around here than he was. Still, she looked familiar. Something about the shape of those eyes or the tilt of her jaw. His body tightened. She interested him, and not just as a member of law enforcement keeping tabs on his beat.

He shook his head, disgusted with the direction of his thoughts. His dick obviously hadn't learned the lessons of the past year.

He didn't do interesting women anymore.